just say when

KAYLEE RYAN

Cover Design: LM Creations
Cover Photography: Sara Eirew Photography
Cover Models: David Santa Lucia & Rachael Baltes
Editing: Hot Tree Editing
Formatting: Integrity Formatting

1

Ava Mae

*A*T THE SOUND of Kara fumbling into the apartment, I close my chemistry book. Glancing at my phone, I see it's after two in the morning. She's later than normal. Kara, my best friend and roommate, has a bit of a wild streak. We were paired as roommates our freshman year and hit it off immediately due to our similar taste in books, music, and clothes. Kara is what some might call a serial dater. She claims that college is a time for her to sow her wild oats. I, on the other hand, am the exact opposite. I'm here to get an education to be able to get a good job. Dating has never been a priority to me. I grew up with an older brother who scared away any potential boyfriend prospects. Even when he joined the Marines, the knowledge of who he was on top of his size kept them at bay. I was used to it, so it didn't really bother me. It also didn't help that he got his size from our father. They are both intimidating as hell at first glance.

From an early age, my parents, especially my father, impressed upon me how important it was to be able to take care of myself. He taught me to change a tire and even change the oil in my car. He said he never wanted me to feel weak or dependent on a man. He's fiercely protective, hence where Brody, my older brother, gets his 'stay away from my little sister' attitude.

I'm pulled from my thoughts as Kara appears at my bedroom door. "I had the best night." She beams at me.

I can tell from her glassy eyes and slower speech that she is a little bit tipsy. Not the worst I've seen her. "I bet it didn't top mine," I retort.

She looks at me in question. I point to the chemistry book on my lap. "The wonderful world of chemistry," I reply dryly.

Kara rolls her eyes. "Ava, you work too hard. You need to take a break every now and then. College is supposed to be the time of your life. You study too much. How long has it been since you went on a date?" she asks.

Shit. It's been months. "Clint." All I need to say is his name and we both shudder. Freshman year, Clint and I had a biology class together. He was a junior and had failed the year before. For some reason, he attached himself to me and wore me down until I finally said yes to a date, as long as Kara came too. The entire night was a disaster. Clint showed up at our dorm with one of his frat buddies and they were already drunk as hell. They took us to a frat party, big surprise there. I spent the entire night trying to keep Clint's tongue off me. Kara, who pretty much loves men, wasn't even feeling his buddy. They were sloppy drunk assholes. I was never so glad for a night to end. Clint continues to ask me out. He's always laughing and smiling telling me it's only a matter of time. It's a game to him, so I just brush him off. He knows it's never going to happen. There are several guys around campus who think Clint and I are an item. He's all hands and doesn't let my insistent glare and occasional elbow to the gut stop him.

"Exactly!" Kara exclaims. "It's time for you to find a real man." She wags her eyebrows at me. I know exactly what she's referring to. Kara is appalled that I turn twenty this summer and I'm still a virgin.

"I have plenty of time for that," I say, waving my hand in the air. "I want to get through school, and then I can worry about settling down."

Kara stares at me with her mouth hanging open. "Ava! We're sophomores. You have two more years and a year of clinicals. Your woo-hoo is going to be covered in cobwebs by then."

I can't hold in my laughter. "My woo-hoo is just fine," I assure her, wiping the tears from my eyes. When I finally have my laughter under control, I focus the conversation back on her. "So tell me about this best night you speak of." And just like that, the subject of my cobwebbed covered woo-hoo shifts back to Kara.

"I met someone, and he's hot, and he trains professional fighters, and did I mention he's hot?" She giggles.

"A trainer?" I question. I immediately think of Nate, Nathan Garrison, my brother's best friend. Just thinking about him causes my heart to skip a beat. His father owns a gym in town and the last I heard,

2

Nate was taking over the reins. The gym is set up for your usual everyday workout, as well as multiple rings where fighters are trained. I've been there a few times with Brody, but he never let me spend much time there. Claimed he was afraid the vultures would descend.

Nodding enthusiastically, she explains that this guy, Tanner, is in the process of training a big name local fighter for a big fight. "Some kind of title," she says. "He trains locally." Her eyes are bright with excitement.

I nod. "Hardcorps," I say the name of Nate's dad's gym. I wipe my sweaty palms on my lounge pants. It's always been this way whenever I think about Nate.

"No way." She smacks my leg. "How did you know that? Do you know him?" The last question is hesitant.

"Not that I'm aware of, but I know the gym. Brody is best friends with the owner's son. They signed up for the Marines together. Nate only did one tour though. His dad had a stroke, so he got out. He runs the place now," I explain.

"I keep forgetting you're the local girl." She laughs. "You hardly go out, so it's easy for me to forget you grew up in this town." She's quiet for a few minutes. "He's so hot, Ava. I mean melt-my-panties hot!" She sighs.

"So, are you going to see him again?" I'm pretty sure by the way she's gushing that she will most definitely being seeing him again. Soon, if she has any say so.

"God, I hope so. What are your plans for tomorrow?"

"Not much. I'm done with all my assignments for next week. We need to clean the apartment and go to the grocery."

Kara picks up my chemistry book and chucks it on the floor. "We, my dear, are hanging out the rest of the weekend. Tomorrow, we will clean and go to the store, and then tomorrow night, we are going out." She raises her hand when I try to speak. "No excuses, missy."

Laughing, I pull her hand down out of my face. "I was going to say that sounds good. I'm ready for a break. I'm all caught up for once. I'm counting down the days until this semester is over," I remind her.

"Are you taking classes this summer?" she asks.

I've been waiting for this question. I know my answer is going to shock her. "No. Mom and Dad, hell, even Brody when he gets a chance to call, have been harping on me to slow down. I'm taking the summer off from school."

"Are you fucking kidding me right now? EEEPPP!" She launches herself at me and hugs me tightly. "This summer is going to be so much fun. Since we have an apartment now, I already told my parents that I'm not coming home. I'm going to go visit for a week or so, but then I'll be back. Hey, you can come with me," she rambles on.

I smile at her enthusiasm. "Sure." Kara is from Florida, so a week on the beach sounds great.

"This is going to be a summer you will never forget, my friend." She places a loud kiss on my cheek and skips out of my room.

What have I gotten myself into?

The next morning, I'm making coffee when Kara stumbles out of her room. I grab another cup, fill it to the brim, and place it on the table in front of her. "Morning, sunshine."

Kara grumbles as she picks up her cup and inhales deeply before taking a sip. I finish making my bagel and pop one in the toaster for her. By the time it's done, she has consumed her first cup of coffee.

"Looks like you started cleaning without me," she says, eyeing the empty sink and shining counters.

"I couldn't sleep; besides that, it's ten o'clock."

I watch as she scarfs down her bagel. "All that's really left is the bathroom and running the sweeper."

"I got the bathroom. Then I'll shower and we can head to the grocery."

She scurries down the hall. I showered already, knowing most of the cleaning was already done. After I run the sweeper, I sit on the couch with my Kindle and wait for Kara.

"Ready," she says from behind me.

Our trip to the grocery store is uneventful. We both have very similar tastes and add items to the cart. We split the bill evenly every time and both eat whatever we want. It's a system that works well for us. We usually go once a week because she and I both like fresh fruits, vegetables, and yogurt. It's hard to stock up on items that have such as short expiration date.

On our way back to the apartment, Kara's phone rings. "It's him," she squeals. I watch from the corner of my eye as she takes a big breath and answers. "Hello?"

I can't hear what he says, but it must be good because it causes her to smile so big I'm afraid her face might crack.

"I'm not sure. My roommate and I were going to hang out," she tells him. "Okay, well let me talk to Ava and I can call you back in a few."

"Ava," she says as soon as they hang up, and I know what's coming. Whatever it is he asked her to do, she wants me to come along.

"Kara."

"Tanner invited us to go to the Underground with them tonight."

"Us?" I question.

"Yes, us. I told him you and I had planned to hang out and he invited you as well. He wants both of us to go."

"I don't want to be a third wheel, Kara," I whine.

"You won't be. It's not like Tanner and I are together. I promise you will not feel like a third wheel. I'll make sure it's you and me all night. Please, Ava, pretty please," she begs.

I think about the smile on her face and how Tanner put it there. She really likes this one. I want nothing more than for my wild and adventurous best friend to find someone to tame her. Maybe Tanner is the one.

"Fine. But I mean it, if I feel even at all like the third wheel, I'm coming home."

"I love you," she cheers, placing her hand over her heart. "I promise you will feel so much a part of the group you will be offering me your first born for convincing you to go," she quips.

I laugh at her craziness. "Let's—" I stop when I hear her talking to Tanner. She wasted no time calling to let him know.

This call is even shorter than the first. "He said his session starts at three and he will train for about three hours." She pauses to send a quick text while wearing a huge-ass grin. "He says he'll pick us up at eight."

I resign myself to the fact we're going out tonight. Don't get me wrong, I'm not a prude. I just like to stay focused, and I don't like feeling out of control. Drinking with people you don't know very well is risky, and I'm not really much of a risk-taker. I blame the men in my family.

After multiple trips, our small galley-style kitchen floor is covered in grocery bags. We both dive in to put everything away. As soon as the last bag is empty, Kara is tugging on my arm, pulling me down the hall toward her room.

"We need to pick out our outfits," she explains.

"Don't you think I should go to my room? You know, that place where I keep my clothes to make that happen?" I ask. I do it to irritate her. Kara loves to dress up. I think the only thing she loves more is when we do it together.

"Shut it. You know how this works." She laughs. She's right, I do. We have the same taste, mine being a little more conservative at times, but we always start in her room. She has kind of a shopping addiction and her closet is bursting at the seams. During our time as roommates, I'm not ashamed to admit, a few articles of clothing that do not belong to me have taken up residence in my closet.

"This," Kara says, holding up a white mini skirt.

"No." I don't want the attention the skimpy sliver of fabric will bring.

"Ava, come on. We need to find you a man."

I laugh at her. "Kara, if I'm going, I am not wearing that."

She scowls at me, and then turns to find me something else. I stand waiting patiently as she sifts through hangers, eventually turning, holding a pair of skinny jeans.

"That will work," I tell her.

Kara decides on skinny jeans as well, since it's late April and the night air can still be chilly. Kara chooses a three-quarter-sleeve shirt made of black mesh. Underneath, she wears a black tank. For me, she chooses a dark grey sweater, which is made to hang off one shoulder, also layering it with a black tank. It's sexy without being slutty, perfect for my taste. We both decide on black knee-high boots, and our outfit selections are complete.

We spend the rest of the afternoon just hanging out. We paint our nails and talk about our plans for the summer. We spend so much time talking that we both end up rushing to get ready.

At eight o'clock exactly, a knock on our apartment door has Kara running from her room to answer it. "Hey," I hear her greet Tanner. I smile at her giddiness over this guy.

Stepping into the living room, I see his large form standing in the doorway. He's a good head taller than Kara, so when he looks forward, he sees me and smiles. "Hey, I'm Tanner." He winks at me. Dear God, please don't let him be a cocky shit. I've had my fill for a lifetime after two years of Clint following me around.

I step up beside Kara, place a smile on my face, and offer him my hand. "Hi, I'm Ava. Nice to meet you."

Tanner shakes my hand and nods. "You, too." Letting go, he turns his attention back to Kara. "You ladies ready?"

Kara gives a quick glance toward me, I nod and she replies, "Yes."

Stepping out into the hall, Tanner leads us out of the building and to what I can only assume is his Hummer. It's black and sleek, and even though I just met him, something tells me this is the perfect vehicle for Tanner.

To my surprise, when we reach the Hummer, a guy who mirrors Tanner's size climbs out of the passenger seat. It was impossible to see him from the dark windows. Stopping in front of him, Tanner introduces us. "Zach, this is Kara and her roommate, Ava. Ladies, this is Zach. He's a good friend of mine and my punching bag."

"Hey now." Zach laughs good-naturedly. "It's actually the other way around." He points to Tanner. "He's my punching bag. It's nice to meet both of you."

"Right, let's get this night started." Tanner claps his hands in excitement. His personality is a lot like Kara's.

Kara and I climb into the backseat, even after Zach volunteered to let her ride up front. She politely declined. Keeping her promise that I would not become a third wheel, or in this case the fourth wheel? Not sure how to classify it. Zach and I are not on a date. Not that I would mind; he's definitely easy on the eyes.

Club Underground is packed, and the line is wrapped around the block. This doesn't seem to faze Zach or Tanner as Kara and I amble along behind them. They walk straight to the front of the line and say hello to the bouncer. After dishing out man hugs, he releases the chain and lets us in. I glance at Kara and, by the look on her face, she is as shocked as I am. We didn't even get carded.

Tanner reaches back to take Kara's hand and pulls her into his side. She easily falls into step beside him. Zach leans down and whispers in my ear. "The crowd can get a little crazy when we show up. Stick close to me until we get through it." With that, he drapes his arm over my shoulders and tucks me into his side, leading me through the crowd. They're all shouting out for Zach, trying to get his attention. He waves, but doesn't stop to talk to them.

This is freaking crazy!

The guys lead us to a reserved section in the back of the club. There are a few others sitting in the same section, but they leave us alone. Not like the vultures we just encountered. "Holy shit." Kara lets out a laugh. "What the hell is that all about?" she asks.

Zach's face flushes. "Zach's kind of a big deal around here. Local boy hits it big. He has a title fight coming up. If he wins, he's the champion in his division." Tanner goes on to explain weight classes and how fights are set up, even the timing in between fights for fighters to heal. Zach scans the crowd, giving me the chance to drink him in without him knowing. He's tall, has brown hair, broad shoulders and from the looks of the shirt he's wearing, he's packing some ridges in those abs.

"Change of subject," Zach talks over Tanner. I can tell he's embarrassed and it's endearing. It's not what you would expect from looking at him. Judging a book by its cover and all that. He turns to me and just like that I'm busted. I give him a flirty smile, no point in trying to hide it now.

"Let's dance," Tanner says, pulling Kara to her feet.

"We can't let them show us up." Zach grins as he holds his hand out for me.

"I would never hear the end of it," I say as I take his hand, allowing him to lead me through the crowd to the dance floor.

Zach spins me around and places my back to his front as we start to move. I feel his lips next to my ear as he asks, "Is this okay?"

I nod my approval and get lost in the beat. Zach rests his hands on my hips, and our bodies immediately sync to a matched rhythm. I love to dance and having a good partner makes all the difference. Zach fits the description. As the song changes, I turn to face him and we continue to rock to the beat. I'm straddling his leg, one hand braced on his shoulder for leverage while the other is in the air keeping time with the beat. His hand that rests on the small of my back pulls me in closer. Glancing up, our eyes meet and he winks. I smile, thinking about my earlier conversation with Kara. She said I would be thanking her. She's going to gloat for weeks that she was right.

This is pretty much how the entire night goes. The four of us laugh, dance, and have a good time. I notice how neither one of the guys drink. Neither one of them seem to need alcohol to have a good time. This fact alone is like a breath of fresh air. Zach and Tanner both seem like great guys, nothing like Clint. It's nice not to have to fight off lips and hands the entire night. When I mention it, Zach's reply is, "I'm training."

He's dedicated to what he does, and I admire him for that. Now, what he does is yet to be determined. How anyone can climb into a ring knowing there is a chance they are going to get their ass kicked is beyond me.

"I hate to be a party pooper, but"—Zach looks down at his watch—"I have to be up in six hours," he says regretfully.

"Why so early?" Kara inquires.

"I run every morning. Five miles." He smacks his stomach as if to prove a point. I've spent the last few hours pressed up against those abs. It takes more than a morning run to make that happen.

"Ugh. Not you, too." Kara points a finger at me. "This girl is like Forrest Gump."

Zach and Tanner erupt in laughter. "That's awesome," Zach says, wiping his eyes. "We should run together sometime."

"Sure." I shrug. I'll just make sure we take a route I'm familiar with, that way when he leaves me in the dust, I won't be lost. The thought of spending more time with him is actually welcoming.

Tanner drives us home, and both guys walk us to the apartment. We try to tell them it isn't necessary, but they scowl at us.

"So, I was thinking you should give me your number so we can do this again sometime," Zach says to me.

"You think so?" I ask as I rest against the wall outside our apartment door.

Zach rests his shoulder against the wall, facing me. "I do. I had a good time."

I also had a great time tonight, more so than I ever expected. I have Zach to thank for that. Giving him a slight nod, I hold my hand out. He grins. Digging into his front pocket, he pulls out his phone, unlocks the screen and places it in the palm of my hand. Tapping the messages icon, I send myself a smiley face text. My phone chimes as I'm returning his and a grin tips his lips. He really is easy on the eyes.

"You ready, man?" Tanner breaks the spell.

Zach slides his phone back in his pocket. "Yeah, five hours and counting," he says, reminding us that he has to be up early.

"Lock up," Tanner says. We nod, wave goodbye, and let ourselves into the apartment.

"Well, what do you think?" Kara asks as soon as the door is shut.

"I think you really like this one."

She nods. "I think you might be right. What about you? Looks like you and Zach hit it off."

"I had a great time. He can move; that's for sure." I grin.

"Yeah, the two of you were burning up the dance floor."

"Like you had time to notice." I laugh. She was in Tanner Land most of the night. I'm suddenly glad Zach was there. My night could have ended up a lot worse.

"I knew you were in good hands." She winks.

My phone chimes with a message.

Unknown: Sweet dreams

I grin, seeing the smiley face I sent myself. I know it's Zach. I quickly program in his name and reply.

Me: Goodnight :-)

"Is that Zach?" Kara asks.

"Yeah, we exchanged numbers. He was just saying goodnight."

Her phone chimes and she grins. "I think I'm going to turn in.

Thanks for coming tonight, Ava."

"Me, too. I had fun," I say, following her down the hall to my room.

The next morning, I wake to the sound of male voices. Reaching for my phone, I see that it's nine thirty. Groaning, I roll out of bed and make my way to the bathroom. I quickly wash my face and brush my teeth. My hair is in a knot on the top of my head and I know there is no use in trying to make it look any different. I slowly pad my way down the hall, trying to see if I can tell who our early morning visitors are. The voices are too low for me to make them out. I continue to the kitchen where I find Kara sitting with Zach and Tanner, having breakfast.

"There she is." Zach grins. "It's about time, lazy bones."

"The guys brought us breakfast," Kara explains.

"Morning, Ava," Tanner greets me.

I'm surprised, but try not to let it show. "Breakfast, huh? What did we get?"

"Bagels from the shop around the corner," Kara tells me.

"Thank you," I say, taking a seat next to Kara. It just so happens to be directly in front of Zach. "How was your run?"

"Good. I did my five miles and then hit the showers to come here."

"Shit, I would be passed out in bed right now if I ran five miles. Better yet, I would probably be keeled over dead somewhere," Kara jokes.

We all laugh at her. "What are you guys getting into the rest of the day?" I ask.

"So, I was thinking the two of you should come by the gym. I have a training session at one," Zach says.

Kara looks at me with pleading eyes. If she only knew what she was asking for. I've avoided seeing Nate since he's been back. Can I do it today? Looking around the table, I see three hopeful faces staring back at me. I need to get over this crush and face the fact Nate and I will never be. Taking a deep breath to tame my racing heart, I answer, "Sounds good." Her face lights up. Tanner and Zach are also grinning like fools. I made the right decision. I need to put on my big girl panties

11

and move on.

"Great, we'll see you both then," Zach says with a smile. "Ava, I'll text you the address." He stands from his spot at the table.

I nod and offer a hesitant smile before Kara walks them out with the promise they will see us soon. I watch the three of them disappear into the living room.

I probably should have told him we don't need directions. I also probably should have told him I know the owner's son. Part of me wants Nate to be there today, the part of me that still harbors a crush for my older brother's best friend. The other part of me wants him to be nowhere near while I'm there. Sadly, that reasoning is also from the girl who has had a lifelong crush on her older brother's best friend. In reality, I'm just me, torn between two wishes.

We're in the car and on our way to Hardcorps and I'm still torn at whether I want to see him. Nate runs the place now and chances are he'll be there. Even though we live in the same town, I spend most of my time at the apartment or campus library, so we don't run in the same circles. I glance at my reflection in the rearview mirror and cringe.

"What?" Kara asks, seeing my discomfort.

"I'm a mess." Kara looks down and smiles. We're both wearing yoga pants and tank tops.

"We're headed to the gym. We can't let them think we're trying too hard," she says.

Easy for her to say, I can potentially run into Nate. I used to have the biggest crush on him and always made sure every hair was in place when I knew he was coming over. Old habits die hard, I guess. Not to mention that Zach is also going to be there.

"Good point," I say as I park in front of Hardcorps. I'm trying like hell to mask my apprehension.

Her phone pings, alerting her to a text. "They're coming out to get us." Just as we round to the front of the car, Zach and Tanner come walking out of the gym. Both well over six feet with lean, muscular bodies that just so happen to be on display. Both guys are in nothing but gym shorts and a pair of slip-on athletic sandals.

"Ladies," Zach says, stopping beside me. He throws his arm over my shoulders. "Glad you all could make it." I chance a glance at Kara to see Tanner has her in the same hold and she's all smiles. Well, all right then. After we've all said hello, the guys lead us into the gym.

I take in my surroundings, seeing a lot has changed since the last time I was here. Nate must be trying to modernize. There seems to be a lot of upgrades, new equipment and things like that. I can't help but scan the area looking for Nate as I fight my internal battle of whether I really want to see him. It also helps to keep my mind off the fact that Zach wants me here, leading me into his domain with his arm around me. What will Nate think? He's going to be calling Brody for sure. I fight the urge to groan at the thought of our future phone conversation.

2

Nate

"YOU DID WHAT?" I stare, dumbfounded, at Zach.

"You heard me. I invited the girls Tanner and I met up with last night to come and watch me train today." He says it like it happens all the damn time.

"First of all, you have never invited a chick to watch you train. Second, how in the hell are you supposed to concentrate with her here, and third, you just met her." I tick off each item with my fingers. "Wait a minute, you said girls, as in two of them?"

Zach throws his head back and laughs. "I'm well aware that this is a first for me. I'll train harder, wanting to show her my skills." He winks. "Yes, I just met them. They seem chill. Not like the usual cage bunnies who run in our circles," he explains.

"You have a huge fight coming up, man. Your fucking title fight. You don't need the distraction," I warn him.

"Chill, Nate. I got this. I'm not going to ask her to marry me. She's coming to watch me train. The four of us had a good time at the Underground last night. She runs, and I just thought she might like the atmosphere is all," he pleads his case.

"So, which one are you after?"

Laughing, he says, "They are both incredibly beautiful women, who will be here"—he checks his phone—"in about ten minutes to watch you run my ass through the gauntlet," he replies, not answering my question.

I clench my jaw, trying to keep my cool. Zach moved here two years ago. He was one of the first guys I took on when I took over the gym. He's usually a pretty laid-back guy, but if he sets his mind to something, there's no changing it. I see that in him now. He wants these girls here. Hell, maybe he's right. Maybe it will inspire him to train harder to impress them. But he needs to stay focused. This is his shot at the title, what we have spent the last two years working toward. He's busted his ass for this shot and I don't want to see him waste it away because of some chick he just met.

I watch as Tanner keeps checking his phone. This time it must be her because a slow smile crosses his face. "They're here. Be right back." He jogs off toward the entrance; Zach is hot on his heels. No doubt they're going out to meet them.

Nothing I can do about it now. If he slacks off, I'm going to have to put my foot down. It's my job to make sure he's ready for this fight. I motion for Trey to hop in the ring. He's one of the best, his skill matching Zach's. Trey has no desire to fight professionally. Tanner is his usual partner, but today Trey's it. I need to mix things up, keep Zach from getting so confident that he thinks he can slack off. Both Trey and Tanner are skilled fighters, just in different areas. Tanner is great with standing, going toe to toe. Trey, on the other hand, focuses more on the takedown. Zach needs a little work in this area, work that he's going to be getting today.

"Here we are, ladies," I hear Zach say behind me. I turn to meet the girl who has him by the balls after one meeting and I'm shocked to see my best friend's little sister standing in front of me. "Kara, Ava, this is my good friend and trainer, Nate."

He turns to me. "Nate, this is—" He places a hand on each of their shoulders.

"Ava Mae," I say her name before he can. I watch as a broad smile lights up her face. Suddenly, my heart is racing, pounding fiercely within my chest. Before I realize it, I'm in front of her in one big step and picking her up in a hug. "How have you been?" I ask, stepping back but not releasing her.

"Good. Just trying to stay focused on school. Looks like business is going well," she says, glancing around the gym, keeping her eyes on anything and everything but me. My fingers tingle from being on her waist. I release her from my hold and take a step back. I take a look around to avoid staring at those big brown eyes. The gym is packed and I feel a sense of pride at how I've been able to keep the family business alive.

"Dietitian, right?" I ask her. She turns back to face me with a surprised look. "Brody." I laugh. He always keeps me updated on what's going on with her. I don't even have to ask. I thrive off every little morsel he throws my way.

She smiles, shaking her head. "Have you talked to him recently?" she inquires.

I nod. "Yeah, just last week. You?"

"Yes, did he mention Sara?" Her eyes sparkle at her delight. I can tell her conversation with Brody was much like my own.

"He did. He seems happy." I never thought I would see the day my best friend would be talking about getting out of the Corps to settle down. Apparently, he met a girl in Hawaii where he's stationed. Her dad is a bigwig on base and my boy fell for her hook, line, and sinker. I asked him how that worked out for him and, surprisingly, he said great. Sara's dad approves of him, how could he not? Brody is a damn fine Marine and an even better person. Sara's a lucky girl.

"I really think he is. He mentioned he might be getting out."

I nod. "Yeah, he's got a year left on this round." I feel a hand come down on my shoulder.

"You two know each other?" Zach says. It's obvious that we do; he's watching me closely. I was pissed at him for inviting chicks to his training, but not now, not with Ava Mae standing in front of me. She was always a pretty girl, but now she's a beautiful woman. The same one who I have fought my attraction to for the last few years. Looking at her now, she's more beautiful than the last time I saw her over two years ago. Ava Mae and her mom came to the hospital to see Dad after his stroke. At that point, we weren't sure what damage had been done. I don't remember many of the visitors, but I do remember her. Those big brown eyes swimming with tears, telling me how sorry she was. She was there to support me and all I wanted to do was hold her and comfort her until those tears left her eyes.

All of a sudden, it hits me that she's the one who Zach seems to want. Tanner is enthralled with her roommate, whose name I have yet to learn. I know Zach introduced us, but I heard nothing but white noise as soon as my eyes landed on Ava Mae. I clench my fists at my sides. No way is Zach dating her. He's not a commit kind of guy, and over my dead body will he hurt her. I'm going to have to keep a close eye on them.

"Ava Mae is Brody's little sister," I explain to him. He knows Brody; they met over a year ago when he was home on leave.

"We grew up together," she says to further explain. She steps back out of my reach and Zach immediately throws his arm over her shoulders. I have to bite my tongue to keep from telling him to keep his damn hands to himself.

"All right then, you ladies can sit here." Zach points to the row of folding chairs beside the ring. "We will be up there." He winks at Ava and points to the ring.

"Actually, Tanner, you can sit this one out. I'm switching this up a little." I point to the ring where Trey is standing. Zach raises his eyebrows but doesn't voice his question.

I spend the next two hours coaching Zach on his takedown technique. I have to admit that he's on fire today, and I'm sure it's because the girls are watching. I'm positive he's doing his best to impress her, just like he said he would.

I fight the need to glance over at her every ten seconds. Every once in a while, I hear the girls laugh along with Tanner's deep chuckle. I can't look, because I can easily get lost in her. Pushing her laugh and beautiful brown eyes from my head, I remind myself to focus, but fuck, it's hard. Having her here isn't what I was expecting. I'm struggling to keep my eyes away from her. It pisses me off that Tanner is the one making her laugh. The fact she's here to watch Zach train . . . fuck!

"Time," I call out. Trey slumps to the floor, as does Zach. They've been at it for two solid hours.

Trey turns his head on the mat and looks over at the girls. "I think I need some loving," he says with a wink.

Kara giggles and jumps up to join him in the cage when Tanner throws his arm around her. "Get your own woman!" he tells Trey.

Trey's responding laugh echoes throughout the gym.

Zach climbs to his feet and exits the ring. He stops in front of Ava, tucking a stray hair behind her ear. "I need to head home to shower and change. How about I pick you ladies up around seven? We can grab a bite to eat before we head to the Underground."

"I'm in," Tanner says, his arm still around Kara's shoulders. She doesn't seem to mind, if her smile is any indication. "You in, darlin'?" he asks Kara.

Kara looks to Ava Mae for approval and I see her give a slight nod.

"You're going to the Underground?" I ask Ava Mae.

"Well, we are now." She laughs. "We had a good time last night." I watch as she looks up at Zach, grinning.

"You're under twenty-one," I say to her, ignoring the scowl I can feel Zach giving me.

"They can still get in, jackass," Zach says. He turns his attention back to the girls. "All right, ladies, I'll see you at seven." I watch as the arm around her shoulders falls so that his hand rests on the small of her back as he leads her out of the building. I will Ava to turn back around, but she doesn't. I want to yell out and tell her she's not allowed to go.

I watch until I can no longer see them, and then stomp off to my office. Ava Mae has no business at the Underground. I contemplate calling Brody to have him weigh in on the subject. I decide against it. I don't want to get him all worked up. He can't do anything about it from Hawaii. I'll just need to keep a close eye on her and make sure all the creepers keep their hands to themselves. Fuck! Looks like I'm going to the Underground tonight.

"What's gotten into you?" Zach asks, storming into my office.

"They have no business at the Underground. They're underage," I seethe.

"Fuck, Nate. They're nineteen, both turning twenty in the next couple of months. They are not underage. Sure, they can't legally drink, but they are old enough to get into the club."

I don't acknowledge him as I slam folders around on my desk.

"If you're that fucking worried about us letting something happen to them, then you should just come with us," he snarls. I let his words sink in. I know they would be safe with Zach and Tanner. My anger at the thought of her with him is clouding my judgment.

I angrily continue to sift through folders, as though I'm too busy to be having this conversation.

"Are you in or not?" he finally asks.

I stop my rant and lift my head so he can see my face. "Fuck, yes, I'm in. I have to keep an eye on her," I explain.

"Them," he counters.

"What?"

"Them, you need to keep an eye on them. They are both under twenty-one, after all." He smirks.

"Yes, that's what I said. Brody would never forgive me if something happened to them." I close the lid on my laptop. "I'm driving, too. I need to make sure sh . . . *they* get home okay. I'll be at your place at six thirty. Be ready." I stalk past him and out of my office.

I'm shocked at my reaction, so I know Zach is floored. For years I've been able to keep my attraction to her under wraps. I've never told a soul that it's Ava Mae who enters my dreams at night.

3

"HOLY SHIT! NATE is sexy. You've been holding out on me," Kara says as soon as she shuts the car door.

"How have I been holding out on you exactly?" I ask, amused.

"You've been hiding him," she exclaims.

I laugh at her. "Kara, I have not been hiding him. Nate is Brody's best friend, not mine."

"He's a hot as hell older brother's best friend whom you forgot to mention existed," she accuses. "Admit it, he's a sexy beast."

"Yes, Nate is sexy, but he's forbidden to me. Brody would have no part of it, and neither would Nate." Brody would flip his shit if something were to happen between us. Not that I ever have to worry about that. Brody and Nate are as thick as thieves, and best friend's little sisters go against the bro code. "Zach and Tanner seem nice," I say, steering the conversation away from Nate.

"Nice? Are we talking about the same guys? Tall, shaggy brown and blond hair, muscles?" she asks.

"What? They were nice. They walked us to the car and everything. Neither one of them even tried to cop a feel," I retort.

Kara bursts out laughing. "Damn it, I know. I was hoping at least one of them would."

"Kara!" I pretend to be offended. We both know I'm not.

"So what are you wearing tonight?" she asks.

"I have no idea."

"You take first shower while I pick out our outfits."

"Okay." I try not to worry about what she'll pick. I rush through my shower, knowing Kara will be chomping at the bit for her turn.

When I open the bathroom door, Kara is in the hallway waiting for me, just like I knew she would be. "I laid your outfit on your bed," she says, rushing into the bathroom and closing the door.

Anxious to see her choice, I make my way into my room. On the bed there is a pair of black shorts and a purple shimmering V-neck top. I've seen Kara wear this outfit before and it's cute. The shorts are short, but not ass cheek bearing, and the top is flowing, just low-cut enough to keep me decent. It's still chilly, but we got so hot last night dancing. I'm sure that's what had her deciding on shorts. Glancing to the floor, I see a pair of black wedge sandals. She did well.

"You look smoking," Kara says, stepping into my room, still dripping from her shower. "Let me get dressed and we'll start on your hair and makeup."

She's gone before I can protest. I'm just going to throw my hair up in a clip and limit the makeup. I looked like a damn raccoon last night when we got home from sweating it all off.

Kara is just finished with her hair when there is a knock at the door. It's ten minutes until seven and Zach is early. Kara scurries off to answer while I grab my license and some cash from my room. I hear Kara and male voices. I stop in my tracks when I reach the living room and see Zach, Tanner, and Nate talking to Kara.

Nate. Shit! I didn't know he was coming.

Zach whistles and I can feel heat creep across my cheeks. Nate smacks him on the back of the head. Zach just laughs and holds his arm out for me. "Ready, beautiful?" he asks. I take his arm and he leads me out of the apartment.

Zach's phone rings and he stops walking. Pulling his phone out, he peers at the screen. "Shit, it's my agent. I have to take this," he says apologetically. I wave him off and continue on to the parking lot.

"You two seem to be hitting it off," I hear Nate's deep voice beside me. He places his hand on the small of my back and leads me toward a Tahoe.

The material of the shirt is thin and I can feel the heat from his hand. It causes goose bumps to break out across my skin. It's not the first time he's ever touched me. I gave him a hug earlier, but this . . .

this feels different.

Intimate.

We reach the Tahoe to see Kara and Tanner already in the third row seat. How did they get ahead of us? "Tanner, I can sit back there," I say through the window.

"I'm good." He raises his hands, which are laced with Kara's, to stop me from climbing in the back.

Opening the front passenger door for me, Nate waits until I'm buckled in before he shuts the door and walks to his side. He climbs in and messes with the radio as we wait for Zach. I can't help but wonder if Zach is going to be mad that I'm sitting up front.

"I can get in the back," I tell Nate.

"No." His voice is gruff and firm. He wants me up front with him. I don't understand what that means and my mind is racing in too many different directions to try and figure it out.

The windows are down, which is why I'm startled when I feel Zach's hand rest on my arm. "Trading me in already?" he jokes.

I turn to face him. "What?" I'm thrown off by the look I see him give Nate.

Zach opens the passenger side back door and hops in. He shakes his head, a slight smirk on his lips, letting me know he has nothing else to say.

I'm so out of my element and the girl in me who has crushed on Nate for as long as I can remember is giddy with excitement to be sitting next to him. Giddy to be going to a club with him, but then I remember Zach, and the adult in me comes crashing back to reality. Nate is looking out for his best friend's little sister.

I'm here because Zach asked me, not Nate. Suddenly, I can't wait for this night to be over.

The drive to the Underground is entertaining. Kara, Tanner, and Zach get on the topic of music and debate back and forth. They try like hell to bring Nate and I into their feud, but we remain neutral. Nate and I make polite small talk about how our parents are and how Brody seems to be falling hard for Sara. We're just two old friends catching up. Too bad this old friend can still feel the heat of his hand on the small of her back.

The line to get into the Underground is unreal. Zach opens my door and helps me climb out of the Tahoe. Throwing his arm over my shoulders, he leads our group to the front of the line.

"Hey, my man." The bouncer reaches out to shake Zach's hand. It's not the same guy as last night, so it might not be as easy to get in.

"Hey. Good crowd tonight."

"Yeah, it's packed in there. How many?" the bouncer asks.

"Five," Zach replies.

The bouncer nods and steps back to let us in. I hear a few complaints from those behind us, but Nate is leading me forward, so I don't have time to dwell on the fact we just received special treatment and cut in line for the second night in a row. Zach truly does have the local celebrity status around here. Once we reach the bar, Zach gets stopped by a group of fans. He hams it up, smiling for pictures and even signs a few autographs. This causes the women to swarm and I get pushed into the back of the crowd.

Standing there watching Zach in his element, I feel a hand grip my elbow. Looking over, I see Nate. He tilts his head, motioning toward the bar and I nod, following him.

"What do you want to drink?" Nate asks me.

He's close.

I can almost feel his lips graze my ear. It's loud in here, so he has to be close. I have to remind myself of this fact so my heart doesn't run off with any romantic notions.

"Water's fine."

Nate orders two bottles of water, pays the bartender, and steps to the side. Tanner steps to the bar and orders the same. These guys really take training seriously.

Tanner leads us to a high top table in the reserved area. Nate excuses himself to go to the restroom.

As soon as he leaves, "Turn Down For What" blares through the sound system. Kara squeals, grabs my arm, and pulls me to the dance floor. We mix right in with the rest of the crowd, bumping and grinding. There's a group of guys standing on the edge of the dance floor where we are. Two of them join us. We're all laughing and having a good time. One of the guys moves in behind me and places his hands on my hips. We start to move in unison to the beat. He's got moves and he's not bad on the eyes either. Kara smiles at me and winks. I close my eyes and feel the music. I love to dance, and as we groove to the beat, I realize my parents, Brody, and Kara are all right. I need to make more time for things like this.

4

*T*ANNER LEADS US to a table and I excuse myself, saying I need to use the restroom. To say I'm livid with Zach is an understatement. He let Ava get lost in the crowd, his fans more important than her. I plan to have words with him, now. I head back toward the entrance where I last saw him. Sure enough, there he stands with a group of girls with their goods on display, vying for his attention.

"Ladies, I need to steal him away for a minute," I tell them. Zach grins and tells them he will be right back.

'What's up, man?"

"Are you fucking kidding me? Do you even know where Ava is?" I force the words through my gritted teeth. He looks around trying to spot her. "Exactly, jackass. Your fan girls are more important."

"Fuck, Nate." He runs his fingers through his hair. I see the relief in his eyes when he spots her at the table with Tanner and Kara.

"Back off, man. If you're not willing to be the man she needs, to put her first above everything else . . ." I take a breath to calm down. "Back. The. Fuck. Off."

I don't wait for his reply as I turn and stalk away.

I reach the table just in time to watch as Kara pulls Ava to the dance floor. They stop right at the edge as if they cannot wait a second longer to move to the beat. We watch them in silence, enjoying the show they're putting on. That is until two guys join them. At first, it looks innocent enough, but when the one closest to Ava puts his hands on her, I know I have to squash this.

"We can't let them have all the fun." I motion to the dance floor. I'm pissed off this guy is mauling her, and I'm pissed off at Zach. I can't believe he let his groupies pull him away from Ava. He doesn't deserve her.

Tanner grins. "You don't have to tell me twice." He places his now empty water bottle on the table and heads straight for Kara.

I'm hot on his heels. I stop in front of Ava and she smiles hesitantly just as the song changes to "Talk Dirty." The guy who was trying to make his move on her is no longer touching her, which is in his best interest. Ava seems nervous as to where she should touch me. This is new for us. I take her hands and rest them on my shoulders as I move my hips to the beat. I keep an eye on the jackass to make sure he knows she's unavailable. I don't want him touching her again.

I pull her tight little body close to mine, not caring that this is Ava Mae, my best friend's little sister. She's forbidden, but for tonight, for this time in which I actually have her in my arms, I don't let it stop me. Instead, I pull her close and pretend she's mine.

Ava rocks her hips against mine and I tighten my grip. Her big brown eyes find mine and her stare is intense. If I didn't know better, I would think that she wants me just as fiercely as I want her. Pulling her as close as I can get her, I bury my face in her neck and match the rhythm of her hips as they grind against mine. I wish like hell she were mine.

As the song comes to an end, Ava mimics taking a drink and points to the bar. I nod, place my hand on the small of her back, and lead her off the dance floor. I notice the guy who was creeping up on her watching us. I make eye contact and give him my 'don't even fucking think about it' look. He must get the message because he looks away.

"Water?" I say against her ear once we reach the bar. With a smile and nod, she lets me know that's what she wants. I raise four fingers and say, "Water" to the bartender. I know Tanner and Kara are right behind us. I look around the room, my eyes searching for Zach. I don't see him. Fucker, I hope this means he took my warning seriously.

"I'm so glad we did this, and two nights in a row," I hear Kara yell over the music.

After settling with the bartender, I turn to give Ava her bottle of water. She smiles and mouths, "Thank you," before taking a long drink.

Handing Kara and Tanner theirs, I take the opportunity to watch Ava as she tilts her head back. Her long slender neck is calling for my lips to kiss her there, to taste her skin. She's sexy as fuck and I have to stop staring at her before I can no longer hide what she does to me. I turn to look at Kara, and nothing. I look back at Ava and my dick twitches. Definitely has a mind of his own, my dick.

"Me, too. I need to get out more," Ava finally replies.

I watch her as she rubs her forehead right between her eyes. "You okay?" Kara asks. Ava nods. "Migraine?" Kara questions.

"I think so, yeah. It's been a while since I've had one," Ava explains.

I place my arm around her and pull her close. "You ready to head out?" It feels good to have her in my arms. I'm still pretending she's mine. I don't want the night to end, to have to face reality, but I know how these migraines affect her. I remember when she was diagnosed.

I watch her as her eyes find Kara. She sucks her bottom lip between her teeth. They seem to be having some kind of unspoken conversation.

It's Kara who answers. "I think we should get her home. This club scene is just going to make it worse."

Leaning into her, I whisper in her ear, "Let's get you home." I walk her to my Tahoe and help her inside. "Can you sit up for me, sweetheart?" I ask her.

She leans forward with the help of my hand on her back. I hit the lever on the side of her seat and help her recline. "Lean back," I softly say the words. I know how sounds and light can affect a migraine. Dad suffered with them for years.

Once I have her situated, I take my phone out and call Zach. He answers on the fourth ring. "Where the fuck are you?" I don't even give him time to say hello.

"I'm in the VIP lounge. Why, what's up?" he asks.

I grit my teeth. "We're leaving. If you need a ride, you've got two minutes to get your ass to the parking lot. Ava Mae has a migraine and needs to go home."

"Shit." He hesitates and that's all I need to hear.

"Just stay. Call me if you need a ride later, but I'm taking her home," I tell him. He lost his chance to have a say when he hesitated. Ava should always come first. He's proven tonight that is just not the case with him.

I hear muffled words and I'm just about to hang up when he says, "Okay, yeah, Mike can give me a ride. Tell Ava I hope she feels better."

I don't even bother to reply. I end the call and slip the phone back into my pocket as I climb in behind the wheel. I glance in the rearview to make sure Kara and Tanner are ready to go. Tanner is grinning from ear to ear and Kara offers me a small smile. The drive back to their place is quiet. Kara and Tanner talk softly amongst themselves while I sit quietly. Every chance I get, I glance over at Ava to make sure she's doing okay. She's sleeping; at least, I think she is. Her eyes are closed and she hasn't moved or made a sound since I strapped her in.

Pulling into the lot, Kara jumps out and has Ava's door open. "Stop." My voice is low, but she can tell I mean business. "Don't wake her." I quickly make my way to the passenger side. Kara steps back and allows me to take her place. I release the seatbelt that I strapped around her and gently lift her into my arms. "Lead the way," I say, my voice softer this time. I can't believe she was going to wake her. Sleep is what she needs. It's hard enough for her to fall asleep when she gets this way, I remember. Kara thinks she's the only one who understands that Ava suffers from migraines. She's not. I can remember many times when I was with Brody at their house and one would hit her. Hell, I remember when the doctors ran her through a gauntlet of tests to rule out all other possible scenarios before she was given the diagnosis of migraines. I was there. I know her, Ava Mae. I remember how scared I was for her, not knowing what was wrong.

Kara unlocks their apartment door, and Tanner and I follow her inside. "Which one?" I whisper.

"First door on the right." She points toward the hallway.

I nod and head that way. Her door is open and the light from the living room is just enough for me to see what I'm doing. I lay her gently on the bed before I take off her shoes. She curls up in a ball and releases a soft moan. I try to pretend the sound doesn't affect me. I pull the covers up over her and gently tuck the hair that is hanging over her eyes behind her ear.

She needs her medication. I stalk back to the living room to find Tanner and Kara kicked back on the couch. "Where are her meds?" I ask Kara.

She looks surprised. "How did you know?"

"Best friend's little sister, remember? I grew up with her. I know she needs them now; otherwise, when she wakes up, it will still be there and worse."

Kara stands from the couch. "I'll get them." She walks off toward the hallway. I assume they are in the bathroom, but I didn't want to go digging through their things. Not with Kara here to do it for me.

She appears a minute later with a bottle in her hand. I reach for it and ask, "What about a bottle of water. I assume she still drinks with them?"

Kara nods and makes her way to the kitchen. I follow her and watch as she pulls a bottle of water from the fridge. I smile in gratitude and make my way back to Ava.

I find her just like I left her, curled in a ball under the covers. I sit on the edge of the bed and gently rub my hand up and down her back. I remember Brody used to do this for her. "Kara," she mumbles.

"No, sweetheart, it's Nate. I've got your medicine. Can you sit up?"

She slowly starts to sit. I wrap my arm around her shoulders to help her, and hand her two pills and the opened bottle of water. I was going to make her take them regardless. I've seen what happens when she doesn't have it.

"Thank you." She takes the pills and a small drink of water.

"Can you drink a little more for me? We need to keep you hydrated."

Tipping the bottle to her lips, she takes a few more large drinks. Satisfied that half the bottle is now gone, I take it from her and help her lie back down. "Can I get you anything else?" I ask.

"No, but thank you. I just need to sleep," she says with a yawn.

I know this. Tucking the covers back around her, I place a light kiss on her forehead, but remain in my spot on the edge of her bed and watch her. I had forgotten about her migraines. Dad used to have them, which ultimately led to his stroke. I feel a vise clench my chest at the thought of something happening to her. I can't picture young, beautiful Ava Mae with the limitations my father has. I don't want to leave her, but I know she's in good hands with Kara. With one final glance, I force myself from my perch on her bed and leave her to sleep.

I don't even reach her bedroom door before I'm turning back toward the bed. I sit gently on the side of the mattress and rub her back again. I want to stay right here in case she needs me. I want to be here when she wakes up.

Fuck!

I never should have allowed myself to pretend she was mine. I take in her sleeping form basking in the gentle glow of the moonlight. I told myself one night, one night to pretend she was mine. I'm going to take full advantage. So instead of getting up and leaving like I know I should, I memorize everything I can about her. The way her hands are clasped together, her head resting against them. The way her brown locks flow over her pillow. The gentle rise and fall of her breathing. I take my time, letting my eyes roam over her, trying like hell to burn the image of her like this into my mind. I want nothing more than to crawl in bed beside her and wrap her in my arms. The urge to do so is too much. I know I need to leave before I do just that. Standing, I lean down and kiss her temple then force myself to leave her room.

My night of pretending is over.

In the living room, I find Kara and Tanner curled up with each other on the couch. "How is she?" Kara asks.

"Okay for now. She just needs to rest. I got her to take her meds and drink a half a bottle of water. Staying hydrated helps," I explain.

Kara nods. "Yeah, her mom told me that as well. However, she usually fights me on it."

I don't bother to comment. Ava Mae knows I won't put up with that. I know what she needs and will settle for nothing less. "Ready, man?" I ask Tanner.

He turns to face Kara. "Later, K. You need anything,"—he nods his head toward the hall—"she needs anything, you call me."

Kara gives him a hug. "Will do. Thanks, Tanner."

I watch as he leans down and kisses her softly on the lips.

I rattle off my number to Kara. "Call me and let me know how she's doing," I tell her.

"Okay, guys, we're fine. This is not the first time she's had a migraine. Just go. I got this."

With one final glance at Ava's door, I nod and follow Tanner back out to my Tahoe.

5

FEELING MY BED shift, my eyes pop open. Kara is sitting on the edge of the bed with a bottle of water in her hand and what I assume to be more of my migraine medication. "Morning, how you feeling?" she asks.

I sit up, taking the water and medication from her hands. I toss back the pills and down the bottle of water. "Not bad. Still a slight lingering, but it's bearable." I'm surprised she's in here. Usually, she just lets me sleep.

"Good, now I can give a full report to Nate so he'll stop calling," she grumbles, pulling her cell out of her back pocket and fires off a text.

"Nate?" I ask, confused.

"Yes! That man is killing me. He's been texting me all morning since about seven thirty, wanting to know how you're doing. I refused to wake you up. He insisted he get a report as soon as you woke."

I glance at the clock, eleven. Damn, I never sleep this late. "I'm fine. He's just like Brody, always worrying." I wish it were more than that. "When I was younger, Nate was around when they started. He was there through all the tests and such. He and Brody would watch me after school. Sometimes Brody would have to stay after, so Nate would bring me home and stay with me. He's like a surrogate brother." One who is sexy as hell and I have not-so-sisterly feelings toward. Don't get me wrong. He's a great guy, but I wish he could see me as more than just Brody's little sister. That's a fantasy of my younger self who always crushed on him. I'm not too proud to admit that even now I still secretly harbor those feelings, just a little . . . or maybe a lot. I push them to the back of my mind, knowing that's never going to happen.

"Well, he's feisty when he wants information," she complains.

Kara is not a morning person, and Nate bugging the hell out of her so early in the day didn't help matters.

"Ugh! Call him, please. Put us out of our misery." She rolls her eyes playfully and stands from the bed. "I'll make you some breakfast. Bagel?"

"Yes, please. Thanks, Kara. I'll call him." She turns to leave and I remember I didn't get to ask her how things went with last night. "Hey, so how did things go with Tanner?"

Kara blushes. "He's amazing. He kissed me goodbye. Just a soft peck, but amazing all the same," she gushes.

I decide to grab a quick shower before I call Nate. I grab some clothes and head to the bathroom that Kara and I share. I just get my hair lathered when the door flies open. "Ava, you said you were going to call him," she scolds me. I don't bother yelling at her for barging in on me. With sharing a bathroom, one of us is usually in the shower while the other is putting on makeup or fixing our hair.

"I will. I needed a shower. What's another fifteen minutes going to hurt?" I continue on with my hair.

"It matters. He's on his way over here. He apparently doesn't believe me that you're fine."

"What? That's crazy." I understand he's worried, well kind of, but Kara is my roommate and best friend. Why is he so concerned all of a sudden? I've been in the same damn town as him for two years and we've not spoken to one another. I don't get it.

"He took control last night. Making sure you had your meds and water. Tanner and I just sat back and let him do his thing."

"He and Brody were joined at the hip growing up. He knows me well, or at least, he used to," I offer in explanation.

"Umhmmm."

I rush through my shower and quickly get dressed. I don't need him barging in the apartment finding me in nothing but a towel. Don't get me wrong, I would enjoy it, but would die of embarrassment for liking it. He will never see me like that. I need to get out more, maybe start to date. My mind flashes to Zach.

I find Kara in my room. She's lying on my bed, but gets up when she sees me. "Did you save me any hot water?" she asks.

I laugh at her. We both know she's the one who drains the hot water. Luckily for me, she usually lets me go first because she feels guilty.

I take her spot on my bed and lie down with my hair still wrapped up in a towel. "I hate how I ruined our night with this damn headache."

"It's fine. You didn't ruin anything. The guys were both fine with leaving. It was getting late anyway," she assures me.

"So, are you seeing Tanner again?"

"We didn't really talk about it, but the kiss was kind of like a prelude to what's to come." She laughs.

"Ava?" a deep voice booms from the living room. I recognize it as Zach's. What's he doing here? How he disappeared last night, I assumed I was a bore to him.

"Sounds like he brought the crew," she says with a smile. "In here," Kara yells down the hall. I wince slightly at the volume. She notices. "Sorry, Ava."

Zach appears in the doorway wearing a grin. "Ava, babe, if you wanted me in your bedroom, all you had to do was tell a guy. You didn't have to fake a headache to get me here," he quips.

"Watch it, fucker." Nate steps in behind him. "Where were you last night?" he grumbles under his breath. He continues his stride until he's standing beside my bed. He sits on the edge and places his hand on my leg. "How ya feeling, Ava Mae?" I can hear the concern in his voice.

"Better, just a twinge of headache, but nothing I can't handle."

"Good, I was worried. I know how bad they can get." He gets a faraway look in his eyes. I can only assume he's remembering how long it took the doctors to diagnose me when I was younger.

"I'm fine," I reassure him. I sit up, feeling uncomfortable lying in bed with the two of them so close.

"See, she's fine. Now let's go eat. I'm starving," Zach whines as he climbs onto the opposite side of the bed.

"What the hell are you doing?" Nate asks him.

Zach puts his arm around my shoulders and I let him pull me against his chest. "Just taking care of my girl."

Nate stands. "I thought you were hungry?" he moans.

"I am, but my girl comes first." Zach pulls me closer to him. "You hungry, Ava?" he asks, a smirk on his face.

"I'm good." Although, I wonder where this sudden concern is coming from. "What happened to you last night?"

"I got held up. Sorry about that. I talked to Nate so I knew you were in good hands," he says.

"Ava Mae, you need to eat. We can bring you something back," Nate offers as his eyes shoot daggers at Zach.

"I'm good. Promise. Kara made me a bagel," I try to reassure him. I don't tell him I haven't eaten it yet. His sudden appearance in my life has me off kilter. "Sleep helps. I think I'll lay back down."

"She's right. Sleeping it off seems to be what helps her the most. I got this," Kara tells Nate. He watches her as if he doesn't trust her to stay with me, which is ridiculous.

"All right, I guess we're going to head out then. You'll call if you need anything?" Nate asks.

I nod. "Yeah, but I'm good. This is nothing new to me. You know that."

Nate stands from the bed, his eyes bore into Zach. "Let's go." His voice is clipped. Zach chuckles and removes his arm from around me. This seems to relax Nate a little. "Ava Mae, take care," he says softly, his eyes now back on mine. Reaching down, he runs his finger across my jaw. "Call me if you need me."

I swallow hard to mask my emotions. "Thanks for stopping by, but I'm good," I reassure him again. He finally nods in acceptance. Zach waves over his shoulder as Nate pushes him out of my room.

Kara and I watch them walk away. "What's up with that?" Kara asks.

"What? Did you want to go get something to eat?" I play dumb. I'm just as surprised as she is about Nate's sudden interest in my well-being.

Kara laughs. "Nice try, smart-ass. You know exactly what I'm talking about, but if you want to play the 'I don't know what you're talking about' card, I'll humor you for now."

I sigh. "He must feel some kind of duty to Brody," I say, trying to define what just happened.

"Nate was . . . intense. Zach seems to enjoy instigating that part of him." She climbs into bed beside me. "Can I get you anything?"

"No. I took my medicine already, so sleep is what I need."

"Sounds good to me. Nate started blowing my phone up at the asscrack of dawn; I could use a nap." She yawns.

"Sorry." I feel bad he woke her up. His reaction confuses me and makes my head hurt even worse. I fall asleep thinking about Nate and his sudden interest in my life.

6

Nate

I PUSH ZACH OUT of her room and out of their apartment. I wanted to rip his head off when he climbed into bed with her. What the fuck? We climb into his truck and I lay into him.

"What the hell were you doing back there?" I demand.

Zach grins. The fucker actually grins at me. "What? I thought we were checking up on Ava?" His smile gives him away. The fucker knows exactly what I mean.

"You need to keep your hands to yourself," I warn him.

"Fuck, Nate. Have you seen her? She's a knockout."

I grind my teeth at his words. Yes, I've seen her and I know she's a fucking knockout. I also know he needs to stay the fuck away from her. "She's Brody's little sister. You remember my friend Brody, right? Big-ass Marine."

Zach chuckles. "Yeah, Brody's cool. I don't think he would have an issue with me stating his sister is a knockout."

"What about last night?" I ask. "She deserves better than that."

The smile slips from his face. "I lost track of time." He shrugs. "I knew she wasn't alone. You were there."

"That's not a fucking excuse," I grit out.

Underneath all the cocky flirting, Zach is a decent guy. He talks a big game, but he doesn't use women. Hell, when he's with someone, he treats her like a queen. He was dating a girl when I met him and he worshiped the ground she walked on. Unfortunately, she was a bitch and left him for another fighter who just signed on with the big leagues. Hence the reason he no longer does commitment. Kara or Ava, either one, would be lucky to find someone like him, should he ever change his ways, but that thought causes my stomach to roll. I don't want him with her.

"Can you please just bow out. Leave her alone?" my voice is pleading. I don't want her with him. Hell, I don't want her with anyone but me. "Can she just be off limits?"

I wait for his reply as I stare out the window. Finally, he says, "Yeah, man. We agree Ava is off limits. I don't want to compete for a chick with you. It's a great idea that we make her off limits."

What? No, no, no. "Well, she . . . I didn't mean . . ." Fuck. I run my fingers through my hair. Not even twenty-four hours after seeing her again and she's got me twisted.

Zach throws his head back and laughs. "Classic, brother. I know exactly what you were trying to say. I was trying to get you to admit it. The anger rolling off you last night . . . How long have you wanted her?" he asks.

Fuck me. There's no point in denying it. "I honestly can't remember. She was just always there, you know? Brody's little sister." I sigh. "She had Brody wrapped around her little finger. He was, is, fiercely protective of her. She tagged along with us since their parents worked a lot. He and I both learned a lot about what we would need to do if she had a migraine." I think back to last night. "I always helped him take care of her. It was scary for a while; they had to run a ton of tests to rule out all other possibilities."

"That explains last night and even this morning," Zach replies.

"Yeah. Old habit, I guess."

"She was a freshman in high school when we left for the Marines. Our parents threw us a combined party, and Ava Mae, she had on this blue sundress and . . . yeah. She no longer looked like Brody's little sister." I pause to think back to that day. I can still remember every detail of how she looked that day. Her sundress was modest, nothing special, but her sun-kissed skin was tempting as ever. Her long brown curls flowing over her shoulders made me itch to run my fingers through them. I remember she hugged me that day, and when she pulled back, there were tears in her eyes. I told myself they were because she knew that me leaving also meant Brody was leaving. I wanted nothing more than for those tears to be for me. I will never forget the way she looked, or the smell of her hair as she hugged me. Zach sits in silence, letting me get lost in my memories of Ava.

"She wrote to me," I finally say. "Once a week, religiously, Brody and I both got letters from her. I was only deployed once, but her letters, they kept me going, kept us both going. Sometimes we would get five or six at a time. Mail was few and far between in the field."

"What's stopping you?" Zach throws the question out there, like me being with Ava would be no big deal.

"She's Brody's little sister." He has to understand she's forbidden fruit to me.

"Talk to him."

I laugh. "Yeah, okay. I don't want to lose my best friend." I can only imagine how that conversation would go. He would be on the next plane home, Marines be damned.

He pulls into Subway and turns off the engine. "I'm fucking starving." And just like that, the conversation is over. I just need a little time away from her and I can get my head back in order. Seeing her again, being around her, dancing with her, she's under my skin. Distance is what I need. I should have never allowed myself to get that close, to pretend she was mine.

It's been two weeks since I've seen her. One weekend of being in her presence and I cannot stop thinking about her. I'm fucked! Brody would kick my ass. I've typed out about a million text messages, but sent none of them. I want her, but I can't have her. It was easier to resist her when she was younger. She was too young for me and Brody was there as a constant reminder. Then he and I went away to the Marines and I had to hide the fact that her letters lit up my world. Brody never questioned that Ava wrote to me. We all grew up together and, well, that's just Ava. She's sweet and loyal to a fault. When Dad had his stroke and I decided not to extend my career in the Marines, the first thing I thought of when I was back in town was Ava Mae. I fought the urge and threw myself into taking over the gym. She and I didn't really run in the same circles, so when I did go out, it was easy to not be in the same place as her. This may be a small town, but for two years I was successful. Two weeks ago, that changed and nothing I do gets her out of my head.

"Again! Damn it, Zach. Do you want this or not? Step in with your left foot."

Zach drops his arms to his sides and glares at me. "What the fuck crawled up your ass? You've been moody as hell. I'm doing it just like I have and all of a sudden it's not good enough? Fuck that. You need to get laid," he sneers at me.

I know I'm being a dick, but I'm on edge. I'm tied up in knots, and as much as I wish it could, a random fuck is not going to fix this. Only Ava can fix it and that, too, is not possible. I need to learn to bury this shit.

"We're done for the day." I stalk off to my office. I drop into my chair and run the palms of my hands over my eyes. I need to get my shit together.

A throat clearing gets my attention; Zach's sitting across from me. "How about we head to the Underground tonight? You can obviously use a drink and a lay, if you're so inclined. I need to jump in the shower and stop by Kara's to drop some CDs off, but then I'm all yours."

At the mention of stopping to see Kara, I perk up for the first time in weeks. "Kara?" I question.

He laughs. "Yeah, Ava has been trying to get her to start running. She says she needs a good playlist first. I'm letting her borrow some of my collection," he explains.

I wonder if Ava's home? Maybe just seeing her will help put these feelings into perspective. I originally thought distance would do the trick. Fourteen days of Ava Mae on constant replay . . . distance has done nothing but make me long for her. "Let's do it," I tell him. Zach nods in agreement, rises from the chair, and heads to the showers. I need to see she's feeling better; maybe that's it. I'm worried about her headaches. When I see she's fine, I can get my life back, my life without Ava.

I quickly check in with the closing staff, letting them know I'm heading out for the day. Zach finds me by the door, keys in hand, waiting for him. He smirks at me and I pretend not to know why. It doesn't take a genius to figure out that my asshole tendencies kicked into play right after Ava Mae was here, and that they are suddenly stalled because I may or may not get a glimpse of her when we stop by to drop off some CDs to Kara. Nope, no intelligence needed. Zach has my number, but luckily for me, he doesn't comment on it.

We make small talk on the way there. Zach talks about the title fight coming up and I ramble on right along with him. It helps to keep me distracted. We pull into their apartment complex and Zach leaves his truck running, telling me he'll just be a minute.

Fuck!

Reaching for the handle, I hop out of the truck and say, "I'll come up with you, say hi."

"Uh huh," Zach mumbles under his breath. I pretend I didn't hear him and follow him into the building. I want to push his slow ass out of the way and rush to their door, but I don't. Instead, I continue to pretend I'm just coming along to say hello to a friend. I pretend the thought of seeing her doesn't make my heart race. I'm calm, cool, and collected with no hidden agenda, nope, not at all.

"It's just Kara. Ava's not home," Zach says as we walk to the door.

What the fuck? "How do you know that?" I ask.

"She told me she was going shopping with her mom today. When I talked to Kara earlier, she said Ava wasn't back yet."

He talked to her? "You talked to her?" My voice is incredulous.

"Uh, yeah. I've talked to both of them at least once a day since I met them," he says, like it's no big deal. I've been trying like hell to stay away from her and he's been cozying up to her. Damn it. He gave me his word.

"So, what, you all are best friends now?" I'm being a dick again and I can't help it.

"Yep," he says, knocking on the door, successfully ending our conversation.

The door immediately opens. Kara smiles when she sees us. "Hey, guys. Come on in." She steps back from the door.

My eyes seek out Ava. I don't see her. Zach must have been right.

"Here are the CDs you wanted to borrow," Zach says.

"Thanks. If Ava insists I run, I at least need to have some kick-ass tunes to keep me company," she explains.

"You guys are welcome to use the gym if you want. We've added a lot of new equipment," I offer. My mouth just opens and spews out words before I can stop it. If they take me up on my offer, I'll see her multiple times a week, maybe every day. I'm not sure how I feel about that.

"Thanks, Nate. I'll talk to Ava and let you know."

My eyes look toward the hall at her bedroom door. Zach saves me from having to ask and make it obvious as to why I'm here. "When will she be home?"

"She went shopping with her mom today. I was going to go, but I'm more of a slacker than she is and I have a paper to finish." She laughs. "Usually, it's an all-day process."

"All right then, well, we're out," Zach says. "We're headed to the Underground if you guys want to stop by later."

"Awesome. I'll talk to Ava; she should be home any time now. Is Tanner coming with you?"

"I'll call him as soon as we leave." Zach winks at her.

We say our goodbyes and head back to Zach's truck. Suddenly, my foul mood is back and I don't feel like going anywhere but home. I don't bother to tell Zach; he'll just drag me to the Underground regardless. I'm ready for this night to be over.

7

Ava Mae

OM WORE ME out today. I think we went to every single store in the mall. It's nice to get to spend time with her. Living on my own, we don't get to indulge in days like today very often. I lug my bags into the apartment, trying not to feel guilty. Mom claims she doesn't need an excuse to spoil her only daughter.

"Hey, need some help?" Kara jumps off the couch to help me with the bags.

"Thanks, we went a little overboard."

"I can tell." She laughs, following me to my room. We drop all the bags on the floor.

"Did you get your paper done?" I ask.

"I was doing really well, pushing through, until Zach and Nate showed up to drop off some CDs. I've been putting them on my laptop and making our running playlist."

I'm relieved and disappointed at the same time that I missed Nate. "Awesome. I'm excited to get back into running."

"This is a first for me, so take it easy on me. Speaking of running, Nate offered to let us come and workout at the gym."

Can I handle seeing him at the gym every day? I think about the last two weeks and how I haven't stopped thinking about him. At least I would be able to see him, even if I can't have him. "What do you think?"

"I think it was very nice of him and exercising in an air-conditioned building is a hell of a lot more appealing than out in the heat."

"True. I guess we should stop by one day next week and see what kind of paperwork we need and how much it will cost."

"I got the impression it would be free, but either way, I'm in. They also invited us to the Underground tonight. I told them I would talk to you and see what you thought."

"I'm exhausted. Mom dragged me to every store in the mall."

"Honestly, as much as I want to go, I really need to finish this paper. Tanner also texted and said he has to help his dad with something tonight."

"Need some help?"

"No, I just need to get my ass in gear." She climbs off the bed. "I'll send Zach a text and let him know we're not coming."

I start emptying bags to put my purchases away. "Have you eaten yet?" I ask.

"I had some cheese and crackers earlier."

"Mom and I ate, but it was earlier, too. How about I make homemade pizza while you work on your paper?"

"You love me. Your pizza is so damn good." I laugh at my best friend. She thinks everything I cook is good. "It's always better when someone else makes it," she defends.

My phone vibrating in my back pocket causes me to jump. I don't bother looking at the screen; I just slide my finger across it and hold the phone between my shoulder and ear so I can keep taking tags off my new clothes. "Hello?"

"How's my favorite sister?" Brody's voice rumbles through the line.

"Hah. I'm your only sister." I laugh. "I'm great, Brod. How are you?" It's so good to hear from him. He's not currently deployed, but the Marine Corps keeps him busy.

"Good. I haven't talked to you in a while. How's school?"

"School's good. Just a few more weeks of classes and I'll have another year down."

"Yeah, and then you have a birthday coming up. Any special requests?"

For as long as I can remember, Brody has asked me this same question around my birthday. My reply is always just a hug. He's been able to come through for all but two when he was deployed. "Just a hug," I repeat the answer to our tradition.

"So, the big 2–0. You have any plans? You and Kara going to hit the town?" he inquires.

"Nope, not really. I'm not much of a hit the town girl, you know that."

Brody laughs. "Yeah, I know, but it's my subtle way of making sure college life isn't changing you."

"Aren't you the sly one?" I laugh with him.

"Just using my kick-ass older brother Ninja skills," he boasts.

"Ninja?" I ask through my laughter. "Last I checked, you were a Marine."

"Semantics. My big brother Ninja skills were honed long before the Marines."

"If you say so. So how are things? How's Sara?" I ask sweetly. The last time we talked, he had admitted he met someone and he was falling fast.

"Sara is beautiful," he replies instantly. "Work is work, same old same old."

"So I spent the day shopping with Mom and she didn't drill me about Sara. I assume that means you are keeping her to yourself for a while?" I ask. If Mom even suspected, it would have been the topic of discussion today.

"Yeah, I mean, not really, I just didn't want Mom to be all 'When are you getting married?' and shit. I just want time to get to know her without any . . . distractions. She's special and I just want it to be us for a while."

"Trust me, I get it. She asked me more than once today if I'm dating anyone."

"Are you?" he asks. Laughing Brody is gone, and serious Brody has taken his place.

"No, but then again, I'm not exactly looking either."

"Just make sure when you do, that he treats you right. Don't put up with any shit."

"Never. He has a lot of competition with the men in my family," I say with a smile.

My response causes him to chuckle. "When you do meet someone, let me know. I'll call Nate and have him meet him. Fill in for me, if you know what I mean."

Nate. Will there ever be a time just the sound of his name doesn't make me long for him?

"Ava?"

"Sorry. I'm unpacking all my purchases from today." It's not a complete lie. I decide I better mention I ran into Nate. If he finds out I didn't tell him, I'll never hear the end of it. "I actually ran into him."

"Ran into who? Nate? When?" Brody fires off questions.

"Yeah. Kara met a friend of his and he invited us to watch him train. Ended up, Nate is his trainer. It was at his gym." I leave out the night at the Underground.

Brody laughs. "He's been back in town for two years and you all are just now running into each other. Times change," he says wistfully.

Not really, big brother. I'm still crushing hard on your best friend. "That they do," I say instead.

"So, are you into this guy? The one who I assume was tagging along with his friend for you?" he asks.

Nope. I'm into your best friend. "No, we're just friends. Kara and Tanner really hit it off. Zach and I are just friends. I don't see anything more coming out of it."

"All right, I just wanted to check in. I'm picking Sara up for dinner."

"When are you coming home?"

"I hope to get a few days off soon."

"Well, make sure when you do that you bring Sara. I can't wait to meet her."

He laughs. "We'll see. I'll talk to you soon."

"Bye, Brod. Love you." With a quick 'I love you too,' he's gone. I miss my brother, but he sounds happier than he has in well . . . ever. Sara seems to be good for him.

"How's that fine-ass brother of yours?" Kara asks.

"He's good. Seems happy. It's still hard for me to believe he's finally met someone"

"Damn it. All the good ones are taken," she whines.

"Like you're ready to settle for just one," I accuse.

"Well, if the right one were to come along, I would. Until then, I'm shopping." She laughs, holding up an empty shopping bag.

"All right, you need to hit the books. I'm going to start on that homemade pizza." I finish hanging up the last of my purchases.

Kara groans as she leaves my room for hers. I swear, if you look up procrastination in the dictionary, you'll see her picture. This isn't the first time I've had to bribe her with cooking.

I busy myself in the kitchen, making the dough for the crust. Mom's recipe calls for letting the dough rise for at least thirty minutes. Just as I cover the bowl of dough with a dishtowel, my phone chimes with an incoming text.

Nate: How you feeling?

Me: ??

Nate: Headaches

Me: I'm good. I don't get them as often as I used to.

Nate: Good. I was worried.

I'm surprised he's texting me. Then I think about my call with Brody. I'm sure as soon as we hung up, he was calling Nate, wanting to get him on board to torture any guy I may happen to set my sights on.

Me: I'm good, thanks.

Nate: Good.

It's hard not to crush on the guy as long as I have and not let my mind make more out of his concern than what's really there.

"Who put that smile on your face?" Kara asks, joining me in the kitchen.

Shit. Might as well spill the beans. "Nate. He was just texting to see how the headaches were." I set my phone on the counter and wash my hands. When I turn back around, she's scrolling through my texts. I would expect nothing less from my best friend.

"He's into you," she says as if we're discussing the weather.

"Brody," is my answer. I want to tell her the feeling is mutual, but I know it's not. Kara doesn't understand how close Brody and Nate are. She wouldn't understand that he's just looking out for his best friend's little sister. Yay me. "Finish your paper?" I divert the conversation to safer waters.

"Ugh! Finally. I just need to do another read through, and then I'm done." She glances at the clock on the wall. "We still have time to make it to the Underground, if you want to go." She points to my cell phone and winks.

"I'm good. Just tired, besides, I'm kind of in the middle of something." I raise my hands covered in dough and wave at her.

"Good point," she laughs. "I'm going to start our playlist."

"Yes, you need to do that. You're not backing out on me," I yell at her retreating form as she leaves the kitchen. She always says she's going to work out. She's more of a gym person. Hopefully, running is something she will stick with. I tried to start yesterday, but she insisted we have an appropriate playlist before we started. That led her to texting Zach, asking him for his suggestions. I hope she keeps her enthusiasm when the work actually beings.

My phone pings with a message. I finish rolling out the dough and washing my hands before checking my message. My hearts beats a little faster at the chance it could be Nate again.

> Zach: You up for a run in the morning?
>
> Me: Sure, I don't have class until 10
>
> Zach: Kara?

"Kara," I yell for her.

"Yeah?" She pops her head back into the kitchen.

"Zach wants to know if we want to run with him in the morning?" I ask her.

"Can't. I have an appointment at eight to have my oil changed. Dad's orders," she laughs.

"Okay, I think I'll go. I've been slacking too much lately."

> Me: Kara's out. When and where?

Zach: I'll pick you up at six and we can run on the outdoor track at the gym.

Me: See you then.

I didn't realize Hardcorps had an outdoor track; at least, it didn't used to. Nate has really made a lot if improvements in the last couple of years.

8

*T*ONIGHT SUCKS ASS. Zach and I went to the Underground, but neither one of us were really feeling it. We each had one beer and then left. We're on our way home and Zach decides to drop a bomb on me.

"So, I texted Ava. She and I are going to run in the morning."

"Zach," I growl his name.

He chuckles. I don't find it the least bit funny. "We're going to be at your gym," he explains. "I told her I would pick her up in the morning on my way in."

He's not only still trying to spend time with her, but he's bringing her to my gym.

My first instinct is to tell him to stay the hell away from her. The only thing stopping me is the fact Ava Mae is going to be at my gym. I take a deep breath and bite my tongue. I'm going to be there to run with them. It's going to be Heaven and Hell, but worth it just to get to see her again. I know I need to keep my distance, so I tell myself I'm just looking out for her. Zach's a good guy, but he's not one to settle down. Ava deserves better.

"What time are you picking her up?" I ask.

"Six. She has a class at ten," he informs me.

What the hell, now he knows her class schedule? We're quiet the rest of the way to my house. Zach drops me off with a "See ya later," and nothing more.

Letting myself in the house, I kick off my shoes and head straight for the bedroom. I'm ready for this day to be over.

The next morning, I'm up way earlier than I need to be and head to the gym. I try to work my way through some paperwork, but end up watching the clock. Finally, at quarter to six, I head out to the track. I'm just starting to stretch when I hear her laugh. Fucking Zach. I need to remind him Ava Mae is off limits.

I pretend not to notice them and continue with my stretching. "Hey, man." Zach smirks, stopping next to me. "Fancy seeing you here."

"Have a ton of paperwork, thought I would get in a run before busting through it and then your training session," I remind him.

"Morning," Ava says cheerily.

"No classes today?" I know the answer because Zach already told me but she doesn't know that. I'm suddenly like a teenage boy trying to coax words out of my mouth to speak to a pretty girl.

"I'm not that lucky." She laughs. "My first class isn't until ten. I've been slacking on my running, which is why I roped Kara into starting up with me."

I look around. "Did I miss Kara?"

"She's not here. She had something else going on. Although, I think she's using it as a stall tactic."

Zach throws his head back and laughs. "I know she is."

"Yep. That's Kara. She's trying to get out of it. I don't mind running by myself, but it's more motivating when someone else is doing it with me." She smiles at Zach.

"It's safer," I say. She nods in agreement.

"Are you running with us?" Ava inquires.

I shrug as if I couldn't care less either way. This of course is a lie. "Sure."

I watch as Ava sits on the ground and starts stretching her legs. It's not until she's on her back and pulling her legs to her chest that I see red. Zach decides that it's his duty to help her. He's leaning over her. He stands over her, places his hand on her legs and pushes into her chest. I've seen it done more times that I can count, but it's never been her, with him. I tighten my fists at my sides and bite my tongue.

Luckily for me, or maybe him, they quickly stretch her other leg and we set off around the track. Ava's fast, but Zach and I slow our pace to match hers. We reach the five-mile mark and all three of us are winded. Ava stops and declares she's calling it quits. Zach and I agree. He's got a three-hour training session ahead of him.

We reach down for a bottle of water, and all too soon, they are saying goodbye. I want to make an excuse for me to take her home, or have her stay longer, but I know that she has to get back so she doesn't miss her class. I watch as they walk away. Zach opens the door for her and waits until she's settled in before shutting it. I grit my teeth and stalk off to the shower.

I hide out in my office for the next few hours, immersing myself in the mounds of paperwork I am behind on. Training is a huge part of what I do here, and I love it, so I tend to let this side of the business slide to the back burner. I may have to break down and hire someone to help.

"Ready, man?" Zach asks as he knocks on the doorframe of my office.

Startled, I look at the clock and see I'm ten minutes late for his training session. *Great.* "Yeah, sorry, I lost track of time."

"You need an assistant or something."

"I know. I was just thinking the same thing."

We spend the next few hours in the zone. Zach is one hell of a fighter and, if he keeps his focus, he can take this title. He spars with both Trey and Tanner. I've decided, and Zach agrees, he needs to work with both of them each day until the fight. Whatever it takes.

After a vigorous session, the four of us are standing outside the ring talking about technique, the fight, you name it. Zach's phone alerts him of a message. Walking to the table, I watch as he swipes his finger across the screen and a smile lights his face.

"What's got you smiling like a fool?" Trey asks him.

"Ava." Zach shakes his head as his fingers fly across the screen. Once he's done, he looks up. "We were talking this morning about how I need to get strict with my diet with the fight coming up. She just sent me a picture of a fucking hot fudge cake." He laughs. "I told her sweets were my weakness."

"We need to start early tomorrow," I snap. It's a dick move, but I'm hoping it will keep him from going out tonight. Keep him from seeing her. He's supposed to be staying away from her.

"Time?" Zach asks. He doesn't seem to be fazed by my demand.

"Six," I snap. "We need to run and work on some cardio before hitting the ring."

Zach laughs. "You keep telling yourself that, buddy." He smacks me on the shoulder and heads to the locker room.

I stalk to my office and slam the door. Resting my elbows on my desk, I rub the palms of my hands against my eyes as if the act can take the stress away. Of all the girls out there, I have to want her, my best friend's little sister. I can't control this . . . jealousy. I've never been jealous, but I can recognize it for what it is. Now I just need to figure out what the fuck to do about it.

The ringing of my cell phone startles me out of my thoughts. Pulling it out of my pocket, I see Brody's name flash across the screen. Perfect timing. I debate letting it go to voicemail, but it's been a couple weeks since I've talked to him. I slide my finger across the screen. "Hey, man."

"Nate, my man, how you been?" he asks.

Your sister has me tied up in knots. "Good, same old same old. How about you? How's life in Hawaii?"

"Good. Good. Just doing my thing." He chuckles. "I talked to Ava the other day and she said she ran into you. Who's this guy she and her friend were with?" he inquires.

"Tanner and Zach." Brody has met them both a couple of times when home on leave.

"Can we trust them with her?"

No, because she's supposed to be mine, but I can't have her because she's your sister. "They're both good guys." The words are sour coming out of my mouth.

"She said they were just friends, but I don't know, man. She sounded off. You think she likes this guy?"

"She ran the track with Zach this morning. I'm pretty sure they're just friends, but I'll keep my eyes and ears open," I tell him. Ava Mae and Zach? No way is that happening.

"Thanks, man. I appreciate you looking out for her."

I feel like a fraud. "Anytime." I force the words out. "So how's Sara?"

Brody sighs. "She's . . . great. I really like her. I think she's the one, man. I'm just not ready to share her with everyone yet," he laughs. "I'm not ready for Mom to have us married with kids on the way just yet." He laughs.

"I hear ya. Mine finally got tired of asking. I haven't done much in the way of dating in the last couple years."

"I get it. You wanted to prove you could handle taking over the business. I think you've done that." He pauses before saying, "It's not all that bad, you know? Having a steady girl. It's definitely growing on me."

"Yeah, I can definitely see the appeal, just has to be the right girl." I want to tell him I found 'the right girl,' but of course I can't do that. "It's good catching up, but I have a session. Keep in touch and stay safe," I tell him.

"You too, Nate. Thanks for looking out for Ava. I owe you, brother."

"No, you don't. Talk to you soon," I say, ending the call. I don't have a session, but I had to end the conversation before I blurted out how I want her, and ruin our friendship.

9

Ava Mae

"I THINK WE SHOULD do it, Kara. It'll be fun."

"Fun? I think you're trying to kill me," she scoffs.

"Hey now. You were the one who said you wanted to start running with me. It's several weeks away, plenty of time to get in shape. Besides, it's just for fun. We aren't trying to win and, hell, you don't even have to finish, but come on." I turn my iPad to face her. "Look how much fun they're having."

Kara pulls the iPad from my hands and hits play on the video again. I watch as a slow smile tilts her lips. "It does look like fun," she concedes. "It's the week before your birthday."

"I know, Happy birthday to me." I laugh. "So, are you in?"

"Yes, but we, like seriously, need to train. I do not want to go out there and only make it freaking five-hundred feet before I'm wheezing like a chain smoker."

"Well, all right then. Every morning we get up before classes and run," I tell her. I agree she needs to train a little, but we're not trying to win. The 5K-Color Run just looks like a fun time. "So you're in?" I ask her. She doesn't answer right away; her fingers are flying across the keyboard of her phone. "Who are you texting?"

"Zach. We need all the help we can get. Besides, it will help keep Tanner on his toes. Can't make it too easy for him." She winks.

I have to give her credit; it's not a bad idea. "He's got a big fight coming up; he might not be able to help us," I remind her.

Kara waves her hand in the air. "Pfft, he'll help and you know it. He's training anyway, so we'll just join him for the cardio stuff. That's what you did today, right?"

"Yeah, I mean, we ran at the outdoor track at Hardcorps. Nate actually ran with us."

"Perfect. This is what he does, trains. I'll have Zach get Nate and Tanner on board as well. This gives me an excuse to spend more time with Tanner without making it obvious. It's a genius plan really."

Her fingers are already flying across the screen before I can stop her.

"Yes! Okay, so Zach says we should take Nate up on his offer to work out at the gym. Said he'll run with us when he can, but if we're at the gym, they can help us."

Can I spend that much time with Nate and keep my feelings hidden? Kara is watching me with an excited look on her face. I've been trying to get her to agree to run with me forever, and if this is what it takes, I'll just have to mask my emotions. I've done it for years. What's a few more weeks?

"I'm in. When do we start?"

She doesn't look up, already tapping away at the screen. Her phone immediately alerts with a message. "Zach says Nate has him running in the morning at six. We can meet them there then." She jumps off the couch.

"Where are you going?" I yell after her.

"I have to get my outfit together. You know, there will be some eye candy there. Besides, Tanner might have mentioned he has an early session tomorrow."

I can't help but smile at her. Tanner has held her interest longer than any other guy since I've known her. It's going to be fun watching this play out.

The next morning, Kara is more bright-eyed and bushy-tailed than I thought she would be. I guess the prospect of seeing Tanner at the gym is good motivation for her. Whatever it takes. As soon as we pull in the lot, I see Nate, Zach, and Tanner waiting outside the front door. They smile and wave, and my heart flips at the sight of Nate. He's wearing athletic shorts and a t-shirt with the side cut out, showing off his toned body. Steeling my resolve, I take a deep breath and walk toward them.

"Hey, guys. Thanks for letting us run with you." My voice is chipper, overly so. They don't comment.

"Let's do this," Kara says, bouncing on the balls of her feet. "Hey, why don't you guys do the Color Run with us?" Kara suggests.

Tanner laughs. "Sounds like a good time. I'm in."

"Me, too," Zach says. He turns to look at Nate. "What about you? You up for a little color in your life?" I can tell by the way he says it, there is an underlying meaning to his question.

My eyes seek out Nate and I find him watching me. Without looking away, he says, "I think I'm long overdue for some color in my life. I'm in."

Zach grips his shoulder. "Hell yeah, let's get started then."

Nate makes sure to instruct us all on the importance of stretching our muscles, and even suggests that Kara and I help each other. After we've all had the opportunity to stretch, we're off and running. Kara and Zach make a game of it. She's bet him she can stay ahead of him for an entire mile. I'm not sure what she's thinking since he's a professional athlete and she hates to run. Her loss. Loser has to buy dinner tonight.

Tanner just trails behind, laughing at their antics. He seems to be really laid back and easy going. That's exactly the personality my best friend needs in a man.

Nate and I take a more relaxed approach. We're not sprinting, but doing what I like to call a heavy jog. We don't talk, because, really, who can carry on a conversation while they're running? Instead, we keep a steady pace side by side.

When we finally reach the mile marker, Kara stops us in our tracks with all her celebrating. I can tell from the smirk on his face, Zach let her win.

Tanner picks her up and swings her around in circles as she cheers for her victory over Zach.

"All right, crazy girl," Zach says. "How about I throw some steaks on the grill at my place?"

Kara studies him before turning to Nate and Tanner. "Have you had his steak?" she questions.

Nate grins at her. "Yeah, he's actually not bad on the grill."

"All right, but if it's not grilled to perfection, you owe me dinner another night." She points her finger at Zach to emphasize her point.

Her ultimatum has all three of the guys doubling over with laughter. "How do you . . ." He takes a deep breath. "How do you deal with her every day?" Zach sputters through his laughter.

I smile at the three of them and shrug. "She keeps life entertaining."

Kara smiles at my words, obviously satisfied with my answer. "I also have a surprise for you," she tells Zach.

"I'm done. I can't run after that." He looks at Kara. "What kind of surprise?"

She laces her arms through Tanner's. "You'll just have to wait to find out." She winks.

"Tanner, she's your girl. Can't you pull it out of her?" Zach asks.

Tanner looks down at Kara. "I could but what's the fun in that?"

We all laugh. Kara is one of a kind and Tanner is perfect for her.

"Let's go hit the bikes for another mile." Zach places his arm around my shoulders.

"Eww, you're drenched in sweat," I scold him, trying to duck under his arm, but he holds tight.

"So are you, sweetheart." He chuckles.

Kara gets a little too close, coming to my rescue. She's not fast enough and he snags his other arm around her.

Seeing my struggle just minutes before, we both give up trying to get away from him and allow him to lead us back to the gym. Truth be told, I'm glad. Zach is great at distracting me from Nate.

"Take it easy on my girl," Tanner calls out.

"You heard the man; take it easy on me." Kara pokes Zach in the ribs.

"Hey, what if he was talking about me?" I pretend to be offended.

"Find your own man." Kara and I laugh as we let Zach lead us into the gym.

10

Nate

I CAN'T TELL IF he's interested in her or if he's just being his usual flirty self. When he put his arm around her, I wanted to rip it off. My anger did come down a notch or two when he did the same thing to Kara. As I watch the three of them walk into the gym, I realize it's not going away. I really like her and I can't just turn it off. In other words, I'm fucked.

Making my way into the gym, I see all four of them are on the stationary bikes. The bike next to Ava is open. Suddenly, my spirits are lifted. Zach has placed himself between both girls, yet again, making it hard to get a read on him. Tanner is on the other side of Kara.

I climb on the bike and listen to their conversation. Kara is asking for details about dinner and Ava volunteers to make dessert.

"Dirt cake?" I speak up for the first time.

Ava turns to me and a smile lights her face. "I haven't had dirt cake in forever!"

"What exactly is dirt cake?" Zach asks hesitantly.

Ava laughs and I wish I could bottle the sound.

"It's yummy freaking goodness, is what it is," Kara chimes in.

"It's a dessert made with Oreo cookies, vanilla pudding, and a few other ingredients. It's so good. Don't try it or you might become addicted."

"Damn it, I just vowed to stick to my training meal plan," Zach pouts.

"Sucks to be you," Tanner goads him.

"It's worth falling off the wagon for, my man. Trust me," I tell Zach.

"You gonna make me a dirt cake, Ava?" He winks at her and I want to punch him.

"Yes. I only have class until two, so that will give me plenty of time to make one."

"Double the batch," Kara requests. "We can leave one at the house and take the other to Zach's."

"Probably a good idea," Ava says. "The last time I made dirt cake, it was gone within twenty-four hours, and it was just the two of us." Ava laughs as she slows down on the bike. "Sounds like a plan. We gotta go, Kara. I have to get ready for class."

"All right, Mr. Grill Master, we'll see you tonight at seven," Kara says to Zach. "You gonna be there?" she asks Tanner.

He nods, not bothering to look to Zach for an invitation.

"What about you?" she asks me.

"Yeah, I'll be there," I tell her. Technically I was not invited either, but Ava Mae will be there, so yeah, I'm in.

"Great, catch ya later," she calls over her shoulder. I stare after them.

"I love to watch them walk away." Zach smirks beside me.

"Which one?" I ask. I try to keep my cool. Maybe it's Kara he's into.

"Fuck, man, have you seen them? Both of them."

I grit my teeth at his answer. "You can't have them both."

"Fuck no, you can't. Kara's mine," Tanner grumbles.

Zach laughs. "Well, damn, sounds like they're both unavailable."

Unavailable? He has to be talking about Kara. "I didn't know Ava was seeing anyone." I've been spending all my time worrying about Zach and looks like some other schmuck might have wormed his way in. Shit!

"She's not." He smirks. "Not yet anyway."

"What the fuck are you talking about?" He's confusing the hell out of me with this word play.

"Ava, she's not technically unavailable, but I have a feeling she will be soon," he explains.

"Who?" I clench my jaw to keep from going off. It pisses me off that he knows something about her that I don't. I know it's irrational but it pisses me off just the same.

Zach chuckles. "You. If you can pull your head out of your ass long enough to see what's right in front of you. I've tried everything I can think of to make you jealous and confess, but nothing I do seems to work. I figured it out that night at the club."

"He's right, you know," Tanner says. "You can slice through the heat in the room when you two are together."

Zach grips my shoulder. "Nate, that girl has it bad for you, almost as bad as you have it for her. Open your damn eyes or she's going to slip out of your reach."

"I can't . . . she's not . . . Fuck! Brody." I sound like a tool, not able to form complete sentences, but he's totally shocked me with his theory. I thought I was hiding how I felt for her.

"Make him understand." He shrugs.

"He'll kick my ass and never speak to me again."

"Maybe, maybe not. I guess you need to decide who you want more. Ava, the girl who you are obviously crazy about, or Brody, your lifelong best friend who you see, what, once a year?"

"I don't want to have to choose."

"See, that right there, perfect example. You have real feelings for this girl. Nate, you two are the only ones who can't see it."

"I can see it, see her. She's all I fucking see. I was able to push it to the back of my mind for the last few years, but now . . . well, now I can't," I confess.

"Look, I get it. You and Brody have been friends forever. I can see you not wanting to mess that up, but answer me this one question. Can Brody keep you warm at night?" He turns and walks away.

Fuck!

No, Brody can't keep me warm at night, but now I'm picturing Ava Mae curled up beside me. I've fought like hell to keep those kinds of images out of my head, but now, fuck me, it's all I can think about.

I stalk to the locker room and quickly shower. When I'm finished, I find Zach ready and waiting in the ring with Tanner. We push through his session. I'm distracted, so he's gets an easy day. It's his fault, after all.

As soon as Zach's session ends, I head straight home. I'm too distracted to be at work. I shower again, then grab a beer and head out to the back deck. My phone rings and I don't bother looking at the screen before answering.

"Yeah."

"Nate?" My father's voice comes across the line.

"What's up, Dad?"

"You okay, son?"

"Yes . . . No . . . Hell, I don't know."

"Is it the gym?"

"No, it's not the gym. Everything there is running just fine. It's a girl," I admit.

"I see. Do I know this girl who has you being short with your old man?" he asks.

I release a heavy sigh. "Yeah, you do actually. It's Ava Mae." I wait for him to tell me how wrong I am, but that's not what happens.

"About damn time you admit it, boy," he booms in his deep voice.

What. The. Fuck.

"Dad? What do you mean, it's about time?" I ask, confused. This seems to be happening to me a lot today.

"Nathan, boy, you've had a thing for that girl for years. You've always just been too damn stubborn to do anything about it."

"What makes you say that?" I'm shocked at this revelation.

"Let's see, how about the fact you were a teenage boy who didn't care if your best friend's little sister always had to tag along. You used to volunteer to bring her home from practice if Brody or their parents were not available. If that's not enough, how about the day you left for the Marines? She hugged you and you held on to her as if your entire world was crashing down. I'm not blind, son."

My mind carries me back to that day. She was hugging me just as tightly, and I pretended it was all for me.

"She's Brody's little sister," I say. This is my only defense and it's also the only obstacle keeping me from pursuing her.

"That she is. She's also a beautiful young woman who, if my predictions are correct, still harbors feelings for you."

"It's against the rules, Dad. You can't date your best friend's little sister. Brody would never forgive me."

"Whose rule? If you were just fooling around with her, not caring about her feelings, I could see it. Brody's a smart man. He trusts you with her. You just have to prove to him he can trust you with her heart. That's what you want, son, right? You want Ava's heart?"

Is that what I want? I picture her big brown eyes and her long brown hair, and I know without a doubt I do. "She already has mine."

"I know she does, son."

Shit! I said that aloud. "Dad, I don't know what to do." My voice is pleading. I'm really at a loss. Do I follow with what I know my heart wants or keep fighting it for the sake of my best friend?

"Nathan, you have to live your life for you. I understand you feel like you're betraying Brody, but once he sees how you feel about her, he'll come around. There is no way he could not be okay with the two of you together. You just have to do good by her, love her right."

"Thanks, Dad." I need time to process all of this.

"Follow your heart, boy."

Love her right . . .

I beat the girls to Zach's place and I'm glad. My conversation with Dad, piggybacking on my earlier conversation with Zach, and my head is jumbled. "Hey, Z, need any help?" I ask.

"Nah, I'm good. Have the steaks marinating, salad's made, and potatoes are wrapped," he says, leading me out to the back deck. "You seem to be in a better mood."

"Yeah." I consider telling him about my talk with Dad, but change my mind. I need to think about what this means. I can't start something with her and not be all in. If I'm going to chance my friendship with Brody, I need to be unwavering in my decision.

"The girls are on their way," Zach says. "Kara called to make sure she approved of what else was on the menu."

I laugh at that. "She does seem to be a handful, doesn't she?"

"Fuck, yes she is. Tanner is in trouble with that one."

I remain in my seat while Zach goes to greet the girls, and by the sound of their voices, Tanner has arrived as well. There is so much going on in my head right now; I can't process it all. I debate whether I should call Brody and just confess it all and see what happens. Then I realize what if they're wrong? What if Ava doesn't feel that way? Then I've lost my best friend for no reason.

"You ladies have a seat with Nate while I throw everything on the grill," Zach instructs as they join me on the back deck. I look up to see, not only is Tanner here, but a third girl. She's a short blonde. I realize this must be Zach's surprise Kara was talking about. I feel a little lighter knowing we're all paired up now. I no longer feel in competition with Zach, even though he reassured me earlier that's not the case.

Kara bounces, yes, bounces, over to the grill, stating she needs to supervise. The blonde is hot on her heels, not taking her eyes off Zach. Ava Mae, she sits next to me. "Hey, Nate."

I briefly close my eyes, letting the sound of her voice surround me before turning to look at her. "Ava Mae, did you guys find the place okay?" Small talk, I'm making small talk.

She smiles and it takes all my willpower to remain seated and not pull her into my lap. "Yeah," is her one word reply. She's twisting her hands together. Is she nervous? Without thinking, I reach over and place my hand over hers. She immediately stills as I run my thumb across her knuckles. Her skin is so soft. "Nate?" Her voice is low and strangled.

Lifting her left hand to my lips, I kiss her wrist. I hear her breath hitch, and my eyes find hers. I see it. She feels this, just like I do.

Decision made, I want her.

"Ava, can I have dirt cake now?" Zach calls from the grill. She immediately pulls her hand from my grasp and looks toward Zach. I watch her as she visibly relaxes; he must not be watching us.

"If you . . ." She clears her throat. "If you want, I can dish you a piece," she replies, her voice stronger.

"No! You need to wait with the rest of us, you big oaf," Kara scolds Zach.

"What about me? Can I have a piece?" Tanner asks her.

Kara giggles.

The four of them join us. "Nate, this is Monica. Monica, this is Nate," Zach introduces me to the blonde.

I tip my head in greeting. "Nice to meet you."

"You too. I've heard a lot about you," she replies. I feel a spark of hope that maybe Ava has been talking to her about me.

"So, where did you learn your grill master skills?" Kara asks Zach.

"My dad. He loved to grill and made sure I knew how as well. We had more dinners on the grill than I can remember."

"It smells amazing," Ava compliments him.

Zach reaches over and squeezes her knee. "Just wait until you taste it, sweetheart." He winks.

I stare him down until he can feel me looking at him. When he finally catches my gaze, he smirks at me. Asshole. He needs to stop touching her, and winking at her, and calling her sweetheart. He's doing it on purpose, and it's pissing me off for more reasons than one.

11
Ava Mae

*H*OLY SHIT! MY heart is beating so hard; I'm sure they can hear it. Nate kissed me. Well, he kissed my wrist, and it was not brotherly. I have no idea what he wants or what it means, but I'm freaking the fuck out! I was hoping Zach would take me up on the offer to serve him some dirt cake so I could get away . . . get some space from what just happened.

What just happened?

"Can I use your restroom?" Kara asks. I jump to my feet and follow her. She gives me a curious look. Yes, we are going together in pairs just like the cliché. I need some space. I hope she got all that from the simple nod I give her.

As soon as we're in the house, she's all over me. "What's wrong?" she asks, concerned. "Your face is flushed. You feel okay?" she fires off.

I nod and pull her down the hall to the bathroom. Once we are both inside, I sit on the edge of the tub and take a deep breath.

"Ava, you're scaring me. What's going on?"

"He kissed me," I whisper. I still can't believe it happened.

"What? Who kissed you?"

"Nate, he, uh, he kissed my wrist," I rush to tell her.

"So let me get this straight. Nate kissed your wrist, which I'm not sure I fully understand, but he kissed your wrist and you're having a panic attack? Do I have that right?"

I focus on breathing for several minutes until I can get myself under control. "Yes." I go on to explain what happened and how I've had a thing for him for years.

"I tried to tell you he was into you. There is no way he would risk his friendship with your brother to play games with you. You need to talk to him."

"I know, and I will. I just needed a minute. I've crushed on him for years. Years, Kara. I just needed a minute," I tell her.

Kara leans down and hugs me. "I've seen the way he looks at you. Take a chance, Ava." With that, she leaves me to compose myself.

Splashing some water on my face, and with one more deep breath, I open the door. What I find surprises me. Nate is standing against the wall, arms and legs crossed. "Ava Mae." He steps toward me. Cupping my cheek with his hand, he says, "Are you okay?" His voice is soft.

I cover his hand with mine, relishing the feel of his touch. "I'm good. Just needed a minute to . . . take a breather."

"I'm sorry if I overstepped." His thumb strokes my cheek.

"N-no, you didn't. I just wasn't . . . expecting it. That's all." Our eyes remain locked.

"I know; I wasn't either. You're beautiful." He pulls me into a hug. "So fucking beautiful, you're all I can think about."

I relax against him. "Nate, what are you doing?" I need to know what this is. Has he been drinking?

"I don't know, Ava Mae. I have no idea. What I do know is I have fought what I feel for you for far too long. I've worried about losing my best friend, but I'm starting to think losing a chance to see what we have could be just as tragic."

"What we have?" Am I hearing him right? I must be dreaming.

"Yes, what we have." He places my hands on his chest above his heart. I can feel the rapid beat. "Every damn time I'm near you, my heart wants to explode. I've been able to push this away for so long. So long I pretended what I felt was just lust or a crush. It's not." He steps closer and our bodies are now aligned; the heat is a jolt to my system. "I want you, Ava Mae. Please tell me you feel this, too. I'm going out of my damn mind with wanting you, and watching Zach and the guys flirt with you, touch you." He brings his forehead to mine. "Tell me you feel it."

I swallow the lump forming in my throat. "I have for years." My voice cracks. "Nate, we need to think about this. We can't just jump into something, and we just need to . . . think about this. Brody will—"

He shakes his head. "I have thought about it, and worried about it, but I'm certain the rewards by far outweigh the risks." He steps closer, our bodies now touching. "You set the pace. Whenever you're ready for this, I'm yours." Leaning in, he places a tender kiss on my forehead. "I can wait for you. As long as I know I'm who you want, I can wait as long as you need."

We stay like this for several minutes. His hands are gripping my hips, keeping my body close to his. "I need to hear you say it, baby. I need to hear you say I'm who you want. Everything else will come later. I just need to hear you say it."

My head is spinning and my heart is racing. For so long I've wanted Nate to notice me as more, and here I am, wrapped in his arms. He's asking me to tell him I want him. I'm scared to take that leap, afraid of what Brody will say, of what our parents will say. Nate moves his hands around my back and buries his face in my neck. I tremble at the contact. I want him. I've always wanted him. I wrap my arms around him, returning his embrace.

This is what I want.

"Yes," I whisper.

I hear him suck in a breath. His lips graze my neck before he lifts his head, and a smile lights his face. "Say it again."

"Yes, Nate, you are what I want. I don't know what that means, or how my brother is going to take it. However, right now, wrapped in your arms, I don't care," I admit. "Besides, you said we'll go slowly, right? That we'll make sure we figure out where this is going?"

Leaning in, he kisses my temple. "Anything you want; you set the pace," he assures me. "Now, I believe we have a steak to eat." Placing his hand on the small of my back, he leads me back outside to join our friends.

I have no idea how long we've been gone, but the four of them don't seem to notice. Kara and Tanner are lip-locked in a lounge chair, and Zach and Monica are talking by the grill.

Nate leads me to the chairs opposite Kara and Tanner. We take separate chairs, even though I want to curl up in his arms. Is it possible to miss that feeling already when I've only had it for minutes?

He takes the chair beside me. Reaching out, he drags me and my lounger a little closer to his. My eyes widen with shock at the move. Leaning into me, he whispers, "I just want you next to me." I pinch my thigh and flinch from the pain. "Ava Mae, what the hell are you doing?" he asks. Looking up, I see he's staring at the angry red patch of skin on my thigh. I feel my face heat with embarrassment.

"I, um, well, I just wanted to make sure I wasn't dreaming," I confess. I wait for the laughter, but instead, I'm rewarded with a bright smile.

"This is real, you and me. I can't fight it anymore. Hell, I don't want to fight it anymore." Reaching over, he gently strokes my reddened thigh.

"Time to eat," Zach yells over his shoulder. He doesn't bother turning around. He's having a hard enough time keeping his attention on the grill. Monica seems to be keeping him quite entertained.

I watch as Kara and Tanner disentangle themselves and head toward the grill. Nate stands and holds his hand out for me. I take it and allow him to pull me to my feet. With his hand on the small of my back, he leads us to the table.

Never in my wildest fantasies did I think this was how the night would turn out. I feel a pang of guilt when I think about Brody. No doubt he's going to be pissed. He should be happy his best friend is interested in me. He trusts Nate with his life, why not mine?

12

Nate

*I*T TAKES WORK. I mean real effort to keep the beaming-ass smile off my face. I know I need to play this cool, but damn, I held her, and she said she wants me too. Zach and Tanner will be able to see right through me if I don't mask this shit. It's not that I want to hide her, or how I feel about her, but I told her she sets the pace. I meant that. I would never rush or push her into something she's not ready for. A few stolen touches and a kiss here and there, and I'm a happy man.

We reach the table and Ava steps away from me, my hand falling from the small of her back. She and her friends are opening containers and getting the table ready while Zach pulls the meat and baked potatoes from the grill. If it were up to me, my body would be pressed next to hers while she does this, but I remain standing where she left me.

"Let's eat," Zach says, pulling my attention away from Ava. Everyone takes a seat around the table. It's a table for four, and there are six of us. Normally, I would complain about this, but not tonight. I can see my boys don't seem to mind either. We all have the girls' chairs pulled close to our sides.

"All right, Miss Kara." Zach's voice is serious. "You get first dibs."

Kara wastes no time choosing a steak and plopping it on her plate. We all watch as she cuts into it and takes her first bite. She moans. "Holy shit, this is delicious."

"Told ya," Zach quips.

The rest of us dig in while Kara continues to eat her steak, not bothering to add anything else to her plate.

"Kara, is that all you're eating?" Tanner asks her.

"Hell no, but this is too good to stop." She laughs then takes another bite.

Tanner nods, satisfied with her answer. I've not spent much time with Tanner outside of the gym, but he seems to be a standup guy. Great fighter. He's not one to brag about girls he takes home, so I don't know that side of him either. I hope things don't turn ugly for them. I don't want anything to stand in the way of what Ava Mae and I started here tonight. I want to see this through, see where it takes us.

Once we all have our plates made, the conversation is easy. Kara continues to rave about Zach's grill master qualities, making us all laugh. Monica asks Zach about his upcoming fight, which leads to teaching the girls the basics. I cut my steak into small pieces and fix my potato just how I like it. Add a little dressing to my salad and, suddenly, I can eat one handed. Brilliant plan, I know. I slip my hand under the table and rest it on Ava's thigh. I'm not trying to push her or make it sexual; I just want to feel her skin. She jumps at the contact and turns to face me. My eyes never leave hers, and no words are exchanged. I softly stroke my thumb back and forth, waiting for her reaction.

She takes a deep breath and I see her relax. She turns back to her plate and continues eating. I can't resist touching her when she's this close. She didn't seem angry, just surprised. We need to talk more later about what she wants. I told her she could set the pace, and I mean it, but she needs to let me know what that is, where my boundaries are. If not, I might push her too far too fast, and I don't want that. I want to do this at a speed she's comfortable with, whatever speed gets us to the endpoint of her being mine. In my eyes, she already is. I just need for her to catch up.

Dinner passes in a blur. I chime in here and there during the conversation, but for the most part, I eat quietly, enjoying being next to her.

"Dirt cake," Zach announces, pushing back from the table.

"Yeah, I need to try this infamous dessert," Tanner adds.

Ava chuckles. I love that sound. "I'll be right back." She glances at me. I take that as my cue to move my hand from her leg. I do so reluctantly. Helping her scoot her chair back, I ask, "You need some help?"

"I got it. I need to use the restroom anyway," Monica answers.

Shit. I was hoping to get her alone, maybe hold her again. Instead, I nod and watch them as they walk into the house. Turning back to the table, all eyes are on me.

"You need to man up and tell her," Zach says. Tanner nods in agreement. Kara is smirking; she knows about earlier. I was standing outside the bathroom when she came out.

"I did. I can't fight it. Brody's going to be pissed, but . . . she's worth it," I confess.

"Make him understand, dude. I've known you for two years and never seen you look at anyone the way you do her. Never seen anyone get under your skin."

"You're right, Zach," Kara agrees. "He needs to make him understand. She's crazy about you, always has been." She looks toward the door. "Make sure she's what you really want and then fight like hell for her. She deserves nothing less."

The patio door opens, keeping me from responding. Keeping me from telling them I've never been more sure of anything in my life. "You ready for this?" Ava taunts Zach and Tanner with the pan she has in her hands.

"Damn right I am." Zach laughs. "I've been on this strict training diet for weeks. It's time I indulge a little."

Monica and Ava dish out the dirt cake. Kara insists the three newbies take their first bite together. Zach and Tanner are practically drooling over their plates.

After everyone has a plate in front of them, Kara gives the go-ahead. "Holy fucking shit! This is amazing," Zach says, shoving another spoonful in his mouth.

"Damn," Tanner says, doing the same thing.

Ava Mae's face lights up. "It's good, right?" she says.

"Good doesn't do it justice, sweetheart." Zach takes his last bite. "You have to take that with you when you leave or I'll devour the rest of it tonight," he says.

"I will gladly take it home with me," Tanner volunteers.

"This is great, Ava," Monica agrees.

"Told you so," Kara pipes in.

My hand, which has once again found its way to her thigh, gives a gentle squeeze. This causes her to turn and look at me. She has just a little dab of dirt cake on the corner of her mouth. I drop my spoon on my plate and lift my hand to her face. I gently wipe it away with my thumb, and bring it to my mouth to lick it clean. Her eyes go wide and she wiggles in her seat. I continue to stroke her thigh as I pick up my spoon and finish my dessert.

This night is one to remember. She wants me, and nothing is better than that. I have an onslaught of emotions running through me and I'm staring them head on. I'm ready for whatever she's willing to offer.

"You all in a hurry to get home? We can head in and watch a movie, or we could build a fire," Zach suggests.

All three girls seem to have a silent conversation. "It's a little chilly," Kara comments.

"Even with a fire, I think it's a little much for me," Monica replies.

I feel Ava shiver and goose bumps cover her skin. "You okay to stay and watch a movie?" I ask loud enough only she can hear.

"Movie then?" Tanner asks.

"Sounds good," Monica and Kara reply at the same time.

Ava turns to me. "Yes," she whispers. This is the second time tonight she's said that one word and it causes my heart to flutter in my chest. I'm not ready to end the night.

"You three head inside while we clean up," I suggest.

"Go ahead and pick out a movie," Zach adds.

The girls waste no time shuffling into the house. I didn't realize the chill in the air, sitting so close to her. I need to pay more attention. Take better care of her.

Standing to clear the table, I see Zach staring at the door. I turn to see what he's looking at and notice Monica standing at the kitchen island talking to Ava as she wraps up the leftover dirt cake. "Looks like Kara brought you a good gift," Tanner says.

"Best gift ever." Zach grins.

We make quick work of cleaning up. None of us admitting that the three beautiful girls in the house are our motivation.

13

"**S**PILL," KARA DEMANDS as soon as the door closes behind her.

"He was waiting for me," I tell her.

"I know. He was there when I walked out of the bathroom," she admits. I tell her what happened as quickly as possible.

"Wow. He's hooked." Monica laughs.

"What makes you say that?" I ask her.

"You can tell by the way he looks at you. His eyes follow you. Like now." She tilts her head toward the deck. Looking out the corner of my eye, I see all three guys looking at us.

"It's all of them," I argue.

"Yes, but he's been doing that all night."

"And, holy shit, when he wiped the cake from your lip and then sucked his finger, the heat between the two of you was off the charts," Kara comments. "No cobwebs for the woo-hoo," she singsongs.

I feel my face blush. "I'm not even going to ask." Monica laughs.

"Ava—" I stop Kara from saying anymore by placing my hand over her mouth. Just in the nick of time because the door opens and the guys walk in. My face heats because they could have heard us.

"What are you three up to?" Tanner questions.

"Just waiting on you," Kara fires back with a wink in my direction.

"Did you pick a movie?" Zach asks as he steps next to Monica.

She gazes up at him. "No, we thought we'd wait on you all and we could pick together."

"Perfect." He throws his arm over her shoulders and leads her into the living room.

"Hey now, we get a say," Kara grumbles as she tugs Tanner behind her, following them. Tanner's laughing at her. I'm glad she's met someone who can deal with her antics.

Strong hands grip my hips and I realize it's just me and Nate left. "Ready, sweets?" he asks.

"Yes." I can't seem to form any other words with him touching me.

"This is going to sound like high school, but I don't care. Can you sit next to me? I promise to be good. I just want to be next to you." He tucks my hair behind my ear.

"Ava, Nate, get your asses in here; we're starting the movie," Kara yells.

Nate's hands are still gripping my hips and his eyes are watching me, waiting for an answer. I nod my agreement. I watch in fascination as a slow smile graces his lips. Leaning down, he kisses my temple before turning me and leading me to the group with his hand on the small of my back.

It doesn't escape me how he hasn't stopped touching me tonight. Is this how it's going to be? Stolen touches and innocent kisses?

In the living room, the only light is coming from the big screen television hanging on the wall. Kara and Tanner are curled up in the oversized chair, and Zach and Monica are sitting on the couch. There is a spot next to Monica on the couch and the loveseat is open. Nate, with his hand still on the small of my back, guides me toward the loveseat. It's in the darkest corner of the room.

Nate sits first, pulling me down beside him. I settle next to him, my body aligned with his.

"Ready?" Zach asks.

"Yep," Nate says, throwing his arm over the back of the loveseat. I want him to put his arm around me and pull me into him. I've thought about it thousands of times.

Zach hits play and I laugh when I see the movie choice. Jerry McGuire. Kara loves this movie. I'm sure she influenced the selection. I don't really care what we watch. I doubt I will be paying much attention. How can I when the guy I've dreamed of being mine for years is sitting next to me. The same guy who not two hours earlier declared he wants me. We could watch the news for all I care. I'm one happy girl, sitting here nestled against Nate.

Not twenty minutes into the movie, I start yawning and can barely keep my eyes open. I try adjusting my position and sitting up straighter to keep from falling asleep. I glance over at Monica and she's out, resting her head against the opposite end of the couch from Zach. He has his hands draped over her legs. Kara is curled up in a ball on Tanner's lap, eyes closed. Tanner holds her, his eyes locked on the screen.

I feel his arm slide around my shoulders and his hand pulls my body close to his. "Lean on me," he whispers in a deep sexy voice. I'm too exhausted to be embarrassed; instead, I take what he's offering and rest my head against his chest. I hear the rhythm of his heartbeat against my ear. Nate strokes his hand through my hair and within minutes, I'm relaxed and starting to doze off.

I'm warm and comfortable. I can smell Nate and I don't want to wake up from this dream. "Ava Mae." He's the only one who calls me that. My parents used to when I was younger and in trouble, but Nate, he always does. It's his thing. I can hear him as if he's right next to me. I squeeze my eyes tightly, not wanting to lose the sound of his voice. I hear a deep chuckle. "Come on, beautiful, open those big brown eyes for me."

My eyes pop open. I'm lying on a chest, Nate's chest. I push myself up and away from him. "I'm sorry. I didn't mean to . . . I'm sorry." I'm humiliated. I fell asleep on him.

"Hey." His hand frames the side of my face. "It's fine. I wanted to hold you."

I melt at his words. I remember now how tired I was and Nate telling me to lean on him. It wasn't a dream.

"You're not the only one who passed out." He points to the others. Everyone is asleep.

"Did you sleep?" I whisper.

He shakes his head. "No way was I going to miss you being in my arms."

Again, I melt. This is a side of Nate I've never seen. He's always been good to me, but this is a whole other level.

He leans in closer, his lips mere inches from mine. "I've tried to resist you. I fought this, but I couldn't escape you. You were suddenly front and center in my life, at the gym, the club. My friends became your friends. I've wanted you for so long; I was afraid if I closed my eyes, you would disappear."

Butterflies. Thousands of butterflies are dancing in my stomach. I clear my throat before I say, "I'm right here," as I lean in closer to his lips.

"I see you," he whispers as he presses his lips to mine.

The kiss is short and sweet, and perfect for this moment. I will never forget this, the first time his lips meet mine. He's completely swept the rug out from under me. I wasn't expecting this, and I'm worried about Brody, but after tonight, after knowing what it's like to have his attention, I can't go back. I don't know what that means and I'm scared to death of what Brody is going to say, but I can't stop this. I don't want to stop this.

14

Nate

I'M COMPLETELY CAPTIVATED by her. I hate that it's time for the night to end, but she needs to get home and get a good night's sleep, and I have to be up early to open the gym. "We should probably wake them," I say, motioning to our friends.

"You're right." She pulls herself off the couch and I have the urge to pull her back. I watch as she shakes Kara awake. Tanner tightens his hold on her and I know exactly how he feels. They mumble softly. Ava nods and Kara snuggles back into Tanner. Next is Monica, she shakes her awake and Zach's eyes pop open. He watches as the girls chat quietly.

Zach turns to me. "You taking her home?" he asks.

Before I can answer, Tanner and Kara stand up. "We're heading out," he informs us. Kara offers us a sleepy smile and a wave as they head toward the front door.

"I guess he's taking her home," I say to Zach.

"She's going home with him," Ava says. "Monica, time to go." Ava shakes her again and her eyes open.

"Kara's going home with Tanner," she says to Monica. "I'll drop you off, or you can sleep in her bed."

"I have to work in the morning." She rubs her eyes.

"Okay, I'll drop you off," Ava agrees.

I look at the time and it's after midnight. I don't like the thought of her out late by herself. "I can drive you. You're both tired and I would never forgive myself if something happened to either of you," I tell them.

"Nate, I can—"

"I can drive Monica. It will give me a chance to convince her to go out with me tomorrow night." Zach winks at her. Monica smiles at him, suddenly wide awake.

"Nate, I need my car," Ava whines.

I stand and hold my hand out for her. She just looks at it. Shit. I'm already in the doghouse. "Ava Mae, I can pick you up and bring you to your car tomorrow whenever you need it," I promise.

"I was planning on running in the morning," she says.

"At the gym?" I ask. Excitement bubbles up that I'm going to get to see her again so soon.

"Yeah, if that's okay."

Is that okay? Hell yes, it's okay. "Yes, you're welcome there anytime you want."

"That means you have to get up early just to come and get me. I can drive," she argues.

Does she not realize that getting up early to see her isn't a hardship? Hell, I've done it the past two days just in the hope I might get to see her. Since she won't come to me, I step next to her. "It's not a problem; I want to. Please let me do this. I won't sleep if I'm worried about you getting home safe." I probably won't sleep regardless; I'm too keyed up from everything that happened tonight. I keep that part to myself.

Ava turns to Monica. "Are you letting Zach drive you home?"

Monica nods and grins at Zach. Ava sighs. "Fine, you can drive me home," she concedes.

This night just keeps getting better and better. I place my lips next to her ear. "Thank you," I whisper.

"All right, well, I guess I'll see the two of you in the morning for our run. I'll text Tanner and let him know in case they want to join us," Zach says, pulling out his phone.

"Don't count on it," Ava mumbles. "That girl takes any excuse she can not to run with me."

"What time do you run, Ava?" Monica asks.

"Six. Nate lets us use the track at his gym."

"Count me in. This Color Run you and Kara have been talking about sounds fun." She smiles.

Zach puts his arm around her shoulders. "The boys and I are doing the Color Run too. I'm helping train them," he boasts.

Monica stands on her tiptoes. "Bring it," she says as she places a loud smacking kiss against his cheek.

This causes all of us to laugh. I slip my hand into Ava's. "You ready to head out?" I'm ready to have her all to myself.

"Yeah." She hugs Monica and, much to my dismay, Zach, goodbye, and we're on our way. I open the door for her, not because she's not capable, but because I want to do nice things for her. Climbing behind the wheel, I glance over and make sure she's strapped in. Reaching over the console, I lace my fingers through hers and bring them to my lips. I place a kiss on the back of her hand before resting our joined hands back in her lap. My thumb rubs over her knuckles. Her skin is soft and I can't get enough.

Neither one of us talk. We ride in comfortable silence. When I pull into the lot of her apartment complex, I shut off the engine, but don't bother to make a move to get out. I don't want tonight to end.

"Nate, what's next?" she asks. I can hear the slight tremble in her voice.

I turn to face her, still holding tight to her hand. "Ava Mae, I have no expectations here. I just . . . want you." I chuckle. "It sounds weird to finally be saying that to you, but I don't know how else to explain it."

"What are we . . . I mean, are we . . . dating? Do we tell Brody? Our families? My mind is racing with all these questions. I still feel like this is all a dream."

"We are what you want us to be. You can tell whoever you want. You set the pace, Ava Mae. I'm all in, no matter what you decide," I try to reassure her.

She's quiet as she processes what I just said. "I think we need to go slowly. I don't want to ruin a lifelong friendship, and then we end up deciding we're not compatible. I say we keep it low-key, see what happens. You might wake up tomorrow and regret tonight." She laughs, but it's not because it's funny. She's nervous.

"I won't, but if that's what you want, I'm okay with that. I do have one request that I can't budge on," I tell her.

Her eyes find mine as she waits for me to tell her. I release her hand, and place mine on her neck. My thumb traces her lips while I lean in close. "Until we figure this out, you're mine. No dating other people, just me and you." I could not handle knowing another man is touching her. "I don't care how you refer to me: a friend, a guy you're dating, your boyfriend." Her breath hitches on that one. "The title doesn't matter. What matters is that no one gets you but me until you're done with me." I lean in a little closer. "Can you do that for me, Ava Mae? Can you be mine?" I ask her.

"Yes," she replies, her voice soft.

I close the distance and kiss her. I mean, really kiss her. She moans in the back of her throat and I slide my tongue past her lips. Her tongue slides against mine and I savor the fact she's here with me. My hand tangles in her hair, trying to pull her closer. I can't seem to get close enough. I've thought about doing this a thousand times and nothing could have prepared me for the taste of her.

Ava pulls back. I don't let her get far as I rest my forehead against hers. I watch as her chest rapidly rises and falls with each breath. It's in this moment I know I will never be the same, not after that kiss. It's not possible. The kiss literally stole my breath.

She's amazing.

She wants me too.

"I better go," she finally whispers. I don't want to let her go, but I know I need to.

I place another chaste kiss against her lips before climbing out and coming around to open her door. Unable to resist, I put my arm around her and tuck her against me as we walk to her apartment. I slow my pace, taking my time. I'm not ready to leave her. When we reach her door, Ava puts both arms around me and hugs me tight. Looking up, her big brown eyes find mine. "Thank you, Nate. I'll see you in the morning."

I lean down and kiss her, one last goodnight. "Night, baby. Make sure you lock the door behind you," I remind her.

Ava nods and unlocks the door. She walks straight in without looking back. I listen for her to secure the lock before heading back to my Tahoe. I'm already counting down the hours until I can see her again.

15

Ava Mae

SLEEP WAS LIMITED last night. It was after one by the time I crawled into bed and I kept running every second of the night through my mind. I'm running on about three hours of sleep.

Nate: Morning, beautiful. I'll be there in five.

I read the message three times before it hits me, five minutes! I'm too busy swooning over the 'Morning, beautiful' part. I need to get my ass in gear. I grab a hoodie and my running shoes. I'm barely finished tying them when there's a knock at the door. Damn, five minutes flies.

I take a deep breath before opening the door. I need to keep my cool. "Good morning," I say when I open to see him standing on the other side. He's freshly showered and sporting a five o'clock shadow. He's sexy as sin.

Leaning in, he places a soft kiss against my lips. "Morning," he says.

I look up at him. "Just one second, let me grab my phone." I rush back to the bathroom and grab my phone from the counter. "Ready."

Nate leads me to his Tahoe. He opens the door for me and rushes to his side. Once he's in, he opens a bag and hands me a bagel. "Cinnamon cream cheese still your favorite?" he asks.

I'm shocked he even remembered. Before I can answer, he hands me a Hardcorps travel mug. "Orange juice. I know you like that for breakfast, or at least you used to." He grins.

"How did you—"

"Ava Mae, this isn't new for me. I've always cared about you. Paid attention to what you liked and didn't like." He starts the Tahoe and pulls out of the lot. "I will have to say things really started to change for me at the going away party," he confesses.

I have no idea what to say, so instead, I take a bite of my bagel. I'm still having a hard time processing that we've both felt this way all this time.

"You hugged me goodbye and there were tears in your eyes. I pretended they were really for me. That you were going to miss me." He takes a drink of what I assume is coffee. "Then you wrote to me. Every week you wrote, just like you did Brody. You kept me going, kept both of us going. When we were deployed . . ." He clears his throat. "When we were deployed, it was . . . hard. Getting your letters, even if they were six at a time after weeks of not having any, they kept us going. Brody and I both looked forward to them."

"I didn't know," I say quietly. "I just missed you, both of you." I take a drink of orange juice and decide to lay it all out there just like he is. "Those tears were for you. Well, both of you, but when I hugged you, those were for you."

Nate nods and places his hand on my thigh. We ride the rest of the way in silence. I finish my breakfast and he's content to leave his hand on my thigh and hum to the radio.

We arrive at Hardcorps and find Zach and Monica standing by his Hummer. "Thought you were going to stand us up," Zach chides.

"Nope, just making sure Ava Mae had breakfast. You guys ready?"

"Yeah. Tanner texted about twenty minutes ago and said he would be here for training, but he and Kara aren't going to make it for the run."

"Why am I not surprised? She better not leave me hanging with this Color Run," Ava says. I can tell she's irritated.

"We got this," Monica says. "We'll drag her ass here if we have to." She laughs.

"I can make it hard on Tanner during our sessions. Bribe him to get her here, if they're going to be spending so much time together," Zach jokes.

"I just might have to take you up on that, Zach," Ava says. "Let's do this. I need a nap."

16

ZACH AND I watch as the two of them jog off toward the track. I want to run after her, but I know she needs her space too. A lot has been said between us in the last twenty-four hours. I have to remember not to push her.

"So, did you talk to her?" Zach asks.

"Yeah, turns out you were right. We still don't really know what it means, but we've both agreed we won't see other people until we figure it out," I tell him.

"What's there to figure out? You're gone for that girl."

"I know, but she's worried about Brody."

"Are you?" he asks.

"Honestly, man, not really. I was, but then I kissed her and . . . yeah, he's just going to have to learn to deal with it. I hate it, I do, but I can't let her go just because he wants me to, you know?"

"I hear ya. He can't keep you warm at night." Zach laughs.

"Exactly," I reply as we start jogging to join the girls.

After our run this morning, both girls went home to catch a nap. Neither one of them have classes on Fridays. When I walked Ava to her car, I told her I would call her later. It's now three o'clock and it's later. I can't wait any longer to hear her voice. I pick up my phone and dial her number.

"Hey," she says after the first ring.

"You enjoy your nap, sweets?" I ask. I know she was exhausted earlier.

"I did. I slept until one. I didn't get much rest last night," she admits.

"I didn't either. There's this girl I've been interested in for a while, and I finally told her how I feel." I smile into the phone.

"Really? Something similar happened to me last night with this guy I grew up with and had the biggest crush on, and then it turned into . . . more than that. He's best friends with my brother, so I was scared to tell him."

"So you came clean, did you?" I continue the charade.

"Actually, he did first, but I can't resist him." She laughs at our game.

"I love that sound," I tell her.

"I don't know what to say when you say things like that."

"Does it make you uncomfortable?" I ask, worried I'm pushing her.

"No, well, not like you think anyway."

I wait for her to elaborate and she doesn't. "Ava Mae," I say her name in warning. She can't just leave me hanging.

"It makes me . . . Gah, I can't tell you," she says.

"Ava Mae, you can tell me anything," I try to reassure her. I think I know what she wants to say, and it's a damn good thing we're talking on the phone. If I was there, I don't know I could keep my hands off her.

"It makes me want you," she says, her voice is soft and low.

"I already know you want me, Ava Mae. We talked about all this last night. Why is that so hard?" I'm baiting her. I want to hear her say it. It's a dick move, but I want to hear those words come out of her mouth.

"It turns me on," she whispers. "It causes this feeling in the pit of my stomach, something I've never felt before with anyone else," she admits.

Just like that, I'm as hard as a rock. "When can I see you?" I need to kiss her. I need to hold her against me and kiss her.

"Well, the girls and I made plans for dinner. I didn't want to assume you wanted to see me."

What? How could she not know? "Ava Mae, always assume, beautiful. Always assume I want to spend every minute with you that you'll let me."

"I don't want to be too clingy. I feel like I could attach myself to you and never let go. I don't want you to get sick of me." She laughs.

"Not going to happen. I hated leaving you last night and watching you leave today. Now that you know how I feel, I want to be with you as much as I can. Always, no matter where it is, I want to be there as long as you're there." After a pause, I ask, "So, dinner with the girls?"

"Yeah. Kara and I are meeting up with Monica and her roommate, Lisa. They were talking about maybe going to the Underground after."

Shit. Dinner I can handle, the Underground not so much. "How would you feel if the guys and I meet you all there? You know, with Zach we won't have to wait in line." I play it off like it will help them. I hope it works. I'm going to be there regardless, if she's there. It would just be easier if she agrees. I don't want to fight with her about this.

"I'm sure they'll be fine with it. Kara was already hinting at asking Tanner to come."

"What about you, Ava Mae? Do you want me there?"

"Yes." No hesitation on her part. Just one simple word.

"Tell me when and I'll be there."

"Okay, I'll text you once we finish dinner."

"Good. I'll be waiting to hear from you. Be safe, Ava Mae."

"We will. Bye, Nate." She ends the call.

Slipping my phone in my pocket, I stand to go find Zach and Tanner. We've got plans tonight.

I find them outside the locker room. "What's got you lit up like a Christmas tree?" Zach asks.

"I just talked to Ava Mae, and the girls are having dinner tonight. She said after that, they're going to the Underground."

"What? Kara didn't tell me that." Tanner reaches for his phone.

"We're going to meet them there," I rush to explain.

Tanner nods and pushes his phone back into his pocket.

"Ava Mae is going to text me when they finish dinner so we can be there when they get there. They're leaving for dinner at six." I look over at Brad. "Monica is bringing her roommate, Lisa. I don't know if she's available, but you're welcome to come. These girls aren't groupies though, so no games," I warn him.

"I'm in, don't have anything better to do," Brad says.

"Sounds like a plan. We can meet at my place and drive over if you want." Everyone agrees to meet at my place at seven. We want to be sure we're ready to go when the girls call.

The guys are all here and we're shooting the shit when my cell alerts me of a new message.

> Ava Mae: We're leaving the restaurant now. About 15 min away.

"Time to go. They're about fifteen minutes from the Underground." It's a twenty minute drive from here, so we need to get moving.

> Me: Okay. Wait for us. We're on our way.

> Ava Mae: Okay.

> Me: Be careful.

> Ava Mae: You too!

Fifteen minutes later, we're pulling into the Underground. I might have broken a speed limit or two, but no way was I letting her go in there alone. I realize I don't know what they're driving so I call her.

"Hello?" I can barely hear her over the noise and music in the background.

"Ava Mae? Where are you?" I told her to wait for us.

"Inside. Lisa has a lead foot and she used to date the guy at the door, so he let us in without standing in line."

"Damn it. Okay, where are you inside?"

"We're standing next to the bar. We'll wait here for you."

"Okay. Stay there, we just pulled in," I say, ending the call. "Damn stubborn woman!"

"Why in the hell didn't they wait?" Tanner grinds out.

"I guess Lisa knows the guy at the door; he let them in. You know what it's like in there. Fucking vultures. We've got to get in there," I say. Tanner and Zach are already in the same mindset, stalking beside me to the door. Brad trails behind. His ass would kick it in high gear if it were his girl.

Zach has no trouble getting us in the door with no wait. We head toward the bar, and when I see Ava Mae, I'm also seeing red. Some jackass runs his hand up her arm to rest on her shoulder. I can tell from her stance, as well as Kara's, this guy was not invited.

Zach clamps his hand down on my shoulder. "Play it cool, man. Don't go over there guns blazing. The gym doesn't need the press and Ava doesn't need to see that shit."

I nod and continue my strides, moving me toward her. I step around the crowd so I can come up behind her. Zach, Tanner, and Brad are right beside me.

Once I reach her, I place my hands on her hips and bury my face in her neck, breathing her in. She stiffens in my arms until I whisper the words, "I missed you, baby," in her ear. She immediately relaxes against me, letting her head rest on my shoulder. Her hands cover my hands, which are clasped over her belly. There is no denying the connection we have from this stance.

"Who the fuck is this guy?" douche nozzle asks.

Lifting my head, I stick my hand out to him, keeping the other around her waist. "Nate, her boyfriend. Who the fuck are you?" I ask him.

He stares at my hand, but doesn't bother to shake it. No skin off my back. I'd rather hold her than shake hands with this fucker any day. I wrap her tightly in my arms and place a kiss on her temple.

"Since when?" he spits at Ava. I've had enough.

"Clint, we are not together. I've told you that. We went on one date almost two years ago. That's it. Get it through your thick skull," Ava snips at him.

"Ava, come on now." He reaches out to touch her arm. *Not on my watch, fucker.*

I step in front of Ava, and she wraps her hands around my waist from behind. I feel her rest her forehead against my back. "Listen up, Clint, was it? This is what's going to happen." I see Zach, Tanner, and Brad flank me, all of them with a girl behind them, protecting them from this asswipe. "You're going to walk away and leave my girl alone. She's made it clear she wants nothing to do with you." I try to be civil.

"Fuck you," he spits. "She was mine first."

I laugh. "You see, that's where you're wrong. She's always been mine; it just took us a while to get where we are today. So unless you want your ass handed to you, I suggest you leave her alone."

"Walk away, man," Zach tells him. His arms are folded across his chest.

Clint's pissed but smart enough to know he's no match for us. "Whatever, she'll come crawling back," he says.

Again, I laugh. "Not happening. Leave. Her. The. Fuck. Alone!" I stress each word, dumbing it down for him. "I will ruin you if you come near her again. Am I clear?"

"What–the-fuck-ever," he grunts and walks away.

I watch until he gets lost in the crowd before I turn to face her. "I'm so sorry," she says as she holds tightly around my waist, her face buried in my chest.

Sorry? "Ava Mae, look at me." I gently stroke her back. She doesn't budge. Leaning down, I try again, this time where I know she can hear me. "Baby, look at me, please."

Hesitantly, she looks up. Her eyes are glassy as if she's fighting back tears. "Why are you sorry?" I ask her. "You did nothing wrong."

"He's just some guy I dated freshman year. One date, Nate. I swear. Nothing happened. He got wasted and I refused to go out with him again."

"He talks big game on campus. Makes all the other guys think Ava's his. He's an ass," Kara chimes in.

Ava still has her arms around my waist, but her big brown eyes are watching me. I cup her face with my hands so I know I have her attention. "I saw him and I saw you. I knew instantly you were uncomfortable. You have nothing to be sorry for." I kiss her forehead.

She nods and places her head back against my chest. I hate she's upset, but I will never complain about having her arms wrapped around me. "Let's grab a table," I suggest. Pulling back, I tuck her against my side and lead her through the crowd. We find a table in the back corner and motion for a waitress. We all order water, which has the waitress looking at us like we're crazy people. The girls aren't old enough to be served and Zach's training. Tanner and Brad take training just as seriously. There's no way I'm going to drink and not be on top of my game if Ava Mae were to need me.

"Shit, Nate, I thought I was actually going to get to see you throw down," Brad says.

"Yeah, that would have been a first," Zach agrees.

Ava looks at me with a raised eyebrow. "Do you not fight?"

"No, I did some in the Marines, but when they told us Dad's stroke was caused by his migraines, which were caused from too many years of being hit in the head, I decided I couldn't do that to my mom or my future family," I say, squeezing her leg under the table.

"I've never seen him throw a punch unless it's at a bag in the gym. Man has control out of this world," Tanner says.

"I just don't want that. I've lived it. My mom and dad are living it, and it's not worth it to me. If I can prevent it by not throwing punches, so be it. I still love the gym and what we do there. Training is what I do, but that doesn't mean I have to be the one doing the hitting," I reply.

The Marines taught me to control the anger, to channel it. Today is the closest I've been to a fight in years. I would have done it without hesitation for her, anything for her.

17
Ava Mae

$\mathcal{S}$OME TECHNO BEAT I've never heard blares through the sound system and has Kara, Monica, and Lisa on their feet. They try to convince me to join them, but I'm not ready, not yet anyway. My emotions got the best of me. I thought for sure Nate was going to be pissed because of Clint. I was worried he would think I wanted Clint. I don't. I never did. I felt bad for always turning him down, which is why I agreed to go out with him, as friends I might add. That's a disaster I wouldn't mind forgetting.

"I'm good, guys. I'll catch up with you in a bit," I tell them.

Kara leans down to give me a hug. "You all right?"

"Yeah, just want to chill here for a while."

The three of them head to the dance floor and I sit nestled into Nate's side and listen to them talk. I've learned a lot. Nate doesn't fight. I just assumed he did because of the gym and, well, his muscles have muscles. He's cut, and I just assumed. I guess that's what I get. Zach took ballet in high school. His football coach said it helps with speed, balance, and even his flexibility on the field. His entire team had to do it. Tanner was a bookworm. He didn't start getting into the gym until after he graduated high school. Never played sports until one day he decided to join the gym just to get fit and walked into Hardcorps. That's where Nate's dad taught him everything he knows. The only thing I learned about Brad is he likes the ladies. We could hardly hold his interest from his head following every female who passed our table.

I'm zoned out sitting next to Nate. He's drawing circles on my shoulder with his index finger. I don't even think he realizes he's doing it. He's always touching me, not that I'm complaining.

"Dance with me?" Nate asks. I nod, allowing him to pull me from the chair. Dancing with Nate and dancing with my girls are two totally different things.

Just as we get to the dance floor, the song turns slow. Dierks Bentley's "Must Be Doing Something Right" begins to play.

Nate wraps his arms around me and holds me close. His hands are resting on the small of my back, before he slips a hand under my shirt and gently strokes my skin, just above the waistband of my jeans. I wrap my arms around his waist and bury my face in his chest, breathing him in. It just so happens, I sigh at the same time Dierks sings about it. I can feel the rumble of Nate's chest as he chuckles. I can't help it. I don't let his laughter bother me. Instead, I burrow in as close as I can and enjoy this time with him. We're barely moving, more like standing with a slight sway as Dierks sings to us. His touch on my bare skin is bringing back that feeling, the one that warms me from the inside out. The fluttering of butterflies dancing causes my heart to race.

Nate kisses the top of my head, and suddenly, that's not enough. I need his lips on mine. Tilting my head up, I find him watching me. His eyes bore into mine. I hope he gets the message. *Kiss me. Please, kiss me.* Deciding he needs some assistance, I stop swaying and stand on my tiptoes. Nate's eyes fall to my lips. I move my hands behind his neck and pull him down to me. He doesn't protest, just slowly moves his lips against mine. He doesn't take it any further than that, just takes his time kissing me.

The song ends and so does the kiss. Nate laces his fingers through mine and leads me from the dance floor. We walk to the edge of the room and stand by the wall. "What's going through that pretty head of yours?" he asks.

"I don't have the words to explain it, Nate. I've wanted this, wanted you, to be with you like this for longer than I can remember. Now that you're here with me, I can't explain how it feels." I decide to be honest with him. I want more than just a few stolen kisses. The more time we spend together, the more obvious that becomes to me. My heart is on the line and that scares me. I'm not ready to be that honest with him. Not yet anyway.

"That makes two of us. I can't say anyone has ever affected me the way you do. I used to think it was because you were off limits, but now . . ." He pulls me tightly against his chest, but I don't dare look away. "Now I know it's you. You make me feel like this. I don't know what it is or what it means, but I know I'm holding on tightly. I'm holding onto you and never letting go. I never want to let you go," he says as his lips find mine. This time, the kiss is more urgent. His tongue duels with mine as I allow him to consume me.

Breaking away, he says, "We have to stop. You deserve better than to be groped up against the wall in a club." Running his fingers down my hair, he gently moves it behind my shoulder. He then buries his face in my neck as his tongue traces from my collarbone to my ear. "That doesn't mean I don't want you." He pushes his erection into me, not that I haven't already felt it just minutes ago. "Just means I want you all to myself. Not for show." He nips at my earlobe then stands to his full height. Lacing his fingers through mine, he leads me back to the table.

When we get there, Zach and Monica are standing to leave. Kara gives her a thumbs up, so I can only assume she's going back to his place or vice versa. "I think I'm going to head out too," Lisa says. She drove us here. "You two ready to go?" she asks.

I'm not ready to leave Nate, but what choice do I have? Tanner speaks for us. "We'll make sure they get home safe." Kara beams at him. Apparently, she's not ready to leave either.

"You think you could drop me off?" Brad says to Lisa. She agrees with a nod.

"And then there were four," I say.

Kara laughs. "I say we head back to our place and have dessert." She wags her eyebrows at Tanner. He grins at her and winks. "I mean dirt cake." She laughs. She totally set him up for that one. "What do you think?" she asks us.

Nate turns to me. "Ava Mae?" Hanging out at home sounds perfect.

"I'm ready when you are," I say to the three of them. Decision made, we load up in Nate's Tahoe and head back to our apartment.

"Who wants dirt cake?" Kara asks as soon as we're through the door.

I smile at her. "You guys make yourselves at home. I'm going to go help her."

"So how are things going with Tanner?" I ask as I set out four bowls.

"Good, great." She beams. "I really like him. We have similar personalities, and he's a great kisser," she gushes.

"Just a great kisser?" I tease her.

She blushes. I don't think I've ever seen her blush. "We haven't got to that just yet. Tanner wants to wait. Said we should get to know each other first. It's a new concept for me, but so far so good. It definitely builds anticipation." She wags her eyebrows. "What about you and Nate? Dusted any cobwebs off the old woo-hoo lately?"

"How are we friends again?" I laugh.

"You love me and you know it," she quips. She's right, I do.

"We're . . . I don't really know. At first I wanted to go slow to see how things played out. I was afraid I would get attached to him and he would decide I'm not really what he wants. I should have known better though. The more time I spend with him, the more I fall," I confess.

"Girl, you were already in love with him; you just wouldn't admit it. You still won't."

She's right. I'm scared to death he'll run the other way. "I'm scared, Kara. I've never had these feelings he evokes in me. My palms are sweaty and my knees are weak. My heart feels like it's going to beat out of my chest."

"Ava, I wish you could see the way he looks at you. He's right there with you. That man is in love with you," she says.

"Kara—"

She cuts me off, "Don't 'Kara' me. Two years we've been roommates. Two years I've watched you stay in, claiming you had homework. Two years I've watched you turn down date after date. You've gone out more and smiled more in the last month than the entire time I've known you. He does that. He brings out your happy." She fills the four bowls with dirt cake. "Embrace your happy, Ava. Let your heart lead you; the rest will fall into place."

"You really think Brody can learn to deal with this?" I ask her.

"Honestly, I think if he loves you, he will accept who you fall in love with. He and Nate are thick as thieves; you said so yourself. He trusts him. He'll eventually come around. You can't let Brody being upset stop you from making your heart happy. Finding someone to share your life with is a gift, one that some never find. You've found yours, Ava. Now the only question is what are you going to do with it?"

"What about you? Is Tanner your happy?" I ask her.

"Let's see, you said sweaty palms, weak knees, and rapid heartbeat." She ticks them off on her fingers. "Yeah, if that's what all that means, then I think I might have. It's too soon to tell. We still have a lot to learn about each other. That's not the case with you and Nate. You've known him your entire life. Take the jump, Ava. Let Nate catch you. He won't let you fall."

She leaves me in the kitchen, holding two bowls of dirt cake, with my mouth hanging open. Kara jokes more than she's serious. I think that's the longest serious speech I've ever heard from her. Even more so, she's right about all of it. That's also something that doesn't happen very often. I think Tanner's going to be a good influence on her.

Sitting in Biology, I try to keep my mind off the weekend. Nate and Tanner hung out at the house after the Underground, and came back Sunday to take us to dinner. It's been three days since I've seen him. He's been busy with the gym and I have been slammed with school. I've been too tired to get up and run in the mornings before class due to staying up late getting caught up on homework. I have a full load and I'm not used to having much of a social life, not that I'm complaining.

Feeling my phone vibrate in my pocket, I slip it out. I smile when I see Nate's name on the screen.

Nate: Missing you

Me: You too.

I snap a picture of my biology notes that I'm no longer taking so I can talk with him.

Nate: Makes me sleepy just looking at it.

Me: Usually I can handle it.

Nate: Usually?

Me: When I'm not preoccupied with a certain gym owner.

I open his reply and it's a picture of him smiling.

> Me: :-)

> Nate: What time is class over?

> Me: Another 30 minutes

> Nate: Call me then. I just want to hear your voice.

> Me: :-)

I send another smiley face, because really what else do you do with that? He has my insides turning to mush. I zone out the last half hour of class. I save the picture Nate sent me and change it to the background on my phone. I smile when I think that he's what I will see every time I unlock the screen. Definitely the highlight of my day.

As soon as class is over, I pack up my books and dial Nate's number before I'm even out of the room.

"Hey," his deep voice answers.

"Hi."

"How was the wonderful world of biology?" he asks.

I laugh. "The last thirty minutes was pretty entertaining."

"Was it now?" He chuckles. "When's your next class?"

"I have an hour."

"Perfect. That's plenty of time."

"Plenty of time for what?" I ask, confused.

"Look up, sweets."

I look up and standing across the lawn is Nate. He's leaning against a brick wall, legs crossed at the ankles, looking like a Greek God. "What are you doing here?" I ask. I quicken my pace to get to him.

"I haven't seen you in three days, Ava Mae. That's longer than I'm okay with. I thought I could take you to get coffee or an early lunch, or hell, we can sit in my truck and just catch up. I just want to see you."

He's no longer standing against the wall. In two more steps, I'm standing in front of him. "You missed me?" I say into the phone, even though he's standing in front of me.

He ends the call and slides his phone into his pocket and I do the same. His hands cup my face. "Yeah, it's safe to say I missed the hell out you." He then presses his lips to mine.

Pulling back, I smile at him. "There's a café on campus. We can go there."

He pulls the bag from my shoulder and throws it over his. Lacing his fingers through mine, he says, "Lead the way."

We spend the next hour sitting at a small corner table in the café. Nate talks about the gym and Zach's upcoming fight. He asks me about school and how Kara has been. It's perfect and comfortable and everything I could want time with him to be. I'm disappointed when I have to head back to class.

"When can I see you?" he asks.

"Probably not until Friday. I have class tomorrow and a huge paper that's due."

He nods in understanding as he kisses my forehead. "Call me then, even if it's just for a few minutes."

"I will. Thank you for the surprise."

"It was more for me than you," he admits with a smile. "But you're welcome." With one more feather-light kiss to my lips, he leaves me at the door for my next class. I watch him walk away, which has me late for class. It is so worth it.

18

Nate

THREE WEEKS. IT'S only been three weeks since the day I confessed my feelings to Ava. Three weeks of phone calls, text messages, runs in the morning, and dinners at night. Three weeks of hugs, kisses, and a whole swarm of emotions that are new to me. To sum it up with one word, I would use bliss. I've smiled so much my face hurts. My mom even noticed and Dad ratted me out. Ava and I still have not discussed what we are, or what we hope to be in the future. I hope we can do that tonight. She has finals coming up and has already warned me I will be seeing less of her until they are over. That's something else I want to talk to her about. I don't care if I can't speak; I still want to see her, be near her. I'm hoping she'll let me help or at least agree to study here. I can cook dinner and she can study. I can drive her home. Doesn't take much for me to be happy, just her . . . time with her. Both of our schedules are busy and going days without seeing her doesn't work for me.

We spend a lot of time with Kara and Tanner or hanging out at the gym. Tonight it will just be the two of us and I can't wait. I left the gym early to come home and get started on dinner. I have Italian chicken and potatoes on the grill and the salad is made. I know she's been stressing out about finals, so I wanted one night with just us before she goes into study mode. Kara has warned me it could be days before I see her. I hope she's kidding. I can't make it an eight-hour shift, let alone days. I started meeting her in between classes to keep that from happening. I hope we can find a solution for this study mode Kara keeps talking about.

Hearing her car pull up outside, I meet her at the door. I'm pulling it open just as she's about to knock. One hand on the door, I put the other around her waist and pull her into me. My lips drop to hers and I kiss her. "I missed you today," I say, releasing her so she can come in.

"I saw you this morning when we ran." She laughs.

"I know; it was forever ago." She just shakes her head and smiles. "Make yourself at home. I have to go check on the chicken and potatoes." I kiss her one more time before checking on dinner.

I got lucky and timed dinner just right. I pull the chicken and potatoes off the grill. I'm just about to yell for Ava Mae to let her know it's time to eat, but I stop in my tracks when I see her in the kitchen. She's in her bare feet, a pair of gym shorts, and a tank top. Her hair is pulled back in some type of twisted knot that leaves tendrils of curls framing her face. She's sexy as hell.

"Salad's out, drinks are made, plates, utensils. What am I missing?" she asks.

I don't answer her. I can't; words have escaped me. I set the platter down on the counter and stalk toward her. Her eyes grow wide as I reach her. Placing my hands on her hips, I lift her onto the counter. Her legs open to allow me to get close, but I can never get close enough. Keeping one hand on her waist, I place the other on the back of her neck and pull her toward me. Angling her mouth just right, I pepper her lips with kisses, teasing her. She wraps her legs around my waist and tangles her fingers in my hair. That's when I know I have her. I mold my lips to hers and she opens for me. I take my time tasting her, stroking her tongue with mine. Tearing my lips from her, I kiss her cheek and let my lips create a path to her collarbone. Using the leverage of her legs being locked around my waist, she pulls herself to the edge of the counter and grinds against me. I have to slow this down. It was not my intent to attack her with my lips before we even have dinner. I just . . . can't resist her.

"Ava Mae, dinner's going to get cold," I say, trying to pull away.

"Don't care," she says, placing her lips against my neck. She's mimicking what I just did to her.

"Really, I worked hard on dinner. I want to talk to you and need a clear head to do it." I plead with her.

With a heavy sigh, she unlocks her legs and allows me to step away.

"You started it." She sticks her tongue out at me.

I laugh at her, with her. I've laughed more in the last few weeks than I can remember in a long time. "I know I did, but it's your fault. I come walking in, seeing you looking all sexy in my kitchen and I needed to kiss you."

"Needed to, huh?" she smirks.

I step back between her legs and place my hands on her hips. "Yes, needed to, just like I need air to breathe. I needed my lips on yours." I kiss her nose and lift her from the counter, setting her back on her feet.

"Sounds serious." She hip checks me.

"It is, trust me." I wink at her.

We eat dinner, telling each other about our day. Ava submitted her last assignments for this semester. Now all she has left is to study for finals. I tell her about Zach's session today. He's doing well and I think he really has a shot at the title. "Other than that, just the same old thing. I'm behind on paperwork, but it's my fault. I need to hire someone else."

"Can I do anything to help?" she asks.

"No, but thank you. I need someone to work the desk and also process all the member applications. That will take a lot off my plate."

"Once finals are over, I'm all yours if you need me. I'm not taking summer classes. I need a break."

"I always need you, but I can't take advantage of you by letting you do my work. I need to hire someone."

"Well, in the meantime, if you need help with anything, I'm your girl."

I place my hand on hers. "I like the sound of that, you being my girl."

"It does have kind of a nice ring to it, doesn't it?" She smiles.

After cleaning up from dinner, we're curled up on the couch in my living room. She's lying in front of me, using my arm as a pillow. "There are a few things I wanted to talk to you about," I hedge. I'm nervous as to what she's going to say.

She turns to face me, throwing one of her legs over mine as she rests her hand against my chest. "I'm all ears."

"Well, first, I want us to be official. I want to be able to call you my girlfriend and know we're on the same page. Girlfriend isn't a strong enough word for what you are to me, but it beats referring to you as the girl I'm crazy about, even though I *am* crazy about you."

"Done. What's next, boyfriend?" She grins at me.

I kiss her softly. That was a hell of a lot easier than I expected. "This next request you might not be as agreeable to," I admit.

"Try me."

"I want to tell our families. I don't want to hide that we're together. I want to call Brody and tell him about us. I don't want him coming home and being blindsided by us being together. Now that we have decided we're official, I think he deserves to know."

"Okay. I can call him, Nate," she offers.

"No, baby. I need to do this. I need for him to understand how much you mean to me. I need to make sure he knows you're special to me."

"Maybe we should do it together?" she suggests.

"No can do. If I know Brody, he's not going to be happy, at least not at first. I don't want you to be on the other end of that anger. I thought I would call him and just put it out there."

"Okay."

That was easier than I thought it would be, too. The next one though, it's sure to trip her up.

"What else?"

I cover her hand, which is lying against my chest, with my own. "Before I ask the next question, I want to make sure you understand that you still control this, us. You set the pace. If I ever take things too far or push too hard, all you have to do is tell me and I'll back off."

"You would never," is her response and my heart swells at the trust she has in me.

"I was hoping . . . that, maybe, you might be willing to spend the night with me?" I see her eyes go wide, so I rush to explain. "I just want to hold you, Ava Mae. I want to know what it's like to fall asleep with you in my arms and wake up the same way. Nothing more."

"Is that your last request?" she asks.

"No. I was hoping that, even though you have to study, maybe you could do it here. I could make you dinner, and I promise I won't disturb you. I can give you a key so you don't have to wait for me to get home from the gym. I just . . . can't go days without seeing you."

She moves her hand to rest on my cheek. "You melt my heart, Nathan Garrison. How's a girl supposed to say no to a request like that?" she asks.

I made two requests. "So that's a yes, you'll study here?" I clarify.

"Yes." She gives me a chaste kiss and climbs off the couch.

My stomach drops; she's leaving. I don't ask her about staying, because I don't want to hear her rejection as well as live it. I stand with her, ready to walk her to her car. Instead, she surprises me. She heads toward the hallway. Turning to face me, she says, "Are you ready for bed?"

She's staying. My heart beats against my chest like a bass drum. She's staying. "Let me lock up." I finally push the words out, they sound muffled from the roar of thunder rolling through my veins.

She's staying.

Once my brain registers, I do a quick walk-through, making sure the doors are locked and turning off all the lights. I find Ava Mae waiting in the hallway outside my room. "What are you doing out here?" I ask her.

"Waiting for you. I thought this was something you wanted to do together."

She knows me so well. Slipping an arm around her waist, I guide her into my room. I watch through the slivers of moonlight as she takes in her surroundings. "Bathroom's through that door. There should be a spare toothbrush in the bottom drawer." She nods and heads that way. I follow her. The master bath has his and her sinks; the hers has never been used. Tonight it will be. I set to work brushing my teeth beside her. I never in a million years would have thought something this simple would make me so happy. Who am I kidding? Anything with her makes me happy.

I catch her watching me in the mirror, and her smile, toothpaste and all, lights up the room. I wink at her, which causes her to laugh. We finish up and head back to the bedroom.

"I can sleep in this." She looks down at her gym shorts and tank top. "But not this." She slides her hands up the back of her shirt and releases the clasp on her bra. I watch as she makes quick work of slipping it off one arm then the other. Her hand goes up the front of her shirt and pulls the bra out from underneath. Turning, she tosses it on the chair in the corner. She surprises me when she also steps out of her shorts and tosses them on top of her bra.

Ava Mae stands in front of me, arms at her sides, full breasts free from confinement, looking soft yet firm through her thin tank top, the thin white tank top that does nothing to hide the outline of her dark pink nipples. My mouth waters at the sight and I want to taste them. Her barely-there panties also don't leave much to the imagination. I know tonight is not the night, and I won't push her, but my dick has other ideas. He's got a mind of his own.

Reaching behind my neck, I pull off my t-shirt and step out of my shorts, leaving me in nothing but my black boxer briefs. Holding my hand out for her, she takes it and follows me to the bed. I pull back the covers and climb in. I hold them up, waiting for her to climb in next to me.

She settles next to me, her body facing mine. I drop the covers around her and she snuggles closer. I put my arm around her and pull her as close as I can get her. Her breasts, only covered by the thin tank top, rest against my bare chest. She slides her legs between mine and her arm goes around my waist. We are wrapped in each other's arms and nothing has ever felt better than this.

"This feels better than I thought it would," I say into the darkness. The window is on the other end of the room, closer to the bathroom, so I've lost the glow from earlier that allowed me to see her. I feel her rise up and place her chin on my chest. All we have now is our voices and our sense of touch. I place my hand on her jaw and gently trace it with my thumb.

"How so?" she asks.

"I've lost count of how many nights I've gone to bed wondering what it would be like to fall asleep with you in my arms. During my time in the Marines, it was usually the only way I could fall asleep at all." Now that we're official, I'm not holding anything back from her. I want her to know this is not new for me. I've always wanted her.

Pulling my hand from her face, she leans back and places it on her chest over her heart. I can feel the softness of her breasts as her chest rises and falls with each breath. "Do you feel that?" she asks.

I take a minute to register what she's asking and that's when I feel it. Her heart is thumping wildly against my hand. "Every time you say things like that, this is what happens. My palms get sweaty and I'm sure, if I were standing, my knees would be weak. I get this feeling in the pit of my stomach like butterflies, thousands of butterflies flapping their wings. You're the only one who's ever made that happen, made me feel this way," she says.

Tilting my head, I press my lips to hers. I want to devour her, but I promised I would just hold her. I'm a man of my word. "Goodnight, my beautiful girlfriend."

She giggles. I love that sound. I want her like this every night. One more soft kiss to her lips and she rolls over. I curl my body around hers, holding her tightly. She relaxes into me and I've found my nirvana. "Goodnight, boyfriend," she says in a sleepy voice. Those are the last words we speak before drifting off to sleep.

I'm having the best dream. Ava Mae is sleeping beside me. My hand traces the soft skin of her belly. I reach the underside of her breast and continue on until my fingers find her hardened peaks, begging for my touch.

"Nate," she moans.

I snuggle in closer and press my hardened cock against her. That feels so real. Memories of last night start to form and my eyes pop open. Suddenly, my dream is a reality. Ava Mae is really in my bed, my dick is tucked up nice and close to her ass, and, yes, my hand is under her shirt and my fingers are caressing her nipples. "Nate," she moans again.

She's moaning for me. Fuck, she's so sexy it's hard to resist her. I'm torn. If she's asleep, she might be angry when she wakes up to find me groping her, but then again, maybe she wants this and is too shy to tell me. Maybe if I can get her to wake up, I can gauge her reaction. Bending my head, I kiss her shoulder, tracing small circles with my tongue. This causes her to moan and push her ass against me. My lips find their way to her neck and I pepper her with kisses. I nip gently with my teeth then soothe the spot with my tongue. I want to taste every inch of her.

19
Ava Mae

*A*M I DREAMING? I feel his rough hands caressing my breast and a slight pinch of my nipple, and I know this is not a dream. Well, maybe a dream come true, but I am most definitely awake, or getting there. I feel his tongue on my neck, his kisses following the path it leaves. He's hard and pressed firmly against my ass. Nate has all of my senses on high alert.

"A girl could get used to this," I say. My voice is laced with sleep. Nate stills behind me. I hold my breath to see what he'll do next.

"Good morning, beautiful," his deep voice whispers in my ear.

I wiggle my ass against his erection and he moans deep in his throat. The sound right next to my ear does nothing to calm the desire I have for him. Squeezing my eyes closed, I take a leap and ask him for what I want. "Please, don't stop." My voice is barely a whisper. I hold my breath, waiting for him to touch me.

"Ava Mae," his deep voice croons as he continues his exploration of my breasts.

Suddenly, his cell rings. I watch as the screen lights up from the dresser. Nate continues kissing my neck, his hand continuing its exploration. "Aren't you going to answer that?" I ask.

"No," he growls. His phone stops ringing only to start up again. "Fuck!" he exclaims.

"Nate, it might be an emergency." I would never forgive myself if someone needed him and he didn't answer.

"Do. Not. Move," he says, climbing out of bed. I enjoy the show; his body is sculpted, rock hard. My eyes drink him in, and when he turns, his erection peeking out of the top of his briefs gets my full attention.

"What?" he says into the phone. "No, we're not coming. Yes, she's with me and we're not coming. I'll be in later." He looks over at me. "I'll be there for your session at one." He doesn't bother saying goodbye as he hits end and places his phone back on the dresser.

I sit up, bringing the sheet with me. "Everything okay?"

Nate stops when he reaches the bed and cups my cheek. "Zach, he wanted to know if we were going to be there to run this morning." He twirls a stray curl, which must have fallen out of my bun while I slept. "Can we take it down? Your hair?"

Reaching back, I remove my ponytail holder and shake my curls loose. I'm sure it looks like a rat's nest after sleeping all night. Nate doesn't seem to notice as he reaches out to touch it.

"So soft, I love your curls," he says tenderly.

He leans in for a kiss and his hands find the hem of my tank. Standing up, he lifts my shirt and I immediately raise my arms so he can remove it. Nate tosses it over his shoulder, not caring where it lands. His eyes rake over my bare chest. With his index finger, he traces the swell of each breast, making sure to run the tip over each nipple. He's driving me crazy. I want his hands on me, but first he needs to know. "Nate."

He climbs into the bed on his knees. "Yeah, baby," he croons.

"I've never . . . I mean, last night was a first for me. I've never spent the night with anyone," I confess. "I've never . . ."

He places his forehead against mine, his hand resting on my back just below my shoulder, giving me courage to continue. "I've never been with anyone. I mean, I've done things, but never actually slept with anyone, I just thought you should know."

He doesn't move, his forehead still resting against mine. "Ava Mae, you're just . . . I don't even . . . You're amazing and so damn beautiful my heart aches when I look at you. You control this, us. You set the pace and I'm here no matter what that is. I'll take you any way I can get you. When you're ready for more, just say when. You tell me what you want, when you want it, and I'll give it to you."

"Nate, I—"

"Shh," he says, touching his lips to mine. "But not today. It's too soon. You just agreed to officially be my girlfriend last night."

116

"I want you. I want it to be you."

"Ava Mae, if that's what you want, then that's how it will be, but not today." He leans over me until my head hits the pillow. "Today, I want to explore. I want to learn every part of you." His mouth drops to my left breast as he sucks on the hardened peak. My hands tangle in his hair. He switches to the right breast and a moan escapes me as soon as his tongue meets my flesh. "I want to taste every inch of you. I want to learn what you like, what makes you crazy for my touch."

"You do that, Nate. Doesn't matter where, when, or what, as long as it's you," I pant.

Releasing my breast with a pop, he settles his muscular frame next to me. His big hands trace the band of my panties. "Has anyone ever touched you here?" he asks. His voice is husky and the sound alone has me rubbing my thighs together.

"Yes."

Slipping his index finger under the waistband, he trails his finger back and forth. "Can I touch you here, Ava Mae?"

"Yes." My voice is pleading.

Sliding his hand underneath, he wastes no time sliding his fingers through my folds. "Look at me, Ava Mae," he commands and I obey. "I want to watch you. I want to commit every moment of this to my memory. I will always remember this day." He leans in for a kiss. "The first time you fall apart at the seams for me," he says gruffly.

"The first time ever," I pant as his fingers continue to stroke me.

"Ever?" he asks, surprised.

"No one else has been able to get me there," I say, feeling my cheeks heat with embarrassment. "I think I always wanted it to be you, waited for you," I add.

His breath hitches and his eyes darken with hunger. "I'll always take care of you," he promises as he slides the first digit inside me.

I fight the urge to close my eyes. The lustful look in his motivates me to keep them open. "You're so wet," he murmurs. I grip his bicep, holding tightly as he slides in another.

"Nate . . ." I'm so close. "I need . . ."

"I know, baby. I've got you." He increases his rhythm. "I can feel it; you're close. You're pulsing around my fingers. Give it up for me,

Ava Mae." Bringing his face mere inches from mine, he utters the words that send me over the edge. "I can smell your arousal. I can't wait to taste you."

That's all it takes for me to fall into the bliss that is Nathan Garrison. He buries his head in my neck and allows me to ride out my orgasm.

"Fuck, Ava Mae, I have no words to describe that. Watching you fall apart from my touch . . . I just . . ." He trails off.

I roll over, needing a minute. I just need to wrap my head around what just happened. Nate pulls me into his arms and rests his chin on my shoulder. I can feel the rise and fall of his chest against my back. I move just a little to get my arm in a better position and he tightens his hold, Like he's afraid I'm going to leave. Neither one of us says anything while we take in the meaning of what just happened. Nate's breathing evens out and I allow myself to relax into his hold.

"I never thought I would be here," he says wistfully. "I never thought I would have the chance to hold you in my arms like this."

I lace my fingers through his on the hand that's resting on my belly. Words have escaped me, even if I did know what to say, I don't think I could push them past the lump of emotion stuck in the back of my throat.

After a few minutes, he finally says, "I'm calling him today, Ava Mae."

"I figured you would. I can do it, Nate," I offer again.

"I know, baby. It needs to be me. I need to make him understand, or at least try to." He kisses my shoulder. "So no classes on Friday's and finals start week after next?" he asks.

"Yeah. I need to start hitting the books."

"Okay. Do you think that maybe you could spend the day with me today? I know I said I wouldn't get in your way for studying, and I won't." He pauses. "Today is the first full day that you're officially mine. I'd like to spend the day with you. If you need to study, I understand," he says in a rush.

My grades are good, great actually, and I know the material. Up until the last month, all I ever did was study. Besides, how can I pass up a request like that? "I would love to spend the day with you," I tell him. He rewards me with a smile and follows up with a kiss. I'm a lucky girl.

20
Nate

I'M SITTING ON Ava Mae's bed in her apartment while she showers. Deciding there is no time like the present, I pull my phone out of my pocket and dial Brody. It rings for what feels like hours before his voicemail finally picks up.

"Hey, man, it's me. There's something I'd like to talk to you about. Give me a call when you get this."

"Was that him?" Ava asks as I'm sliding my phone back into my pocket.

"Yeah, well, not really, no. It was his voicemail. I left him a message."

She fidgets from one foot to the other; I can tell she's worried. Holding my hand out for her, she takes it. I guide her to stand between my legs. She rests her hands on my shoulders and I wrap my arms around her waist. "I want him to approve of this, Ava Mae. I really do, but I have to be honest with you. If he doesn't, it's his loss. I can't and I won't let you go. I just got you."

"I don't want to cause problems between the two of you. You shouldn't have to choose."

Reaching up, I cup her face with my hand. "Baby, there is no choice. He either accepts that we're together or he doesn't. It's you and me, no matter what." I study her. I can still see the worry in her eyes. "Do you still want this, Ava Mae? Are you having second thoughts?" I force the words, even though I'm afraid to hear the answer.

"No, but I—" I shush her by placing my index finger over her lips.

"No buts. I want you. I want us, and he needs to understand I would never hurt you. I understand you're his sister, but you're my girlfriend." I grin at her. She laughs, which is a good sign. "There is no choice for me. You're not some random girl I just met and started dating. You're the girl I grew up with, the one who's always been there so close, yet so far away. I can finally reach you." I slide my hand, which was resting on her back, underneath the hem of her shirt. "I can finally touch you." Lifting her shirt to bare her toned stomach, I kiss her right above her belly button. "I can finally kiss you. I won't let him take that from me, from us." I pull her shirt back down and pull her down onto my lap. "So, no buts. If you still want me, we're in this together. You and me, Ava Mae." I press my lips to hers.

I have to break the kiss before I get carried away. "Now, let's grab you some clothes and your books so we can start our day."

"Clothes?" she asks.

"Yeah, I was hoping you would spend the weekend with me."

Her mouth drops open in mock horror. "Nathan Garrison, what would your girlfriend have to say about that?" And just like that, the tension in the air is gone.

Wrapping her in my arms, because I just can't not touch her, I say, "She would say that she would love nothing more than to spend the weekend with me." I kiss the tip of her nose. "Today, we just enjoy being together. The rest of the weekend, I'll spoil you while you study." I raise my hand in the air. "Promise." She leans her forehead against mine. "No expectations, Ava Mae. I'm just not ready to be away from you yet." I've watched her, wanted her for as long as I can remember. Now that I have her, well, let's just say I feel like attaching her to my hip.

"You had me at 'grab some clothes,'" she teases. Kara is obsessed with *Jerry McGuire;* I think it's starting to rub off on Ava Mae.

I tickle her sides, which causes her to jump off my lap. "What can I do to help?"

"Nothing, just give me ten minutes and I'll be ready to go."

I lean back against the headboard and revel in the fact I'm here with her like this. Waiting for her outside the bathroom at Zach's was the best decision I ever made. It led us here, and here feels pretty damn good.

"Okay. All set." Her words bring me back to the present.

She has two bags sitting at her feet. "I'm not high maintenance, I swear. This one," she points to her left, "has my laptop and books. This one," she points to her right, "has my clothes, toiletries, and things like that," she explains.

Hopping off the bed, I pick up both bags. "You could pack everything you own for all I care; that means you'll be there longer." I lean in and kiss the tip of her nose. "That would make me a very happy man." I stand to my full height, bag in each hand, and stroll out of the room.

I place her bags in the backseat and rush to open her door, but she's already in the passenger seat and strapped in. She blows me a kiss through the window and I can't stop the grin that turns up my lips.

"So, what do you want to do today?" I ask her.

"Really, we can just hang out if you want. Seems like we're always rushing, or at least it does to me. School, running, and meeting up with friends. A nice quiet day," she reaches over and places her hand on my thigh, "with you sounds perfect."

One hand on the wheel, the other covers hers. "Anything you want." I give her hand a gentle squeeze.

When we get back to my place, I grab her bags from the backseat, set the one filled with her books down in the living room and carry the other to my bedroom. I have two spares she can use if she decides that's what she wants, but I want her in mine. The thought of closing my eyes with her in my arms and waking up the same way causes my heart to flutter. Emotions I've never felt before consume me when it comes to her.

I find Ava sitting on the couch, digging in her bag. I stop and lean against the doorway just to watch her. She pulls out her laptop and plugs it in. Reaching back in the bag she retrieves a stack of books and places them on the coffee table. I notice her Kindle sits on top of the stack of books. She always did love to read. My chest swells at the sight of her making herself at home here, in my home. I never want her to leave.

No longer able to resist the pull her body has on mine, I push off the wall and head toward the couch. Standing behind it, I place my hands on her shoulders and gently rub. "How about some lunch?"

"Aww, you really know the way to a girl's heart," she teases.

If feeding her is what gets me her heart, I will make sure she has three hearty meals a day and snacks in between. "Why don't I throw some hamburgers on the grill?"

Ava Mae tilts her head back and looks up at me. "Perfect. I'll see what else I can scrounge up in that kitchen of yours to go with it."

Bending down, I kiss her forehead, which is still turned up to me. "I'm gonna go fire up the grill."

Ava hops off the couch and follows me into the kitchen. I head out the patio door to get the grill started. It takes a minute to get it to light. I think it's about time to upgrade this old thing.

Walking back into the house, I find Ava Mae making hamburger patties. "Hey." She smiles. "These are almost ready." I watch as she finishes the last one and places it on the paper plate with the rest of them. "I think I'm going to make some baked beans, well, not baked exactly. We don't have time for that, but you know what I mean." She laughs.

After washing her hands, she grabs a can of beans from the pantry and begins pulling open drawers to find the can opener. I can't take my eyes off her as she moves freely around my kitchen. Once she gets the beans on the stove, she pulls a cucumber from the crisper in the refrigerator. I went to the store this week and bought some of the foods I know she used to like. I was hoping I would be able to convince her to spend the weekend with me. I got lucky.

Ava reaches above her head to pull down a bowl. She's on her tiptoes, but can't quite reach. I catch my reflection in the window and I'm grinning like a fool as I move in behind her. I place a hand on her hip and she yelps in surprise. Tilting my head so my lips are next to her ear, I nip at her lobe. "Let me help you." I pull her body against mine then reach up and grab the bowl she was reaching for, setting the bowl on the counter in front of her. She spins around to face me.

"Hey, I could have got that," she pouts. She's fucking adorable and I have to kiss her.

21
Ava Mae

*N*ATE SMIRKS. HIS hands, which are resting on my hips, grip tightly, and the next thing I know, I'm being lifted up on the counter. I hear the bowl he just retrieved wobble on the counter behind me. I don't have time to do anything about it because his lips are on mine. His tongue traces the seam of mine and I open for him. His tongue slides against mine and causes me to moan. I grip his shirt and pull him closer. My legs wrap around his waist and as his erection hits my core, Nate is the one releasing a moan.

With my legs gripping his waist, I slide to the edge of the counter, lining us up perfectly. Nate breaks away from the kiss and buries his face in my neck. "Ava Mae." The way he says my name causes my heart to flutter in my chest. His lips find my neck and I tilt my head, allowing him better access. We're wrapped up in each other in our own little world, which is why we don't hear the door open. We also don't hear his parents enter the house. It's not until we hear the words, "Oh my," that reality comes crashing back around us. Nate lifts his head and kisses my lips.

"Busted." He grins, discreetly reaching down to adjust himself. "I'm gonna need some help hiding this, baby," he whispers, still grinning like a fool.

Nate turns and rests against the counter, bringing my legs to latch around him, my feet resting at his crotch, hiding his erection. His hands rest on my legs while his thumb lazily draws patterns on each one, and even though it's simple and not meant to, it fuels my desire for him.

"Mom, Dad," he says. "I didn't know you were stopping by today." I can hear the amusement in his voice.

"We were in town and stopped by the gym. Zach was training alone. Said you took the day off. Your mother was worried about you," his dad explains. "Not like you to take off, let alone miss training before a big fight," he adds.

His mom continues to stand there, eyes wide, just watching us. I take the cowards way out and rest my forehead against the back of his neck, effectively hiding my face. Maybe they won't notice it's me. Brody doesn't know yet, neither do my parents. Are we ready for this?

"True," Nate agrees. "However, if you get a chance to spend the day with your girlfriend, work has to take a backseat." His mom gasps. "Besides, Zach knows the routine, as do Trey and Tanner. Me missing a day"—he grips my legs to pull them tighter around him—"or two is not going to set him back," he replies.

"Girlfriend?" his mom questions.

"Yep," Nate chirps. "You see, I've had my eye on her for a while, and a wise man once told me I need to follow my heart." He shrugs. "Best advice I ever got."

"It's about damn time," his dad's booming voice replies.

Shit. This is not good. When they find out it's me hiding behind him, they will not be impressed.

"Ava, you gonna hide back there all day, girl?" his dad asks.

Lifting my head, I look over Nate's shoulder just in time to see his mom smack his dad on the arm. "You knew. I can't believe you didn't tell me." She turns and points at Nate. "And you, Nathan Garrison, think you're so smooth, keeping secrets from me. Well, guess what, a mother knows these things. You've loved that girl for as long as I can remember." She walks closer, placing her hand on his jaw. "I'm happy for you." Her other hand pats my leg, which is still tightly wrapped around her son. "Good to see you, Ava." She smiles at me.

Nate chuckles. I can feel the rumble in his chest. This is not how I expected this to go down. "You too," I croak out.

"We were just fixing lunch. Would you like to join us?" Nate asks.

"Is that what you kids are calling it these days?" his dad jokes. I feel the heat creep up my cheeks.

"Times change, old man," Nate fires back. I relax my legs and let them hang against the counter. Nate leans back, resting his arm on my leg, his hand covering my knee.

Mrs. Garrison smacks her husband's arm again. A smile lights her face. "We'll get out of your hair. I just wanted to make sure you were feeling all right."

Looking over his shoulder at me, he raises his eyebrows in question. The look on his face is . . . hopeful. Who am I to say no to him inviting his parents for lunch? I nod my agreement. "It's fine. We have plenty. The grill is probably nice and hot by now." He chuckles.

I poke him in the side. "Hey, what was that for?" He stands, turning to face me.

"Really, Nate?"

Smiling, he leans in and kisses me. It's just a quick peck on the lips, but it still causes my breath to hitch. Not to mention his parents are standing right there.

With his hands on my hips, he lifts me from the counter and sets me back on my feet. He pulls me into a quick hug and I can't help but wrap my arms around him.

"Dad, want to help with the grill?" he asks, releasing me.

I watch as Nate picks up the plate of hamburger patties, his dad following him. "What can I help with?" Mrs. Garrison asks me.

"I think I'm good." I glance over to the stove. Luckily, I had not turned the burner on yet. "I have some beans on the stove." I walk over and turn them on. "Then I was just going to cut up this cucumber in some vinegar and water. We have chips as well," I tell her.

"Sounds perfect," she says. I smile and get to work peeling and slicing the cucumber. "So, how long have you two been official?"

"Uh, well, we've been dating I guess you could say for about a month now. We made it official last night." Heat creeps up my cheeks. "Brody doesn't know yet. Nate tried to call him today, but didn't reach him."

She nods. "Ava, I watched you a minute ago when my son kissed you. You lost your breath," she says warmly. "When that happens, when you find someone who can do that to you, you latch on and never let go." She pats my hand. "Your brother will come around. We've all seen this attraction between the two of you for years. My guess is, in the back of his mind, he always knew this was a possibility. Honestly,

I'm surprised Nathan held out this long," she confesses.

I don't reply. It's still hard for me to wrap my head around the fact that as long as I watched him from afar, wishing he would see me as more, he actually did. He was fighting his feelings for his best friend's little sister. It's funny how life works sometimes.

The patio door opening saves me from the silence. Nate enters, carrying a plate of hamburgers, his dad trailing behind with the grilling utensils. I quickly grab the mayo, mustard, and pickles from the fridge, setting them out on the counter.

"Babe, can you grab me a tomato?" Nate asks.

The term of endearment just rolls off his tongue, like we've been together for years. Then again, if you want to get technical, we have. Pulling open the crisper drawer, I grab a tomato and join Nate at the island, handing it to him.

He leans over, kisses my temple, and proceeds to slice it into thin, even slices. It all feels so . . . domestic. I thought I would be able to steel my heart. I know I love him. I've always loved him. What I didn't expect was to fall in love with him to the point where my heart would never be the same.

22
Nate

"**W**ELL, WE BETTER get out of your hair," Mom says. I love my parents, and I'm glad they caught us. However, I'm glad they're leaving. I just want to spend some alone time with my girlfriend.

"Thanks for stopping by to check on me." I grin.

Mom shakes her head and Dad's grin matches mine. Sure, it's not the ideal situation to be introduced to my girlfriend, but this is Ava Mae. Not to mention, I don't want to hide this, hide us. That reminds me, Brody hasn't called back yet. I'll need to try him again later on.

"Ava, dear, it was good to see you. I'll call Nathan to set up a time for dinner at our house in a few weeks," Mom says, giving her a hug.

"Take care of your girl, son. We'll see you soon," Dad says. He kisses Ava on the cheek, and then they are gone.

Ava slumps down on the couch and buries her face in her hands. "I can't believe they caught us like that," she says.

Taking a seat next to her, I pull her hands away from her face. "I'm glad they know. I don't want this to be a secret." To further my point, I reach in my back pocket for my phone. I dial Brody's number. After the sixth ring, his voicemail picks up. "Hey, man, just thought I would try to catch you again. Call me when you get this." I end the call and place my phone on the table.

"I don't want to hide it either, but I would have preferred that your parents not find us . . . like that." She points to the kitchen.

"True, but I'm glad they know." I lean in for a kiss. "Now, what would you like to do the rest of the day?" I ask just as a bolt of thunder cracks, causing us both to jump.

"Well, I don't want to go out in that," she says with a chuckle.

"Movie?" I suggest.

"Yes. Sounds perfect."

I stand from the couch, pulling her with me. "Let's watch it in bed; there's more room to stretch out."

"Uh huh." She smiles.

"What? You think I have ulterior motives?"

"More than likely."

"I'm a tall guy; I just want to be able to stretch out," I defend myself, trying hard not to let my smile show.

Patting my chest, she says, "I know, big guy, come on," and leads me to the bedroom.

If she only knew that I would follow her anywhere. If the guys could hear me now, my man card would be revoked, permanent ban on privileges. Hell, if Brody could be inside my head for any amount of time, he would be okay with this. That is until he got to the file that contained all the thoughts about what I want to do to her, with her, over her, under her, all of the above. As long as it's with her, I'm good.

Ava Mae grabs her bag from the bed and opens it up. She digs until she pulls out a pair of gym shorts and a t-shirt. "I'm going to change, be right back."

"Wait," I call out to her as she heads toward the bathroom door. Opening my dresser drawer, I pull out a Hardcorps t-shirt and throw it at her. "This might be more comfortable." I wink.

She catches the shirt, smiles, and then disappears into the bathroom. I decide to follow her lead and change into a pair of basketball shorts. We might as well be comfortable for this Saturday afternoon.

A few minutes later, Ava emerges wearing what looks like only my shirt. It hits her mid-thigh and covers her shorts completely. I see nothing but her toned legs, those of a runner. I can't take my eyes off her as she walks toward me and climbs into bed. "What are we watching?"

Grabbing her by the hips, I pull her toward me as close as I can get her. "I was waiting on you," I say next to her ear.

The next thing I know, she's grabbing the remote from my hands. I don't even put up a fight. Instead, I take advantage of both hands being free and wrap my arms around her. Resting her head on my chest, she snuggles in close as she flips through the channels. She settles on a re-run of a sitcom. I don't care what she watches. I'll only be watching her.

The room is shaded in darkness due to the weather outside. The only light is from each bolt of lightning as it flames through the sky. The rain is hitting the windows, along with the occasional roll of thunder. Ava Mae is curled up in my arms where she belongs. Nothing gets better than this.

"I love to sleep in the rain," she says with a yawn.

"Me, too. I think it just got better though," I admit.

"How so?" Her voice is soft. I can tell she's fighting the battle of falling asleep.

"I have you in my arms, baby. That makes everything better," I declare.

"Always wanted to be here," she mumbles. My chest swells at her words. I've always wanted her here.

Her breathing becomes deep and even, and I feel myself being lulled by the storm raging outside. I don't fight it. Instead, I hold my girl a little tighter and let sleep take me.

I don't know how long we sleep, but I wake to the feel of her lips on my neck. "Morning, baby," I murmur. I slide my hand under her shirt, my shirt, and what I find surprises me. The shorts I thought were hiding are not there. The little minx never put them on. I'm not sure I could have fallen asleep knowing that.

"Ava Mae." My voice is strangled. "Where are your shorts, babe?" I ask as my hand runs over the silk of her barely-there panties, which are attempting to cover her ass.

I feel her shrug. "I decided against them."

"Decided against them?" I croak. "Jesus, woman, are you trying to kill me?"

She giggles. "Tempt you is more like it."

Grabbing her hips, I flip her on her back and hover above her. "All you have to do is breathe to tempt me, Ava Mae."

"I'm breathing," she purrs.

Fuck me! I capture her lips with mine. Pushing my tongue past her lips, I have to taste her. She opens and gives just as much as I take. I allow myself to get lost in her kiss, her taste. However, I need to slow this down. As I do so, my lips trail down her neck to the hollow of her throat.

"Nate," she says breathlessly.

I answer her with the trace of my tongue against her lips. Before I can take it any further, the house phone rings. Thinking it might be Brody, I reluctantly break away from her and reach for the phone on the nightstand.

"Hello?"

"Hey, Nate. It's Cassie. Sorry to bother you on your day off, but the power's out. I called it in and they said it'll be four hours before it's back on at best. Didn't know what you wanted me to do." Cassie is one of my desk clerks that I just recently hired.

I look over my shoulder at Ava Mae lying on my bed. Her soft brown curls spread across my pillow. "Close shop," I tell Cassie. "Push them out and lock up."

"Okay, are you sure? Zach said you would probably want to come in and start the generators," she questions.

"Nope, not coming in. Close up shop." I feel Ava's hands slip under my shirt and rub my back. "Tell everyone to report tomorrow at normal time. Thanks for calling, Cassie." With that, I hang up.

"Nate, you can go if you need to. I can stay here, or go home—"

"No." I slide my body next to hers. "I'm staying here. You and I have plans. I'm spending the entire day with my girlfriend." I kiss her nose and she smiles, her eyes bright with an emotion I can't name.

"Lucky girl." Her hands run through my hair.

I hover my lips over hers. "I'm the lucky one." Brushing a loose curl out of her eyes, I softly place my lips on hers. Yeah, I'm not going anywhere.

23
Ava Mae

TODAY HAS BEEN amazing. There is no other word to describe it. We spent the afternoon curled up in his bed, watching TV, napping, kissing, and just being. Even with the way his parents caught us earlier, I wouldn't change a single minute of it.

We just finished dinner. Nate ordered pizza and we ate it on the living room floor. I pick up our paper plates and am carrying them to the kitchen when the power goes out. "Well, that sucks."

Nate laughs, his deep voice carrying through the darkness of the house. "I got you, babe."

I hear him rustling around and the click of a lighter, and then a soft glow of a candle lights his handsome face. "I see you." I grin.

Chuckling, he walks to me, pizza box in one hand and the candle in the other. He tilts his head toward the kitchen. "Let's throw this stuff away and go back to bed. It's hard to tell how long the power will be out. We're lucky it just now happened since the gym's went out hours ago."

We quickly get rid of our trash. Nate grabs my hand and leads me to each door to make sure they're locked. Stopping by the living room, we pick up a few more candles and head back to his bedroom.

Nate places the lit candle on the dresser across the room, along with the other two that are not lit. "I don't think we need those," I voice my opinion.

"No?"

"No, we're just going to sleep. I say blow them out, but we'll know they're there if we should need them."

"What if I was trying to set the mood?" he replies.

I decide to throw his words from earlier back at him. "You're breathing; the mood is set. Now blow out the damn candle and get in bed." I place my hand on my hip, trying to be sassy. It's a feat because all I want to do is laugh at his reaction.

He immediately blows out the candle, then runs and jumps on the bed, causing me to flop around. Once I finish laughing, he hovers above me, sliding his hips between my legs. I wrap them around him and bury my fingers in his hair.

"Now that I'm here, what are you going to do with me?" he goads.

Not able to help myself, I say, "I thought we could just go to sleep." I fake a yawn as best as I can without laughing. "It's been a long day." I'm able to get the words out, but I have to bite my lip to hinder the laugh that is dying to escape.

Nate gives a gentle thrust with his hips. "Tired, huh? That's too bad." He rolls to the side of where I'm lying and wraps me in his arms. "I guess we'll just sleep then."

Rolling over, I push him back on the bed and straddle his hips. "I don't think I'm tired anymore." I rock against him for good measure.

His hands grip my hips. "You sure, babe?"

"Um hmmm." I rock again. This time it's not to drive him crazy; it's for me. We're lined up just . . . right and the feel of him against my core is driving me crazy with want.

Keeping one hand on my hip, assisting me with the steady rhythm I've created, Nate slides his hand up my shirt. Slowly tracing my ribcage, he stops at the underside of my breast. He traces the outline with his finger. He tests the weight in the palm of his hand before massaging my now hard nipple between his thumb and forefinger. The sensation, along with my hips rocking against him, sends a flood of desire through me.

Nate changes tactics, and within seconds, my shirt is off and thrown somewhere into the darkness. Sitting up, he nips and sucks each nipple while gently massaging the other. "Nate," I moan as I tilt my head back, allowing the sensations running rampant through me to take over.

"What, baby?" he asks. His mouth goes right back to my breasts, feasting on them, never missing a beat.

"I need . . ." The words are clipped as I press myself a little harder against him.

"Ava Mae, tell me what you need," he coaxes.

"You, Nate. I need you."

One arm wraps around me, while the other hand is still massaging a nipple, his mouth breaking to pull out of me what I want, what I need. "I'm right here, beautiful," he says tenderly.

Gah! I'm on the edge, just to the point where I can fall off at any time, but then again, not quite close enough. "Please," I beg. A girl has to do what a girl has to do.

"Please, what? What do you need, Ava Mae? I'll give you anything you want." His teeth nip at my nipple just as a strike of lightning flashes through the sky. The sensation races through me as though I've been struck by the force of the bolt.

"Touch me, Nate," I plead with him.

"Show me where, Ava Mae. Where do you want me to touch you?"

I'm teetering. I'm so close and forming coherent words isn't an option. Gripping his wrist, I pull his hand from my breast and pull it down my abs, stopping to rest where my body meets his.

Nate leans in, his lips next to my ear. "Here, baby?" He slides a finger through my folds. "Jesus, Ava Mae, your soaked," he murmurs.

I don't reply; I can't. I'm too close. Nate senses this and finally does what I've asked for as his thumb finds the spot, the one that aches for him to touch.

Seconds, it takes seconds for me to finally fall, screaming his name, "Naate!" I ride the wave of pleasure that takes over my body before falling against him.

Nate, still sitting with me in his lap, wraps both arms around me and buries his face in my neck. "I . . ." He stops. I want to tell him to finish, but I can't speak just yet. "You're perfect, Ava Mae. Perfect and so fucking beautiful coming apart in my arms." He kisses my neck.

Nate holds me, letting me come down from the bliss that just captured my body. Once our breathing is back to normal, he lies back on the bed, pulling me with him. He tucks me into his side and holds me close. I'm sated and so damn comfortable here with him that I can't keep my eyes open.

I feel Nate kiss the top of my head and say, "I'm never letting you go."

This is the second time he's taken care of my needs and I have yet to take care of his. I need to think of a way to seduce him into being the one on the receiving end. All kinds of thoughts flood my mind as I let sleep claim me.

24

I WOKE UP THIS morning wearing a smile. It has yet to leave my face as I sit here on the couch with Ava Mae's feet in my lap while she studies. I'm watching TV, but have the volume turned down low. She says the noise doesn't bother her, but I don't want to distract her. I know how important school is for her. I'm not really watching it anyway. I've spent the last half hour massaging her feet, just watching her as she chews on her pen and making notes on the notebook in her lap.

A knock at the door pulls me from the memory of last night that has been on constant replay since it happened, even in my dreams. "Come in," I yell.

Ava Mae doesn't even look up. She just continues to flip through notes and study her cute little ass off.

"Hey, man, where in the hell have you been?" Zach's voice booms as he enters the living room. "Ah, never mind. I see what has you so pre-occupied," he quips.

"Zach, have you met my girlfriend, Ava Mae?" I ask him.

This gets both of their attention. Ava Mae looks up, a smile lighting her face. I wink at her. Zach throws his head back and laughs. "Hand them over," he says.

"Hand what over?" I ask, confused.

"Your balls, dude," he retorts.

I don't let his comment faze me. Instead, I decide if you can't beat them, join them. "I'd love to, man, but I already gave them to Ava

Mae." I try to keep my face as stone cold serious as possible.

Zach falls into the recliner laughing so hard he can barely catch his breath. Watching him makes it impossible to keep a straight face. I let the laugh I've been fighting go as well.

Ava Mae just shakes her head at our antics and goes right back to studying.

"Did you forget you were supposed to help me move the weight bench today?" Zach asks.

Shit. "I did."

"Well, let's go then. The faster we get it done, the sooner you can get back here to your girl."

I look at Ava; I hate to leave her alone. Hell, I hate to leave her, period. Her eyes find mine and my breath hitches. Finding my voice, I say, "It will only take an hour, tops."

She waves her hand in the air. "I'm good here, if that's okay with you. Or you can take me—"

"No," I cut her off. I know she was going to offer to let me take her home, and that is not happening. Not yet. It's only one o'clock and she promised me all weekend. In my eyes, that means she's staying again tonight. "I'll be back soon. You need anything before I go?"

"No. My ass is going to be glued to this couch and my nose buried in this book."

I stand and stretch, grabbing my phone from the coffee table. I'm still waiting for Brody to get back to me. Bending over, I brace one arm on the back of the couch and the other on the arm, blocking her in. "I won't be gone long," I say as I briefly touch my lips to hers. Any longer than that and Zach will have to drag me away from her.

"Be safe, Nate."

Dropping a kiss on her forehead, I stand and turn away from her. "Let's do this," I say to Zach.

He smirks as he walks toward Ava. Leaning down, he kisses her cheek. "Good to see you, sweetheart," he says.

Grabbing the back of his shirt, I pull him up. "Keep your lips off my woman." Zach roars with laughter all the way to his Hummer.

"Seriously, man, why do you rile me up like that?" I ask, exasperated.

"Nate, buddy, that girl only has eyes for you. What are you so worried about?"

I think about what he said. I know he's right, but I just got her. For years I sat on the sidelines wishing she could be mine. It all still feels like it could disappear at any minute.

Zach starts talking about the fight that's just a little over a month away and that consumes our conversation all the way to his place. When we get there, I leave my phone in the console. I'm wearing gym shorts and have no pockets. I shouldn't need it anyway, not to move a weight bench.

Turns out, Zach needed more than just the bench moved. We ended up rearranging the entire basement. I've been gone for over two hours. Luckily, I made him let me call Ava Mae and tell her what the holdup was. Calling to check in and having someone at home waiting is a new experience for me. I fucking love it. You will never hear me complain about having to check in with my girl.

Climbing back into his Hummer, my phone beeps. Picking it up, I see I missed Brody. Fucking figures. I've packed this damn thing like a pistol the last two days and the one time I leave it for two hours, he calls. Swiping the screen, I put the phone to my ear to listen to his message.

"Hey, man, it's me. I got your message. Things have been crazy here. I'll try you again soon."

Checking the time, I see he called fifteen minutes ago. I almost hit send and call him back, but I don't want to have the conversation with Zach sitting beside me. It will just have to wait until I get back to the house.

Zach drops me off. I don't invite him in, a dick move, but he was headed to the gym anyway. Apparently, my dad is coming in today to 'check his form.' I'm glad my old man still comes to the gym. The stroke keeps him from moving around like he used to, but he's lucky.

Entering the house, I realize it's not only eerily quiet, it's also dark. Did the power go out again? I call out for her, but she doesn't answer. I reach the living room and her books are lying on the couch, but no Ava Mae. My heart starts to race and I call out for her again. I head down the hall to the bedroom and flip on the light. "Argh," she moans and I immediately turn the light off and stalk to the bed.

I sit on the edge and softly stroke her back. I tuck her mass of curls behind her shoulder so I can see her face. "You okay, babe?"

"Headache," she mumbles.

Shit. "Did you take your medicine?" I ask her.

"Yeah," she whispers. "I felt it coming on. It's not too bad."

I exhale. I hate how she suffers from this and it scares the hell out of me. Ava's been stressing out over her finals, and even though she acts tough, it worries her about what Brody is going to say when he finds out about us. She's stressed.

"Hey." I trace a finger on her jawline. "Can you take your shirt off for me? I'll be right back."

I hop from the bed and retrieve a bottle of lotion from the bathroom. I'm going to give her a massage and see if that helps.

Taking my seat on the side of the bed, she removes her shirt. "Roll over on your belly," I instruct. She does without question.

I unclasp her bra and pull it down her shoulders. She lifts and I pull it from underneath her. Pumping some lotion in my hands, I rub them together to get them warm. As soon as I begin to knead her shoulders, she sighs. That's all the confirmation I need. I continue to massage her shoulders, moving down her back. I get lost in the feeling of her skin under my fingertips. Once I feel her body is completely relaxed, I wash my hands and head back to help her with her shirt. Instead, I realize she's fallen asleep.

I want nothing more than to wrap myself around her, but she's peaceful and the rest will do her some good. Deciding not to disturb her, I cover her with a sheet and retreat to the living room.

I need to try and call Brody again anyway.

25
Ava Mae

FINALLY! I JUST took my last final. I feel good about them; of course, my study routine was very different this go round. Nate made me dinner every night and would rub my feet, my back, and any part of me he could reach as long as I studied. Believe it or not, the plan worked. He says it was a purely selfish way to keep his hands on me. Little does he know I had the same motivation.

I'm sitting on a bench outside the library, waiting to meet up with Kara. I feel like it's been ages since we've actually hung out together. I've been spending a lot of time at Nate's, but even on the nights I'm home, she's not. She and Tanner have really seemed to hit it off and she spends just as much time with him as I do Nate. I'm mindlessly scrolling through my Facebook feed when someone sits down beside me.

"Hello, Ava."

Clint.

"Where's your guard dog?" he asks.

"If you're referring to my boyfriend, he's at work," I snap. I am so sick of this guy. It's my fault. I used to be able to ignore him, until Nate. Now ignoring him isn't enough. I just want him to leave me alone.

"I forgive you for spending so much time with him," he says, picking up a lock of my hair and twirling it around his fingers.

I quickly smack his hand away and stand. "Don't touch me. As far as forgiving me, you're nothing to me, Clint. Find someone else to use your advances on."

"Why are you being such a bitch, Ava? You think now you have some hotshot pretending to be your boyfriend that you can just brush me off. You know he feels sorry for you, right? Being your brother's best friend and all." He smirks.

"Fuck you. You don't know anything about Nate, or our relationship. Just leave me the fuck alone." I turn to stalk off.

I run straight into what feels like a brick wall at the same time I feel my arm being pulled behind me.

Brick wall guy pulls me into his side. "Keep your fucking hands off her," he seethes.

Tanner.

I relax, knowing I'm not clinging to a complete stranger.

"You okay, Ava?" he asks.

"Yeah, I was just leaving," I tell him.

"The fuck you were," Clint spews. "I'm not done talking to you." He reaches for me.

Tanner moves me in behind him. "I told you to keep your fucking hands off her," Tanner reminds Clint. He crosses his arms over his chest. He's a big dude. Clint doesn't seem to be fazed.

"Look, man, I don't know who you are, but I just need to talk to my girl," Clint tries to reason.

"Look, man," Tanner spits his words back at him. "Ava is *not* your girl, and she doesn't want you touching her. I'm not against using whatever means necessary to make that happen," he says, stepping closer to Clint.

"Fuck you. This isn't over, Ava," he seethes before turning and stalking away.

Tanner keeps his stance until he can no longer see Clint. Turning, he places his arm around my shoulders. "You okay?" He studies me and I nod. "Want to tell me what that was about?" he asks.

"He's an ass," I reply.

Tanner laughs. "I got that. What's his deal?" he asks

"I have no idea. I went on one date with him almost two years ago. Kara and I went out with him and a friend of his. They were drunk when they picked us up. We spent the entire night fighting off their drunken advances. Neither one of us ever went out with them again. Clint continued to ask me out and tell people I was his girl. I used to ignore him, but he saw me with Nate and now he's not impressed. Normally, I'm just with the girls and he would let it go. Today was different."

"You sure you're okay?" he asks again.

"Yes, thank you. What are you doing here anyway?"

He smiles. "I was coming to surprise Kara. She mentioned she was meeting you here. I just wanted to stop and say hello, and maybe steal a kiss before I head to the gym," he says sheepishly.

"Hey," Kara says, walking up to us. Her eyes take in Tanner's arm around my shoulders. "What happened?" she questions. I love my best friend. I love how she knows me better than anyone. Never once did she assume Tanner and I were up to no good from the hold he has on me. I love that girl!

"Hey, sweetheart," Tanner says, releasing me and pulling her in for a kiss. "Some jackass was putting his hands on her and wouldn't take no for an answer," he explains.

"Ava?"

"Clint. He was acting stranger than usual. He tried to tell Tanner we were together. When I went to walk away, he grabbed me. Luckily, I plowed into this guy." I point to Tanner and he grins. "Tanner scared him away," I reassure her.

"What a fucking psycho!" Kara exclaims.

I smile at her outrage on my behalf. "I'm fine. Luckily, your man here was stopping to steal a kiss."

Kara looks up at Tanner and grins. "You were, huh?"

He answers her with a kiss to her lips. "Heading to the gym from here." He sighs. "Ava, you know I'm gonna have to tell Nate," he informs me.

"It's fine, nothing happened," I tell him.

Tanner shakes his head. "Doesn't matter. He'll be pissed if he finds out we kept this from him. What if I wasn't here, Ava?" he asks.

Damn it. I know he's right. "Fine. I guess I'll catch a ride with you to the gym."

"I'll drive you and we can catch up on the way," Kara offers.

And just like that, we're on our way to Nate to tell him what happened. He's going to be pissed.

26

Nate

ZACH AND I are standing at the back of gym waiting for Tanner. He was supposed to be here already. He's usually punctual. I glance at my phone, making sure I didn't miss him. Wouldn't surprise me. Somehow I've missed Brody three times. We are playing a never-ending game of phone tag. I'm about to just drop the bomb in his voicemail and call it good. If he wasn't my best friend and my girl's brother, I already would have. Just as I'm getting ready to call Tanner, he strolls in with a girl under each arm, one of them being mine. Any irritation I felt at him for being late floats away as Ava Mae walks toward me. That is until I see her face.

It takes me two strides to reach her. She breaks free from Tanner and wraps her arms around my waist. Something's wrong. "What's wrong?" I say low enough for only her to hear. I don't know what it is, but she might not want to air it among our friends and the rest of the gym.

"Ava?" Tanner says. It sounds like he's warning her. I scowl at him over her head and he scowls right back. "Tell him or I will," he says.

Placing my finger under her chin, I lift her eyes to mine. "Baby, what happened?" My voice is soft and soothing. That's how I feel on the outside. On the inside, I'm flipping the fuck out. Something happened that has Tanner concerned enough to bring her here, Kara too. It also has her clinging to me.

"Can we go to your office?" she asks.

I nod and lead the way back to my office. I hear footsteps behind us. I assume that means Tanner and Kara are following. We file into my office, Zach and Trey included. I scowl at them. "Guys, can you give us a minute?"

"No," Ava Mae says. "I don't want to have to say this twice. Once I do, it's done, over." She looks around the room making sure everyone understands. I don't commit to that statement. I need to know what happened.

Resigned, Ava Mae begins to tell us what happened this afternoon while she was waiting for Kara. I tighten the hold I have on her as she tells the story. I'm able to school my emotions and not show the anger that is racing through me from what this guy said to her. I'm controlling it, not wanting to scare her.

"And," Tanner prompts her.

"When I went to walk away, he grabbed me, but I bumped into Tanner and he scared him off. End of story," she rushes to say.

It takes a few minutes for my brain to catch up. "What the fuck? He put his hands on you?" The beast in me is ready to unleash. "Ava Mae," I growl when she doesn't answer.

Tanner speaks up. "I walked up on her moving away from him. He was grabbing her arm when she plowed into me," he explains.

I reach for her arms and inspect them. There's the slight outline of what looks like a thumbprint on her wrist. "Motherfucker!"

Ava Mae flinches away from me. Taking a deep breath, I reach out and snag my arm around her waist. I slowly pull her into me, wrapping her in my arms. I bury my head in the crook of her neck and focus on deep, even breaths, just breathing her in. She's safe; he didn't hurt her, not like he could have. She has a small bruise, but Tanner was there. I repeat this over and over in my head. Fuck! What would have happened if Tanner hadn't been there?

Lifting my head, I look around the room. "Out," I say. I'm not trying to be a dick, but I need a minute with her. "Please, just give us a minute." My voice cracks at the range of emotions swarming me.

I don't bother to make sure they leave; instead, I bury my face back in her neck.

Breathe in.

I hear the shuffle of feet and then the click of the door closing behind them. Pulling back, I lead Ava to the chair in front of my desk.

I sit down and pull her onto my lap, clinging to her as if my life depends on it. My head rests against her chest. I feel her run her fingers through my hair and slowly I start to relax.

"Nate, I'm fine. He's an ass. He didn't hurt me. Tanner stepped in," she says soothingly. She continues to run her fingers through my hair as I work on matching my breathing to hers.

Breathe out.

I don't know how long we sit like this. Time seems to creep by as I hold tightly to her.

"Nathan?" Her voice is hesitant.

The sound of her sweet voice saying my name does something to me and the floodgates open. "I used to admire you from afar," I tell her. "You would tag along with whatever it was Brody and I were getting into and I used to watch you, closely. The day before we left for the Marines, I hugged you and pretended you were mine that day. I pretended you were going to be waiting for me when we got home. When I got your letters, I continued to pretend—you kept me going. When Dad had his stroke and I came home for good, I fought the pull to seek you out. I battled with myself to stay away from you. You were his little sister and off limits to me. Each night I would wish you were lying beside me, and each morning wish you were the first thing I saw. Years, Ava Mae. For years I've longed to be with you."

Lifting my head, I focus my gaze on those big brown eyes of hers. "Now I know," I whisper. "I know what it feels like to fall asleep with you in my arms. I know what it's like to open my eyes and you are the first person I see. I don't have to pretend anymore." I wipe the lone tear that falls from her eye with my thumb, bringing it to my lips to taste. "The thought of anyone hurting you, his hands on you, cuts me. I want to protect you from that, from the Clints of the world. I know it's irrational and caveman, but that's who I am with you. I'm that guy. The one who would give his life to protect his girl."

I want to tell her what she means to me, that she's the only one who can keep my bed warm at night that I'm in love with her. The only thing stopping me is my best friend, her brother. I want him to know about us. I need to tell him what she means to me before I tell her. I need him to understand so when I tell her, she can accept it. She will do that if she knows he has as well. She tries not to let it bother her, but I know it does.

"How is it possible we wished for the same thing and neither one of us knew? Everything you just said is like you're inside my head, reading from a script." Leaning in close, she says, "It's always been you," before molding her lips to mine.

Breaking away from the kiss, I study her face. She still has that worried look in her eyes. "Talk to me."

"I don't want you going after Clint. He's not worth the trouble. I'm fine." She places her hand against my jaw. "I'm here with you. Can we please just let it go? Tanner scared him off. He's smart enough not to mess with me anymore. He's seen the three of you. He gets it. How could he not? This was his last ditch effort, and now it's done. Promise me, Nate."

"I might be willing to consider letting him live with a few stipulations."

"And what might they be?"

"First, you stay clear of him. No more walking around campus or anywhere by yourself. Not for a while at least. Let's make sure he's really going to leave you alone."

"Done. What's next?"

I cup her face in my hands and lock my gaze on to those big brown eyes of hers. "If he ever so much as breathes in your direction again, he's going to suffer the consequences. There will not be anyone who can stop me from teaching him a lesson."

"Nate—" I cut her off.

"No. This is non-negotiable. He's lucky this time it was Tanner and not me. Regardless of who it is, if there is a next time, I get to handle it."

"Okay," she softly agrees. I can tell she doesn't like it, but I won't concede on this. If he comes near her again, he answers to me.

27

Ava Mae

*I*T'S BEEN A week since my run-in with Clint. Now that classes are over for the summer, I've been spending time with Nate at the gym. I work out and often help at the desk if one of the receptionists is running late or needs time off. It's really a win-win for me. The job is easy, I get to see Nate, and it makes me feel . . . worthy. I don't want to be seen as the clingy girlfriend. My parents insisted I take this summer off. I took classes the summer after high school and last summer. This is the first real break I've had in a while. With no job, no classes to go to or study for, I have a lot of free time on my hands.

Currently, I'm sitting in Nate's office and just finished entering in a few invoices. He tried to talk me out of it, but really, I'm going crazy with nothing to do. I close down the program and log in to Facebook. Nate and Brody have been playing phone tag for weeks. I've decided a little cyber stalking is called for to try and track down my big brother. I know he's busy with his job, but really, it's never been this hard to get a hold of him. He's not deployed; he's in Hawaii for goodness' sake. I told Nate last night that we should just hop on a plane and go visit him. He thought I was kidding and said if he's getting me on a plane, he's taking me to Vegas so Elvis can tie us together for the rest of our lives. I know he was kidding. I, however, was not. My heart was also not kidding when it skipped a beat at the suggestion of marriage. We're not there yet, but I hope one day we will be.

Pulling up my brother's name, I find nothing that will lead me to what he's been up to. His last post was three months ago and it was of him and some of his Marine buddies having a drink after work. So much for cyber stalking.

"Hey, babe," Nate greets me.

147

I look up to find him leaning against the frame of his office door. "Hey. You finished with Zach's session today?"

"Yeah, I just need to stick around for a few more minutes and make sure Cassie shows up. She's supposed to close tonight."

Glancing at the clock, I see it's almost four o'clock. "Sounds good." I point to the computer screen. "I finished entering the invoices and sent a few reminders out to late members. I also tried to cyber stalk Brody to see what has him so busy, but that was an epic fail."

"It is a little weird that we keep missing each other. I'm beginning to think your 'hop on a plane' idea might have merit."

"Don't tease me, Nathan Garrison." I mock glare at him.

This causes him to laugh and stride toward me. Suddenly, he's right in front of me, leaning down, bracing his arms on the desk. "We can make a stop in Vegas on the way there. That way he'll have to accept it. Legally, we'd be bound together and there is nothing he could do." He leans in and places his lips next to mine. This kiss is quick, and before I know it, my lips feel bare without his. He stays in this stance, eyes boring into mine. "Then he couldn't take you away from me," he says before standing to his full height.

"Nate?" I know he can hear the question in my voice. I watch him as he runs his fingers through his hair. He walks around the desk and pulls me out of his seat, his ass replacing mine; then he tugs me onto his lap. Leaning my back against his chest, I rest my head on his shoulder. He moves my hair away from my neck and buries his face there. I feel his hot breath against my skin.

"Tell me he won't make you change your mind. The longer we play phone tag, the more my anxiety rises. I know how close the two of you are, and it scares the hell out of me that he's going to tell you we"—he wraps his arms around my waist—"are not an option."

"What about you? You guys have been best friends since kindergarten. Bros before hos and all that," I fire back.

He chuckles. "See, that's where you're confused. Bros before hos is part of the guy code. However, the code says nothing about bros before the forever girl. That's what you are, Ava Mae. You're everything, the only one who means everything. No guy code can touch that."

His words warm me. The butterflies that are always present when he's around are going crazy in the pit of my stomach. I would have thought they would have calmed down by now, but no. He can cause them to take flight from simply looking at me.

"You melt my heart, Nathan Garrison," I say, turning my head to kiss his cheek.

"That's good, baby, because you own mine," he confesses.

My breath hitches in my throat. If I wasn't sure before, he just sealed the deal. I'm head over heels in love with him. A deep, all-consuming, love that changes you. The kind of love that is beyond comparison to anything and everything else. But I'm not ready to tell him just yet.

"It won't matter," I say softly. "It won't matter what he says, how mad he gets. He's not changing my mind." I stop there before I blurt out my all-consuming declaration of love.

His lips press against my neck causing me to moan in appreciation.

"Son, are your lips ever not attached to that girl?"

Hearing his father's voice causes me to jump from Nate's lap. "Not if I can help it." He laughs as he stands.

Reaching over, I smack his arm. This causes them both to chuckle. "Your mom's out in the car. We just stopped to see if you kids would want to come over for dinner?"

Nate smiles and looks at me. "Babe?" he asks. Nothing like being put on the spot in front of the parents.

I nod, letting him know I'm okay with it. "Sure, I'm just waiting for the night closer to get here and then we'll head over."

"Do we need to bring anything?" I ask.

"No, sweet girl, just your appetite and my son. I don't, however, foresee that being an issue as long as you're going to be there." He winks and walks out the door. A pang of guilt hits me that my parents still don't know about us. We've been waiting to tell them so we could tell Brody first, but I'm tired of waiting for him. He's going to find out regardless.

"Nate, maybe after we leave your parents' house we can stop by mine," I throw it out there.

"What about Brody?" he questions.

"I hate how I'm keeping this from them. I don't want to hide us, not that we've really been hiding. I want them to hear it from us, not some random acquaintance who has seen us together. Brody has to find out one way or the other. Maybe we can ask them not to say anything since we're trying to get a hold of him so we, or you rather, can tell him."

Placing his hands on my hips, he pulls me close. "Does your dad still have that shotgun?" I can tell he's joking.

I laugh. "Yes, but lucky for you, he's always liked you, and besides, he doesn't like to see me cry. Shooting you would most definitely make me cry," I fire back.

"Then it's settled. Call them and see if they're going to be home. We can stop by after dinner."

In just a few hours, my parents will know exactly what's been keeping me so busy the last couple of months. I'm not worried, not really. They love Nate and know he's a good guy. The only obstacle we face is Brody, if we could just connect with him.

28

Nate

INNER WITH MY parents was great. They have accepted our relationship with open arms. Not that I thought they wouldn't. Dad ratted us out to Mom that he found us kissing again in my office. Her reply was, "I remember those days." This, of course, prompted my dad to lay one on her. I took the hint and we called it a night. Now we're on the way to Ava Mae's parents' house. They've always been great to me. I practically grew up there. That doesn't mean they will approve of me for their daughter. I've been so wrapped up in wanting to tell Brody that her parents never really crossed my mind.

Ava Mae called them on the way to my parents and asked if she could stop by a little later. Told them she had someone she wanted them to meet. One look out the window as we pull into the drive and they will know I'm that someone. My Tahoe is easy to spot with the Hardcorps' logo casing the windows. She didn't say meet her boyfriend, just someone she wanted them to meet. They probably assume she's just bringing me by for a visit. It's been too long. I avoided them to avoid her, because I wanted her. They're in for a surprise.

"Ready for this?" she asks.

"Yeah. Let's do it," I say, squeezing her hand.

As we walk to the front door, Ava Mae laces her fingers through mine. I've dreamed of this exact moment so many times, being with her here. I take a deep breath and hold it as she opens the door and leads us into the house. Here goes nothing.

"Mom, Dad, we're here," Ava Mae calls out for them.

"In the kitchen, sweetie," her mom calls back.

"Here we go, boyfriend." She grins at me. Just like that, the smile on her face calms my nerves. We got this.

"Hey . . . Nate! It's so good to see you," her mom says as soon as she spots me. She comes around the counter to embrace me in a hug. I try to release Ava Mae's hand, but she holds tightly. Stepping out of the hug, she turns to embrace my girl. "Ava, it's been weeks. What have you been up to?" she asks.

Her mom steps back around the counter and continues working on mixing what appears to be cookie dough. "Where's Dad?" Ava Mae inquires.

"Right here, baby girl," he says, engulfing her in a hug. This time she has no choice but to let go of my hand as he lifts her in the air, squeezing her in a hug.

Setting her back on her feet, he finally sees me. "Nate, son, how are ya?" He holds his hand out for me to shake.

I shake his hand, making sure my grip is firm all the while keeping eye contact. "Good. It's been a while," I say.

"So what brings you kids by?" he asks, stealing a bite of cookie dough.

"I thought it was time to introduce you to my boyfriend," Ava Mae replies.

They both stop and stare at her. "Did you make him stay in the car?" her mom asks.

"Let me get my gun before you invite him in," her dad laughs. I watch as her mom smacks his arm. Searching their faces, they are both smiling. Okay, so far so good.

"Why would I make Nate sit in the car? It's not like you all don't already know each other," Ava Mae just throws it out there. Reaching over, she laces our fingers together.

I'm momentarily frozen from the smile that lights her face, causing those brown eyes of hers to sparkle. She winks at me and I can't help but chuckle. Tearing my eyes from her, I chance a look at her parents who are watching us with their mouths hanging open.

"Before you say anything, please let me talk." Ava Mae finally gets serious. "About three months ago, Kara met a guy who just so happens to be one of the fighters who Nate trains. He invited us to watch him train. He was training at Hardcorps and Nate and I saw each other for the first time in over two years." She squeezes my hand. "We fought it, both of us fought against it. We didn't go into this lightly. When we finally decided that becoming a couple was what we both wanted, we decided Brody should be the first person we told. Unfortunately, Nate and Brody have been playing phone tag for weeks. Nate's parents know. They stopped by when I was at his place." She leaves out what exactly we were doing at my place. "We were trying to wait for Brody before we told you, but we were tired of hiding it."

She steps next to me and I put my arm around her, pulling her close. It's not until after I've already kissed her temple that I remember her parents might not approve of my display of affection for her, too late to worry about that now. I keep her in my arms, curled against my chest. "We wanted you to find out from us, not some random person on the street. We would like to ask that you not mention it to Brody. We want to be the ones to tell him, if we can ever make a connection," she requests.

"Nathan, I trust you'll do right by her," her dad addresses me.

I look down at the gorgeous girl in my arms. She smiles up at me as her arms give a gentle squeeze of comfort. Resting my chin on top of her head, I respond. "Yes, sir. Always." I keep my eyes locked on him, letting him see how serious I am.

He smiles. "Good, let's have some cookies." He swoops in and steals another ball of cookie dough.

"Stop that," her mom says, moving the pan a little to the side. "Have you all had dinner? We have some leftover spaghetti if you're interested," she offers.

"We just had dinner with Nate's parents," Ava Mae confesses.

"Good thing I'm making dessert." She grins. "Let me get these in the oven and we can sit and catch up."

"Nate, let's grab a beer on the deck while the girls make us some cookies." He grins at his wife.

I nod once, kiss my girl on the forehead, and follow him outside. He takes an oversized lounge chair and points to the one beside him, handing me a beer. "She seems happy."

So am I. "I hope so," I say instead.

"You seem pretty happy yourself," he adds.

I smile. "I'm not sure happy is a strong enough word. Ava Mae is . . . my world." The words fall off my tongue before I can stop them.

He chuckles. "I can see that too. If I didn't, I wouldn't be okay with this." He smirks. "Brody's going to need some time when he finds out."

"I know, but I won't hide from this, from what I feel about her," I say honestly.

"I know my son, and he will adjust . . . eventually." He takes a sip of his beer. "What if he asks you to choose?"

"Impossible. He's my best friend and I would do anything for him, anything but give her up. I love them both, in very different ways." Holy shit! I just told her dad in so many words that I'm in love with her. I take a long drink of my beer, letting that sink in. "If he made me choose, if there was no other option, I would choose her. It would be impossible to do, to think that our friendship would be over, but she's . . . yeah, it would be her." I figured I might as well lay it out for him.

"That's all I can ask for from the man who holds my baby girl's heart."

"I hope it doesn't come to that, to him telling me I have to pick."

"He'll adjust. He'll need some time, but he'll come around."

The patio door opens and Ava Mae walks out holding a plate of cookies in her hands. Her mom is right behind her. She sets them on the small table between the two loungers and then sits down beside me, snuggling close. Never able to resist her when she's near, I pull my arm around her. That's how we spend the next two hours. Sitting outside enjoying time with her parents as a couple, as Nathan and Ava Mae.

29
Ava Mae

"Hey, Brod, it's me. Call me when you get this." I leave yet another message for my brother. It's not that he's not calling back, but the times are just not matching up. He called me back yesterday while I was in the shower. It wasn't even five minutes later when I called him back, only to get his voicemail. I toss my phone in frustration into my bag that's sitting just a little ways from me.

I'm currently perched on an exercise ball. I should be using it to 'strengthen my core'; instead, it's softer than the floor, so it's my chair. Nate had an initial meeting with a new fighter who wants Nate to train him. They are sitting across from me just shooting the shit it looks like. I started out in Nate's office. I got his paperwork caught up, and then I got bored. Once the gym officially closed, I locked the doors and began wiping down equipment. Thinking about Brody is what led me here, to the ball. It's not only comfortable but it gives me a great view of his potential client and Nate. Nate's wearing athletic shorts and a shirt that has the sleeves cut out of it. I can see his toned arms and abs through the side of the shirt. Every once in a while, he'll glance over and his face softens when he sees me watching him.

He looks good enough to eat, among other things. I'm more than ready to take our relationship to another level, but Nate seems to be content with where we are. I blame my brother. I know Nate better than he thinks I do. He's refusing to sleep with me until Brody knows about us. Like he needs his blessing or something. I can see it now. "Brody, I'm dating your sister and I want to have sex with her." Yeah, that conversation would go over like a turd in a punch bowl. Although I'm sexually frustrated, I get it. He wants to be straight up with him, make his intentions clear before we take that last step. Let's face it, that's all that's left.

We've shared our bodies with one another. I know where to touch him that brings chills to his skin. I know he likes it when I kiss his neck just under his ear, among other places. I can catalogue it all. Blindly, I could tell you which part of him I'm touching. What I can't do is tell you what it feels like to have him inside me. What it feels like to be connected as one with him. I want that, no, crave is more like it. The need to share that with him is almost overwhelming. I've yet to come out and ask for it. I can tell he's holding back, and even if I asked, he would turn me down. So, instead, I take what he's willing to give.

"Comfy?" His question pulls me away from my naughty thoughts about him, well, that is until I look at him. He's settled on the floor in front of me. You can tell he's been running his fingers through his hair. "I didn't think he was ever going to leave." He sighs.

Reaching out, I run my fingers through his hair, just because I can. He catches my hand and places a kiss on the inside of my wrist. "It was hard for me to focus with you sitting over here on that damn ball, looking all sexy." His voice is gruff.

He places my hand against his cheek. "I was willing him to leave. I guess he finally got the message I was sending."

Dropping my hand, I rest my elbows on my knees, bringing my face close to his. "He's gone now." I softly kiss his lips. "I locked the doors earlier; we're all alone," I tell him.

He runs his hands up and down the calves of my legs. "So soft," he murmurs.

Just the simple glide of his hands against my skin is driving me wild. "Touch me, Nate," I whisper.

His slow stroke starts at my ankle, leading up to my knee. This time he keeps going as his big hand slides across my thigh. When I feel his finger slide under my panties, I can't stop the moan that escapes me. "Nate."

"What, baby? You asked me to touch you. Do you want me to stop?" he asks, although he makes no attempt to stop. Instead, he traces the outside of my folds with his finger.

"No, don't stop."

"Are you sure?" I can hear the cockiness in his voice.

"Positive," I pant.

"Stand for me," he says, removing his hand. I whimper at the loss of contact. Standing, I brace my hands on his shoulders; my legs are weak. Nate remains sitting on the floor. With a hand on each hip, he grasps the corner of my shorts and panties, and tugs.

"Step." I do as I'm told and step out, one foot at a time.

"Sit." Again, I do as I'm told and take my place back on the exercise ball. Nate rises to his knees. "Open for me." With one hand resting on each of my knees, he pushes my legs apart. His hands roam my thighs, gently caressing. He brings his lips close to mine. "You are so fucking beautiful."

"Nate." My voice is pleading, begging him to touch me.

He answers my plea by tracing his index finger over my folds. Teasing, taunting me. My hands are gripping tight to his shoulders. Each barely-there stroke sets my nerve endings on fire.

"Please." I'm not above begging him if that's what it takes.

Nate chuckles and slides one finger through the wetness that his teasing has caused. He takes his time exploring with just that one finger. He doesn't apply pressure where I need it. He doesn't push it inside me. No, he's playing with me. It's complete torture and pure bliss at the same time. Only Nate can do that to me. Make me feel so many emotions from a single stroke of a single digit.

"More," I moan at the same time he pushes his digit inside me. I tilt my head back, close my eyes, and let the pleasure he's creating wash over me.

I feel him move in close. He traces my collarbone with his tongue, trailing up my neck. Stopping at my ear, he whispers, "I need to taste you." Slowly moving down my body, the anticipation of what he's about to do has me vibrating with need.

"Hold on tight, babe." He dips his head between my legs and it takes every ounce of balance I have to stay on the damn ball at the first swipe of his tongue. Taking his advice, I grip his shoulders, holding on for the ride.

He slides his finger back inside me along with the slow, even stroke of his tongue and I rock my hips, seeking more. The sensation of my movements is heightened by the ball. It takes little effort on my part to continue the bounce/rock sensation that it creates. "Don't stop. Please, don't stop," I beg him. I'm so close. He adds a second finger, and within three pumps, I'm screaming out his name. He continues to stroke and lick until my body ceases to spasm. Within minutes of his mouth leaving my body, he has me off the ball and in his arms.

Molded against his chest, I can feel the heavy rise and fall of his breathing. "Jesus, Ava Mae. That was the hottest fucking thing I've ever seen in my life," he rasps.

"Hmmm," is the only reply I can manage. He chuckles at this.

His lips touch my temple. "Let's get you dressed and head home." Luckily, this is something he helps me with. I slowly stand with Nate keeping a tight hold on me. He holds my panties and shorts, allowing me to step back into them. Once I'm dressed, he stands and engulfs me in a hug. I love the feel of his arms around me. His arms, however, are not the only thing I feel. His erection is still standing loud and proud. Reaching down, I trace the outline of him with my hand.

He growls in my ear. "We can take care of that later. Let's go home," he says again. "I want you in my bed," he whispers.

Hearing those words has my feet moving toward the door.

30

Nate

I BREAK MORE SPEED laws than I care to mention getting us back to my place. As soon as I pull into the drive, Ava Mae has her door open and she's walking toward the door. My first instinct is to chase after her. I want to throw her over my shoulder and carry her back to my room. I ache to be inside her. I'm beginning to wonder if it's worth holding out until Brody knows about us. Honestly, the idea of waiting so I can tell him I love her and have yet to be inside her, seems like wasted effort when she's like this. I know she wants more. I can see it in her eyes. I can hear it in the way she sighs as soon as she realizes I'm once again not letting things go as far as she would like. She doesn't mention it, but I worry how many times I can stop it. How much longer can I resist her without her thinking I'm rejecting her.

Once I'm in the house, I throw my keys and phone on the table. Looking around, I realize she's not in the living room like I assumed she would be. "Ava Mae?" I call out for her.

"Bedroom," she calls back. My dick seems to understand her words as he rises to the occasion. In reality, he's been at attention, ready and waiting to get here. I reach my bedroom door and my mouth waters at what I see. Ava Mae is lying on my bed on top of the covers wearing nothing . . . she's completely naked. Her head is propped up on her elbow and her silky brown curls are hanging over her shoulder, causing her breasts to play peek-a-boo. Leaning against the frame of the door, I soak in the sight of her. My eyes rake over every inch of her skin as I commit it to memory.

"You're too far away." She smiles at me.

"You think so?" I ask, buying myself some more time to look my fill of her.

"Yeah, I do." Her voice is husky. "It's your turn, Nate."

I watch as she licks her lips. Sweet baby Jesus, I will never get enough of her. Leaving my perch on the doorframe, I slowly make my way toward her.

'"Strip," she commands.

I do exactly that, pulling my shirt over my head and tossing it across the room. "Pants," she says with a smirk. She's enjoying this, being the one in control. If she only knew what I would do for her . . .

I stop beside the bed and slide out of my shorts, pulling my boxer briefs down at the same time, kicking them both to the side. Reaching down, I grip my hard cock and begin to stroke. "What now, baby?" I ask her.

She pats the bed beside her. With another long stroke, I release my aching cock and climb into bed beside her. Her small hands reach out and grab me. "It's your turn, Nate," she murmurs in a soft voice next to my ear.

"Ava Mae, you don't have to."

I watch as she licks her lips. "It's only fair I get to taste you, too."

Squeezing my eyes shut, I try to think of something other than those luscious lips being traced by her tongue. I try to ignore the fact her soft hands are pumping me, slowly increasing their rhythm. "Ava Mae." Her name is a plea from my lips.

With my eyes still tightly shut, I miss the fact she's there, and that her mouth is there. I'm alerted to the fact when I feel her hot tongue against me, tasting me before she takes me deep. Nothing could have prepared me for what it feels like to have her mouth on me. I fought against her, wanting to do this for weeks. Tonight, I've lost my willpower. I can't resist her; I don't want to. That's been the struggle all along. I've never wanted to, but thought it was the right thing to do.

My hands find the back of her head and I grip her hair. She moans and the vibration against my cock has my eyes rolling in the back of my head. I would love to watch her as she moves her hot mouth over me, but the pleasure that's coursing through me is too much. It's taking every ounce of control I have not to thrust into her mouth.

I feel her adjust positions, and then her mouth opens wide and I slide deep. So fucking deep. No way is this going to last. "Ava Mae . . . you need to stop," I force the words. Fuck, I don't want her to stop. I want to let go and have her take every bit of me, but I don't know how she feels about that. We've never talked about it and I feel like an ass for not having that conversation. I spent so much time trying to avoid being in this position before talking to Brody that I don't know what she wants, what she expects in this scenario.

"Ava Mae, baby, I'm close." I take a deep breath when she moans, causing that same vibration that drives me wild. I tap my hand on her shoulder, trying to get her attention. She grabs my hand and places it on the back of her head, never missing a beat. "I'm going to come, babe," I warn her and she takes me deeper. Fuck, I grip her hair and lift my hips as I coat the back of her throat.

Her mouth doesn't leave me until the last shudder rocks through me. My hand falls away from her hair as she crawls up my body. "Thank you," she whispers in my ear.

I turn my head to face her. Why is she thanking me? I raise my eyebrows because my brain has not recuperated from the mind-blowing orgasm she just gave me.

Sensing my question, she responds, "For not stopping me this time. I want to be able to share this with you. To be able to make you feel the pleasure I do every time you touch me."

Still unable to speak, I wrap an arm around her and tug her close. I kiss the top of her head. This sexy, beautiful creature just rocked my world and now she's telling me how much she enjoyed it. How the fuck did I get this lucky?

"You're amazing," I say, finally finding my voice.

Raising her head off my chest, she looks up at me. Licking her lips, she smirks as she says, "So are you."

That's all it takes for me to be ready for round two. I never see myself having my fill of her.

Not able to contain the smile on my face from her innuendo, I lean into her and kiss her forehead. Reaching behind her, she brings the covers over us as she settles back against my chest. The words are on the tip of my tongue. I bite back the urge to tell her. I need to get a hold of Brody. I know she was joking, but if I have to fly to Hawaii to do it, I will. Something has to give.

31

Ava Mae

"TIME TO WAKE up, beautiful." Nate kisses my bare shoulder, which is not helping his case to pull my ass out of bed. We pretty much stay with each other every night now. Either his place or mine. We try to split our time so Kara and I still get to spend time together. Tanner is usually there as well, so it's a good thing we all get along. Kara and I do a girls' day once a week and we still run every morning. I'm surprised she's kept with it. I think Tanner is a big part of that. The Color Run is today, so I know I need to get up, but I'm warm and surrounded by his scent. It's hard to leave that.

"Come on, babe. You need to get up and give yourself time to eat. You can't run on an empty stomach," he says, tugging at the covers.

Knowing he's right, I don't fight him. "I'm getting in the shower," I say, climbing out of bed.

"We need to save water," he says, standing up to follow me.

I put my hand up to stop him. His arms are longer than mine, making it easy for him to still reach out and grip my hips, pulling me close to him. "Not happening," I inform him.

He sticks out his bottom lip, pretending to pout. "Pwease?" he says.

I can't help but laugh at him. "That's not working on me, Nathan. I want you, but you won't let me have you. You can shower when you learn how to share," I tell him as I twist out of his arms and bolt for the bathroom door. I know he's not following me, but I'm not taking the chance of him catching me.

Nate is still refusing to have sex with me. I'm frustrated as hell about it. He has this idea in his head that we need to tell Brody first. I tried to explain to him that it doesn't matter. If Brody knew the things he's done to me . . . it just doesn't matter. In reality, it's Nate. He has it in his head that he wants to be able to tell Brody we haven't slept together. We may not have had sexual intercourse, but we most definitely have slept together. What we do is just as intimate, if not more, but I want more regardless. I've never met someone who can make my body ignite for them with just a simple touch. I wasn't saving myself for marriage. I was just saving myself for someone who could light my fire, so to speak. In the back of my mind, I think I might have always been waiting for Nate. I'd imagined it being him more times than I can count. Now he's mine, now that I can make that dream a reality, he's making me wait. I'm not a fan of waiting.

I find Nate in the kitchen. He has a cup of coffee and a bagel with cinnamon cream cheese ready and waiting for me. "I just talked to Tanner; they're on their way here. We're going to ride together."

"Have you heard from Zach?" I ask. He was supposed to run with us, but he had to fly to New York to meet with his agent. He's moving up in the world. He had still planned to meet us at the event and run, but his flight was delayed due to weather.

"Yeah, his flight lands at noon. He was pretty bummed."

"That sucks. This started with him training just Kara and I, and then it became a group thing." I take a sip of my coffee. "We'll just have to plan to do another one so he can be there."

Nate laughs. "I think Kara will have something to say about that."

"You might be right. I'll just have to recruit Tanner to use his sexual persuasion to convince her."

"Hmpf. Didn't work for me," he mumbles.

I point my finger at him. "You, Mr. Garrison, have no room to complain."

"It's never been this hard to connect with him," he says in defense.

I shrug. "He's got a girlfriend now. That on top of the Marines keeping him busy, there just aren't enough hours in the day. I don't see why you're letting that stop you from being with me."

"Ava Mae, I'm not." He reaches over and places his hand on top of mine. "You're here with me, where you belong. Regardless of how he feels, I'm in this."

"Do you hear yourself right now?" I ask him. I'm so damn frustrated with his reasoning. "You are letting it stop you. I want to know what it's like to make love to you." His eyes soften at my words. "You refuse to give me that until you talk to him." I pull my hand away from his. "You are letting him stop you, stop us." I'm upset, but trying to keep my emotions out of it. It feels like rejection, even though I know it's not. It's still hard to swallow.

Nate stands and rounds the table. Grabbing my hand, he pulls me from my chair. His hands clutch my cheeks, his eyes boring into mine. "I need you to listen to me, Ava Mae. I want nothing more than to make love to you." He takes a deep breath. "I also need Brody to understand what this is. He's been my best friend for twenty years. I know it doesn't make sense to you, but trust me on this. He's going to ask me if we've slept together. He's going to want to know that. I can't lie to him; I won't lie to him. When I tell him I've never had sex with you, I need it to be true."

"Why, Nate? Explain it to me. Because from where I'm standing, it feels like rejection." My voice is soft and pleading. I need to understand why this is so important to him.

"No, baby. That's not what this is." Leaning in, his hands find my hips as he rests his forehead against mine. His grip is tight and his breathing rapid. My eyes are glued to his chest as it rises and falls with each breath. Finally, after what seems like an eternity, his low voice surrounds me. "When I tell him I haven't slept with you, he's going to understand what you mean to me. Most guys, me included, would not be with a woman and not be reaping the benefits the relationship can provide unless she was more." Raising his head, he lifts my chin with his index finger so we are once again looking eye to eye. "Ava Mae, you are so much more. You're my past." He kisses my forehead. "You're my present." He kisses my nose. "And I hope like hell you're my future," he says, his lips pressing lightly against mine.

The kiss is soft and sweet and has all those damn butterflies taking flight yet again. "I want you, baby. I ache with want for you, but, as a guy, when I can honestly tell him that, he'll understand. Maybe not immediately, but trust me. He will understand what this is, what I want with you. I . . . just please be patient with me." He wraps his arms around my back and hugs me tight.

I understand what he's saying, and it makes sense to me. I still hate waiting. Not to mention, my brother is about to be hounded by his baby sister. I am going to blow his phone up until we reach him. Operation Hound Brody is now in process.

Our hug is interrupted by a knock on the door. "Are we good?" he asks me.

"Yeah." I stand on my tiptoes and kiss him. "I need to finish getting ready," I say before bounding down the hall to his room to get ready. Color Run, here we come.

32

Nate

I WATCH HER WALK away, ignoring the second knock on the front door. I almost told her. This is the closest I've come to just blurting it out. I can see she feels it too. It's in her eyes every time she looks at me and in her touch every time my body makes contact with hers. Another knock on the door draws my attention and has me rushing to answer it.

"What the hell took you so long? Dusting off the cobwebs?" Kara laughs.

"Kara!" Ava Mae shouts from behind me. This causes Kara to throw her head back in laughter.

"Hey, man," Tanner says with a grin. "You ready for this?" he asks.

"As I'll ever be." I've never done a Color Run. It looks like a fun time. Maybe Ava Mae will let me wash her back when we're done.

"Let's do this," Ava says as she links her arm through Kara's and they walk out the door.

"We're taking the Tahoe!" I yell after her. Tanner and I follow the girls to my Tahoe and they both climb in the back. I know she misses spending time with Kara. They meet up one night a week, but that's nothing compared to what they used to do. I don't want her giving up her friends for us, as long as I end up in the same bed as her at night with her in my arms, I'm good. Next Saturday is her birthday. I need to talk to her about what she wants to do. I thought about surprising her, but Ava Mae likes to keep things low-key. Glancing in the rearview mirror, I see the girls chatting away, not paying any attention to us at all. I decide to do it now; it's not like it's a surprise.

"Hey, babe." I wait until I have her attention. "What do you want to do for your birthday?"

Her eyes meet mine in the rearview mirror, a smile lighting her face. It's a struggle to keep my eyes on the road. Every time I look at her, she takes my breath away.

"I thought we could just hang out," I hear her say. I can't look at her again. It's too dangerous. I should have let Tanner drive.

"Who is 'we'?" Kara asks. "I better be included in that equation," she warns.

Shit. Maybe I should have talked with her when we were alone. I didn't mean to put her in a difficult situation.

The sound of her laugh eases my guilt. "Yes, you and Tanner. Zach and whomever he wants to invite, and us," she says as she leans forward, resting her hand on my shoulder.

Leaving one hand on the wheel, I reach up and cover her hand with mine, giving it a gentle squeeze. She makes no effort to remove her hand, which is fine by me. I lace our fingers together, taking full advantage of the situation.

"Anything specific you want to do?" Tanner asks.

"No. Just keep it simple. We can maybe grill out, hang by the pool, and build a bonfire. Nate, if you don't mind, maybe we can get together at your place?"

Like she even has to ask. "Anything you want, Ava Mae."

"Nate, you take care of the bonfire and the grill. I got the food covered," Kara informs me.

"Kara, you don't—" She cuts me off.

"Zip it, Garrison. I got this."

"That was so much fun!" Ava exclaims as she jumps in my arms, wrapping her legs around my waist. We're both completely covered in . . . color. "We have to do that again. Zach needs to do this." Her eyes are sparkling with happiness.

"Yeah, he would have got a kick out of it."

"Hey, you all want to grab something to eat?" Kara asks.

Ava nods. "I just need to talk to the event coordinators. I want to know when and where the next race is that's close to us." She releases her legs from around my waist and slides to her feet. "That's her standing over there." She points to the registration booth. "I'll be right back." She kisses my cheek and bounces off toward the booth. I watch her go, her yoga pants showing off her curves, curves that were just wrapped around me.

"What time was Zach's flight getting in?" Tanner's question has me pulling my eyes from her.

I pull my phone out of my pocket. "He should be landing now."

"I wonder if he needs a ride?" he inquires.

"No, he left the Hummer at the airport. I asked him last night when I talked to him."

"Kara, you let me know if you need anything for next weekend. I can cover the food too," I tell her.

"No, I want to do this. I know what she likes, so I'll take care of it. You just have some firewood and the grill ready."

"Okay, but if something changes, you let me know." I want this to be a great day for Ava Mae. I've already got her gift, or gifts, planned out. I can't wait to see her reaction.

"What's taking her so long? I'm starving," Kara whines.

I glance over my shoulder toward the registration booth and don't see her. I scan the area around the booth and nothing. "I don't see her," I say, pulling my phone back out of my pocket to see if I might have missed a call from her.

Nothing.

"I'm gonna go look for her," I tell them, but my feet are already moving in the direction of the last place I saw her. I reach the booth and the lady behind the table greets me.

"Hi, can I help you?" She smiles.

"I'm actually looking for my girlfriend. She was headed this way to ask about the next race, but it's been a while. I'm starting to get worried," I explain, trying not to let the worry show through my voice. My eyes scan the area.

Still nothing.

"Would that happen to be Ava?" she asks with a smile.

I feel my body relax a little. "Yes. Do you happen to know which way she might have gone?" I ask.

She hesitates for a minute. Tanner and Kara step up beside me. "Hey, did you find her? I'm seriously starving right now," Kara complains.

I look back at the lady behind the table. "Do you know which way she went?" I ask her again.

"Look who I found." Ava's voice washes over me.

Immediately, the tension leaves my body. Turning to face the voice, I reach out and pull her into me. "Hey, man," I say to Zach.

"Flight got in early." He grins. "Ava said we're going to eat; I'm starving."

"Good, we all agree. We found her, now let's roll." Kara tugs on Tanner's arms, pulling him toward the parking lot.

"You found me?" Ava raises her eyebrows in question.

"You were gone a while. I looked over here"—I point behind us to the registration booth—"and didn't see you. I started to worry."

"Aww." She grins. "That's so sweet." She's mocking me.

"Is that jackass still bothering you?" Zach questions her.

"No, I haven't seen him since the day Tanner ran him off." She shrugs. "I think he got the message."

"Let's eat," Zach says, ending the conversation. I feel her relax at the change of subject.

"The sooner we eat, the sooner we can shower." Ava wags her eyebrows.

"Let's get you fed," I say with a wink. She can tease me all she wants. I'm not giving in on this one . . . not yet.

33

"SO ANYONE ELSE you want to invite next weekend?" Kara asks around a mouth full of French fries.

I smile at my best friend. "I can't think of any." I've never been one to make a big deal out of birthdays. My only routine is the hug I ask Brody for every year. He has yet to let me down. Although, this year I have a feeling might be the first.

"You sure you don't want to hit the Underground?" Zach asks.

"Positive." I smile. "It actually sounds perfect," I say, my gaze landing on Kara. She nods, letting me know she gets it. I'm more of a homebody. I don't need to go out every weekend. My best friend knows me well. A simple night with friends sounds like the perfect way to spend my birthday. Kara's still looking at me, so I mouth "Monica" to her. I don't want Zach to feel like the outcast.

"Done," Kara say, setting her phone on the table.

"What's done?" Nate asks.

Kara winks at me. "I texted Monica and let her know about your birthday plans." She looks over at Zach. "You good with that?" She smirks.

Zach doesn't answer her, but the grin on his face says it all. He really likes Monica, but he's fighting the pull. Been there, done that.

"That's what I thought," Kara quips, causing us all to laugh. "Ugh, I need a shower."

"Yes, please," Tanner agrees.

"It looks like you all had fun, but I'm glad I don't have to deal with all of that." He waves his hands at us. We're a mess.

"My place or yours?" Nate asks low enough for only me to hear. I love how he does that. Let's me know he wants to be with me. He doesn't care where we are. I feel the same way.

"You coming home?" Kara asks me.

"No, we're going to Nate's. I'll probably just stay there tonight," I tell her.

She looks up at Tanner. "My place?" He nods his agreement.

After saying goodbye, Nate and I climb into his Tahoe. "I can't wait to take a shower," I tell him.

"I know. It was a good time though." He reaches over and places his hand on my thigh. "You had a good idea, babe."

"It was fun. I wish Zach could have been there, and Monica. I think she has been avoiding Zach."

"Why?"

"She likes him, but he keeps throwing her mixed signals. She's just trying not to fall."

"Hmmm," he says, not bothering to comment. He doesn't really need to. I know what he's thinking. We went through the same thing. The only difference is that we've known each other for years. I can't speak for the pull Monica feels toward Zach, but the one Nate has on me is all consuming.

Nate lets us into the house at the same time he pulls his shirt over his head. "You can take the master bath. I'll shower in the guest room. I need to get this shit off me," he says, heading down the hall.

I want to chase after him. I want to tell him he can shower with me and I'll wash his back, his front, and every inch in between. Instead, I bite my tongue, remembering his reason for resistance. I understand it, but that doesn't mean I agree with it. Stripping down in his bathroom, I decide to leave the door open. I'll break through his resolve eventually.

Much to my disappointment, Nate doesn't join me. He's not even in the bedroom waiting for me like I thought he would be. Grabbing some clothes from the drawers he cleaned out for me, I slip into yoga pants and a tank. I assume we're in for the day. Nate and I are a lot alike in that way. We're both more than happy to spend the day lounging. Just being together. Although it's good that we have similar interests, it's hell on my heart. I fall just a little more in love with him each day.

I find Nate kicked back on the couch, remote in hand. As soon as he sees me, he lifts his arm, inviting me into my favorite spot, curled up against his chest. No further prompting needed, I settle in beside him. He wraps his arms around me and kisses the top of my head. "Anything you want to watch?" he asks.

"Not really. I'm good with whatever."

He flips through the channels, searching for something that catches his eye. He finally settles on a satellite music station. "Let's stretch out," he suggests.

Yes, please! I stand, allowing him to lie down. Once he's settled, I lie down beside him, resting my head on his chest. He runs his fingers through my hair. "Your hair is so soft," he murmurs.

"Mmm." It's too damn comfortable lying here in his arms. I'm beat from the run and could fall asleep in no time.

He chuckles softly. "Am I boring you, babe?" he teases.

"I'm worn out," I say with a yawn.

His fingers continue to glide through my hair as he says, "I called Brody again, had to leave another message. I feel like I'm missing something. It's never like this, never been this hard to get a hold of him."

"You think he's okay?" I didn't want to say it aloud, but this is out of the ordinary. It's almost as if he knows what we want to tell him so he's avoiding us. "Do you think he already knows?" I ask Nate.

"Nah. He would've already called and ripped into me. I'll keep trying him until we get him."

"You're probably right. It's just weird how we keep missing him."

"Doesn't matter." He brings my hand that's resting on his chest to his lips and kisses my knuckles. "I want him to know. I need to explain to him what this is, but other than that . . . it doesn't matter. I would like to think he will understand, that I can get him to listen." He lays our entwined hands on his chest against his heart. "If not, he's going to have to learn how to deal."

This isn't the first time we've had this conversation. Nate continues to reassure me, that regardless of what Brody says or does, it will not come between us. I can't help but feel the heaviness of the situation bearing down on me. I don't want to come between them. I also don't want to give up what we have, what we're building. I think I'll call my mom tomorrow and get her in on the action. Maybe she will have better luck than we do.

34

Nate

*Y*OU'D THINK I would be used to this by now, waking up with her in my arms. I'm not. I don't know if I ever will be. Ava Mae is still napping, lying in my arms. Her hand grips my t-shirt as her soft breath hits my neck as she slowly breathes in and out. I could hold her like this for hours.

My phone beeps, indicating a text message. The sound causes her to open her eyes. "Hey, beautiful." I kiss her temple. "You feel better?"

"Yes, did you nap?" she asks, propping her chin up on my chest so she can look at me.

"I did." My phone beeps again. Ava Mae starts to move and I tighten my hold on her. "I have something for you."

She looks at me, eyes sparkling. "You do?"

"Yes. It's your birthday week after all."

"Birthday week?" She sits up on the couch. This time I let her.

"Yeah. Your birthday is one week from today. It's your birthday week." I'm taking any excuse I can get to spoil my girl.

"Nate, that's crazy talk." She laughs. "Who celebrates the entire week of their birthday?"

Sitting up beside her, I slide my hand behind her neck and bring her mouth close to mine. "We do, baby." I kiss her quickly. Releasing her, I jump off the couch and head to my room where I've hidden her first gift. I have them in the top of the closet. Pulling down the box, I reach in and pull out the small gift with the Post-It labeled Day 1. I quickly close the box and place it back on the shelf.

Ava's still sitting on the couch where I left her. Putting my hand behind my back, I approach her. "Close your eyes," I instruct her. I watch as a shy smile tips her lips and she closes her eyes. "Hold out your hand." Her smile grows bigger as she does as she's told and holds out her hand. I place the card in her hand, and then take a seat on the couch beside her. Leaning in close, I place my lips next to her ear. "Open."

Pulling away from her, I watch as she slowly opens her eyes and sees the card I've just placed in her hand. "Nate, this isn't necessary." She says that, but her smile is saying something different. I know she's never had this, a relationship. Never had someone to show her what it's like to be loved. I haven't told her yet, but I know she feels it. I make damn sure I show her every time I touch her, look at her . . . taste her.

"It is. It's your birthday week. You're my girl and that means we have to do this up big." I point to the card. "Open it."

"Thank you."

I chuckle. "Babe, you haven't even opened it yet. You might hate it."

Shaking her head, she looks at the card in her hands. "No, that's not possible." Her eyes meet mine. "It's from you."

I want to kiss her so fucking badly, but this isn't about me. This is about Ava Mae and making her feel special and loved. It's about showing her what she means to me. "Open."

Slowly, she slides her finger under the seal of the envelope and pulls the card out. She opens the card and the fifty-dollar gift card I got her for her Kindle falls out. I watch her eyes as she reads the card. It's when they shine with unshed tears that I know she's reading my message.

Ava Mae
I hope this will help
feed your addiction
one story at a time.
Just make sure you
remember you have the
real thing ☺
XOXO
Nate

She chuckles as she reads the words aloud to me. "This is too much."

"None of that," I tell her. "I want to give you . . . everything. Please don't fight me on this." I tuck a loose curl behind her ear.

"Okay." I watch as she slides the gift card back inside the card, which is returned to the envelope, and places them on the table. Turning toward me, she leans in and presses her lips on mine. "Thank you, Nathan." Her voice is soft.

"You're welcome."

"I'm going to make us a sandwich." She climbs from the couch and heads toward the kitchen.

I can see she wants time to compose her emotions, so I watch her go. By the time this week is up, she'll understand this is me, me with her and there is nothing I wouldn't do to put that smile on her face.

Remembering my phone was beeping earlier, I dig it out of my pocket.

Brody: Hey man, I know we keep missing each other. A lot going on here I need to tell you about. Things are slowing down. We'll talk in the next few days.

Me: Yeah, you're harder to get a hold of than the president. You okay?

I'm still waiting for his reply when Ava Mae joins me with two plates in her hands. "Brody texted me earlier." I take my plate from her and hand her my phone so she can read his message. "Thank you for this." I hold up my plate.

She nods as she sets my phone on the coffee table. "Well, Brody's not one to go back on his word, so it looks like we only have to wait a few more days before the cat's out of the bag."

"You change your mind?" She looks worried and that bothers me. As much as I want her, as much as she means to me, I would never force this on her. We can wait as long as she needs. The alternative is letting her go, and I know I can't do that. I couldn't live here with her in the same town. That would slowly kill me.

Her eyes find mine. "No, Nate. I haven't and I'm not going to. I'm worried his response is going to make you change yours."

I start to speak but she holds her hand up, stopping me. "I know you say it won't, but the two of you are like brothers, thick as thieves. My stomach aches every time I think about coming between the two of you. On the flip side of that, my heart actually hurts at the thought of not being with you."

Taking her plate from her hands, I set both of them on the table in front of us. Reaching over, I pull her into my lap. Lifting her chin with my index finger, I gaze into her eyes, begging her to see what I want so badly to tell her . . . *I love you.* I watch as her big brown eyes well with tears. "Ava Mae, I . . ." I stop myself before I blurt it out. Instead, I kiss her. I capture her lips with mine and slide my tongue against hers. I take everything she's willing to give and then some. Nothing else matters, nothing but her.

My phone beeps, causing her to pull away. Her eyes are no longer sad, mission accomplished. Holding onto her, I reach over and grab my phone.

Brody: Yes. I'm good. More than you know. Talk soon.

I turn the screen so she can read it. If I don't talk to him before her birthday, I'm buying both of us a plane ticket and we're flying to see him. I cannot keep resisting her like this. It's taking its toll on both of us.

35

ATE HAD TO go in to the gym today. Zach's fight is only two weeks away. Nate says he's ready, but they can't slow down on his training this close to the event. That leaves me with a few hours of nothing to do. I swept and mopped his kitchen and dusted the living room. I threw a load of towels in the washer and cleaned the bathroom. With nothing else to clean, I decide to text Kara and see if she wants to grab some lunch.

> Me: Hey! Want to grab some lunch?
>
> Kara: I'm party shopping today. My BFF has a b-day coming up.
>
> Me: :-) I can help.
>
> Kara: Not happening. I'll text ya later.

All right then, looks like I get a little me time today. I make myself a bag of popcorn and curl up on the couch with my laptop and Kindle. I load the gift card Nate gave me last night and start one-clicking.

Once all of my new books are loaded, I settle on the couch with my bowl of popcorn and get lost with my new book boyfriend. This is where Nate finds me a few hours later.

"Hey, babe." His smile lights up his face. Bending over, he kisses me. "New book?"

"Yes, my boyfriend gave me an early birthday present."

"Hold that thought." He takes off down the hall toward the bedroom. He's back in front of me in no time, holding a gift bag. "Birthday week, day two," he says, handing the bag to me.

"Another present?"

"Yes, you will get a present every day this week." He raises his eyebrows, daring me to argue. I don't bother. I know I won't win. Instead, I take the bag from his hands and say thank you.

Nate sits on the edge of the couch, facing me as I start digging tissue paper out of the bag. Reaching in, I feel something soft. Taking it out of the bag, I see it's a soft throw blanket, just like the one I have at my apartment. This one is a dark gray color. The material is so soft I immediately place it against my cheek.

"I know you use the one at your place a lot. I thought you might need one for here." Setting the bag on the floor, he takes the throw and lets it fall open. Standing, he places it over me, handing me my Kindle. "Now you look like you're home."

Leaning down, he kisses my forehead before picking up the trash from my gift. "I'm hopping in the shower; I smell like the gym."

I reach out and grab his wrist before he gets too far away. "Thank you." He nods and leaves the room.

Bringing the throw up to my neck, I relax into the couch. I fight tears yet again at the thoughtfulness of his gift. He knows me, really knows me. Growing up, he was always nice to me. Even if Brody was being a brat, Nate would say something like, "Let's just leave her alone," but I never got to see this side of him. I've never had the chance to see the side of him that gives with his whole heart. I never got to see the guy who can tell you more with a look or a single touch than words would ever be able to relay.

With every look and every touch, I fall a little harder.

Monday morning, or day three of my birthday week, I wake up alone in Nate's bed. Rolling over, I see an envelope propped up on the nightstand with my name written across the front. Giddy with excitement to see what he's done today, I sit up and grab the envelope, sliding my finger under the tab to open it. It's a letter.

Ava Mae
Morning beautiful. You looked so
peaceful I didn't have the heart
to wake you up.
Not only that, but you work too
hard. You deserve to sleep in, and
lounge for the summer.

Today is day three of your
birthday week and I think you
need a little pampering.
Kara will be at the house at noon
to pick you up. The two of you
are having a spa day.

Enjoy it, babe. Everything has
been paid for, just relax and
enjoy.
                    xoxo Nate

Glancing at the clock, I see it's just after eight. An idea hits me and I'm climbing out of bed and heading toward the shower.

An hour later, I'm pulling into Hardcorps. I'm on a mission. Walking through the door, I acknowledge the receptionist with a wave of my hand. She says something, but I don't know what. I'm focused on the guy standing across the room . . . Nate. He's standing beside the mats, which have been placed on the floor. I hear the deep rumble of his voice saying Zach's name. He's wearing athletic shorts and a tank top, and it does nothing to hide his muscular frame.

My feet carry me to stand behind him. I wrap my arms around his waist and rest my forehead against his back. I know he knows it's me. I can do the same with him. He places his hands over mine, which are locked around his waist. He continues to instruct Zach and Trent on the mat, never missing a beat.

I'm getting what I came for. I wanted to wrap my arms around him, just be next to him. His gifts are stirring all kinds of emotions in me. The biggest one being love. The thought of not seeing him until this evening just wasn't enough. I could have used my few hours before

Kara picks me up to read or even sleep a little longer, but all I wanted to do was see him.

"Break," Nate calls. This has both Zach and Trent falling to their backs on the mat. Nate slides his fingers through mine and pulls them from his waist. He guides me in front of him, where he settles both of his hands on my waist. "This is a nice surprise." He brushes his lips against mine.

"I wanted to say thank you."

He smiles. "You're welcome. Has Kara called yet?"

"No, was she supposed to?"

"No, I told her not to call before eleven. I wasn't sure how long you would sleep. I didn't want her to wake you."

There he goes being all sweet. "You're too good to me." I lock my hands behind his head and bring his lips to mine.

Our kiss is interrupted by Zach yelling at us to get a room. This causes Nate to laugh against my lips. "I need to get back to work. Have fun today."

Placing my arms around his waist, I hug him tightly. He holds me close, never once trying to break away, once again giving me what I want. "I'll see you later?"

"You going to come back to my place, or do you want me to come to yours?"

"Yours." His place is starting to feel like home to me.

36

*T*ODAY IS DAY four of Operation Show Ava Mae You Love Her, AKA: My girl's birthday week. As soon as I finished with Zach's session today, I rushed home for the day. I've been doing that a lot lately. Rushing out of there to spend time with her. I've hired two additional trainers in the last several weeks so I can free up more of my time. The gym is doing well, so financially I can afford to do it. I've never had anyone to come home to, and now that I do, work is not going to keep me from her.

"Thanks for making dinner, babe." I push my plate away from me. She made homemade chicken pot pie and it was delicious.

"You're welcome." She winks as she stands to clear the table.

"I got this, you cooked."

"We can do it together."

It takes no time for us to clean up. It's time for present number four. I try to mix it up each day, keep her guessing. "Present time," I announce once we are back in the living room. Ava Mae sits cross-legged on the couch wearing a grin, a grin I put there. Reaching behind the couch cushion, I pull out the envelope I placed there when I got home today.

"Happy birthday week, Ava Mae." I hand her the envelope.

"Thank you." Her smile is still lighting her face.

Sliding the envelope open, she peeks inside. "No way!" she screams. This causes me to laugh. "When? When is it? I can't believe you bought me Sam Hunt tickets!" Tickets and envelope still in hand, she launches herself at me across the couch. Her arms wrap around my neck and she holds on tight. Pulling back, she kisses me on my nose, my cheeks, my forehead, all the while saying, "Thank you. Thank you. Thank you."

I knew she would like them, but I didn't expect this. "You're welcome, babe," I laugh.

"You're going too, right?" she asks, finally pulling the tickets out to look at them.

"There are two tickets. You can take whoever you want. I wasn't sure if you wanted to take Kara."

"Nope, I want you to go." Holding the tickets up so I can see them, she says, "EEEPP! This is so awesome."

"There's nowhere else I'd rather be," I tell her honestly. If she's there, so am I. It's that simple.

Reaching over, I turn off my alarm. It's supposed to go off in ten minutes, but I don't want it to wake Ava Mae. I slip out of bed as quietly as possible, trying hard not to disturb her. I even go to the extreme of showering in the guest bathroom. Today is Wednesday, birthday gift number five. This one is more personal. After we had dinner at my parents, Mom stopped by the gym the next day and handed me an envelope. When I questioned her, she just told me to shush and open it. What I found inside was a gift that is irreplaceable. Inside the envelope was a picture of Ava Mae and me after my high school graduation. It was taken at the party the day before Brody and I left for the Marines. She hugged me goodbye that day, and I was so wrapped up in her that I didn't realize there were eyes on us. To hear my mother tell it, she and Ava's mom were standing together when Mom snapped the picture. She said they knew then that we would end up together.

In the picture, Ava Mae is standing on her tiptoes with her hands on my shoulders. My hands are resting on her hips. The picture paints an intimate scene, more so than what I remember. Then again, all I could think about was leaving, and wishing in that moment she was mine, pretending she was mine.

We're both so focused on the other, with sad smiles on our lips. You can see people standing around us, but we're lost in our own little world. I remember that moment. Have thought about it several times over the years. Even more so in the last several months with her back in my life. I didn't want to let go of her that day. If I'm being completely honest, I was in love with her then. They say a picture is worth a thousand words. This time it sums it up in three. I love you.

To have this picture, to have physical evidence of that moment, it gets to me. Man card be damned, I got a little choked up. Mom just smiled her coy smile and headed back home. Leaving me with my past, present, and future in one four-by-six piece of paper. When I got the idea to celebrate Ava Mae's birthday each day of the week for seven days and then her big gift day eight on her actual birthday, the picture immediately came to mind. I know that day meant a lot to her as well. We've talked about it. We were feeling the same thing, wanting the same thing, but fighting it. I didn't tell her about the picture. Selfish I know, but I wanted to keep that moment in time just for me. However, when I was contemplating gifts, I knew this had to be one of them.

I took the picture to a local photography store and had it blown up into an eight by ten. I also had it framed at a custom frame shop. This is why I've been in stealth mode all morning. I don't want to wrap it. I want to display it on the nightstand so she'll see it when she wakes up. Very carefully, I arrange the picture on the nightstand. I'm tempted to kiss her goodbye, but I don't want to chance waking her. With one last look, I leave her to sleep peacefully.

I'm in the kitchen eating a piece of banana nut bread Ava made yesterday, before heading to the gym. Checking the time, I make sure I'm not going to be late for Zach's session. I need to get moving. I shove the last bite of bread in my mouth and stand to rinse off my plate. This is where she finds me.

"Nate." Her voice cracks.

Surprised she's awake, I turn to look at her. She's wearing nothing but one of my Hardcorps t-shirts. Her hair is in a knot on top of her head. Loose curls hang on either side of her face. The picture I placed on the nightstand just minutes ago is clutched tightly against her chest. Tears are falling from her eyes as she bites down on her bottom lip.

"Where . . . where did you get this?" She looks down to her chest. "How did you . . ." Her voice cracks. "This is the day, the day you both left. The day I was so afraid I would never see either one of you again."

Removing one hand from the picture, she wipes her cheeks. "This is the day I thought it was over. That I would never get the chance to tell you how much I cared about you."

I'm standing in the same spot, leaning against the sink. Her reaction has shocked me. I thought she would be happy, and now all I've done is make her cry. It takes me two long strides to reach her. I wrap my arms around her as she buries her head in my chest.

I hold her.

Taking a deep shuddering breath, she asks again. "Where did you get this?" She pulls away from me, so she can see my face. I explain Mom brought it by the gym. She smiles when I get to the part about her mom being there as well and their theory on us ending up together.

Guiding her to the living room, I sit on the couch and pull her onto my lap. I gently pull the picture away from her chest so we can look at it. "I remember every minute of that day. I'll never forget how it felt to be in that moment with you." Tucking a loose curl behind her ear, I bring my lips in close. "It's always been you, Ava Mae."

She doesn't say anything else and neither do I. Instead, I hold her. When her breathing evens out, I know she's fallen back to sleep. Very carefully, I slip my phone out of my pocket and text Zach to let him know to start without me. I'm not ready to let go of her just yet.

37

Ava Mae

I WAKE TO KISSES on my neck. "Ava Mae, it's time to wake up." His soft words whisper against my ear. Nate informed me last night when he got home that he's taking off the rest of the week. Zach was fine with it. He, Tanner, and Trey know the routine and he's ready. Now it's just about keeping up his endurance. Nate also spent some time yesterday with one of the new trainers he hired to sit in on Zach's training while he's gone. I felt bad and was worried about it affecting Zach's chances to win the fight. Nate tried to reassure me, but it took him calling Zach and having him tell me before I relaxed. I still feel guilty about it, but they both assured me it's not an issue.

"I made you breakfast," Nate murmurs as he kisses my neck.

Not a bad way to wake up I might add. "Mmm, what did you make me?"

"French toast." He smacks my ass. "Rise and shine, baby. It's day number six."

His words cause me to smile. So far, his gifts have been perfect. Yesterdays is by far my favorite.

"Avaaaa," he whines. This causes me to chuckle.

"Fine, I'm up. You're worse than a kid at Christmas," I scold him.

"I can't help it. I'm nervous about today's gift."

"Aww, that's sweet, babe." I pat his leg. Nate reaches out and tickles my side. "Okay, okay, I'm sorry," I laugh. "Uncle!" I yell.

He stops. "Eat, woman." He kisses my forehead and jumps off the bed to get the tray he has sitting on the dresser.

"It smells amazing. Thank you."

"You're welcome." He sets the tray down and my eyes pop out of my head.

"There's no way I can eat all of this." The plate is piled high with slice after slice of French toast.

He picks up the syrup and covers the plate with the gooey goodness. He then reaches for a fork and cuts off a piece. "Open," he says, holding the fork to my mouth.

I do as I'm told and take the bite he's offering. It's delicious.

"You're not going to eat it all. We're sharing." He proves his point by taking the next bite. We continue this way, him feeding us, bite for bite until the plate is cleared. "Close your eyes."

Not able to contain my grin, I close my eyes. I hear him climb off the bed and set the plate back on the dresser. I hear the sound of the closet door open, and then a few seconds later close. The bed dips as he sits beside me. "Open."

When I open my eyes, Nate is sitting on the edge of the bed holding a photo box. "I'm not sure how much of a gift this is for you; it's more for me. Each one etched into who I am. The gift is me showing you what they meant. What you did for me, what *they* did for me." At first I think it's more pictures, but I know that can't be right. Not in a million years could I have guessed what was in the box before he took the lid off.

"I wanted to show you that you're a piece of me," are the words he speaks as he lifts the lid.

I stare at the box in confusion. "They're all there, Ava Mae. Every single letter you ever wrote to me while I was away. I kept them with me, kept you with me. This was the one thing I made sure was always with me. No matter where I went, you were with me."

Cue the waterworks. There's no fighting off the tears that fall from my eyes. There is no way to control the rapid rise and fall of my chest as my heart beats to a rhythm that is Nathan Garrison.

"I can't believe you kept them. I mean, I have all of yours, but I never thought you would have kept them."

Pushing my hair back over my shoulder and then wiping the tears from my cheeks, he offers me a shy smile. "They were important to me. You are important to me."

"Lay with me?" My voice is thick from my tears. "I just need to be next to you."

"Anything you want, baby."

He crawls up the bed and pulls me into his arms. "I want to read them, my letters to you. I never expected you to keep mine either, so I kind of know how you feel right now," he confesses.

"How do you feel?"

"Like my heart could burst from happiness. Like I can't breathe unless you're in the same room. Like every wish I've ever had has come true."

"Glad to see we're on the same page," I tease him. Throwing my leg over his, I burrow into him. "I'd like that though, to go through them together." Sounds like an emotional day for both of us, but I want to do it. "Not today, I feel a headache coming on, so not today, but soon. If you're willing, I'd like to do it soon."

"You need your medicine," he says, sliding out from under me.

"I'm good, just need to rest a minute."

"Not taking any chances, babe. It's been a while since you've had one. We want to nip this thing in the bud. It's your birthday week after all. I need you well."

He disappears through the bedroom door. I hear him rustling around in the kitchen. I hope he found the pills in my purse. I need to clean that thing out.

A few minutes later, he's sitting on the edge of the bed holding my migraine medicine and a bottle of water. I sit up, take the pill he shakes out into his hand, and drink down half the bottle of water. I know he won't settle for any less.

Nate lies back down and pulls me into his arms. "I'm sorry I've overwhelmed you the past few days."

"I've cried a lot, but I wouldn't change a minute of it. It's not too bad right now; taking the meds and lying back down will help."

He runs his fingers through my hair. "Rest. I'll be here when you wake up."

I close my eyes and allow the feeling of him softly stroking my hair to lull me back to sleep.

38

Nate

WE SPENT THE day yesterday just lounging around. When we woke up for the second time, Ava Mae's headache was gone. I still insisted we take it easy. She tried to argue it was my day off and we should do something fun. I spent the day convincing her that anything I do with her is fun, especially in the bedroom.

We haven't heard anything else from Brody this week. Tomorrow is her birthday and he never misses giving her the hug she always asks for. She tries not to let me see that it bothers her. I know better.

"Nate!" Ava Mae calls out for me.

"Yeah," I call back. I've been in my home office taking care of a few invoices while she was reading.

"Do you have cards?"

"Yes," I say, sneaking up behind her.

"Shit!" She jumps. "You scared me to death." She laughs.

Pulling her back against my chest, I bury my face in her neck.

"Cards?" she says again as she tips her head to the side, giving me better access.

I trace my tongue over the length of her neck. Nipping at her ear, I whisper, "In the drawer to your left."

I slide my hand up the front of her shirt. I've almost reached my destination when her cell rings. "That's probably Kara," she breathes.

I stop my journey, but leave my hand where it is. "Hello?" She barely gets the word out. I slide my hand back down her toned stomach and slip my finger under the waist of her shorts.

"Yeah, no." She clears her throat. "I'm fine."

My tongue once again traces the line of her neck while my hand hovers over where we both want it to be.

"N-no, I think we're good. See you in a few." She hits end and lays her phone back on the counter. "No fair," she whines.

I remove my hand from her shorts and turn her to face me. "They on their way?"

"Yeah. Stopping to pick up the pizza then heading this way. Wanted to make sure we didn't need anything else."

"Call her back and tell her we need . . ." I look at my watch. "At least an hour."

She chuckles and smacks my chest. Grabbing her hips, I lift her to sit on the counter. "Today's day seven," I say as I lean in for a kiss. "I need to give you your present."

Her arms rest on my shoulders and she automatically closes her eyes. Bringing her hands down, I pull her gift from my back pocket. Placing it in her hand, I close her fingers around it. "Open."

Her eyes pop open and zero in on her hand. I watch as she opens her fingers and spies what I've given her. She's confused; I see it when she looks up at me. I pick it up so I can explain. "This is an infinity keychain. I know you're worried about Brody and how this is all going to play out. This is a symbol of how I feel about that, about you. I can't put a time limit on how long we'll be together, because there isn't one. The amount of time I want you by my side is infinite."

She smiles as a lone tear slips down her cheek. Cupping her face, I capture it with my thumb. "The key, well, that's just as important. You see, I love you being here. I love falling asleep with you in my arms and waking to your warm body tucked against me. This key is to my house. I want you to be engrained in every part of my life. I want you to feel like this place is yours, come and go as you please. I hope one day this will be your home, your home with me." I wrap her fingers back around the set. "In a way, with the two of them linked together, it's like you hold the key to my heart."

"Nate," she chokes out the word.

Resting my forehead against hers, I'm going to tell her. I can't wait any longer to tell this beautiful, smart, amazing girl how much I love her. "Ava Mae, I—"

"Knock, knock. Look who pulled in behind us," Kara's loud voice booms through the living room.

Releasing a heavy sigh, I pull away from her. "Nate!" Kara yells.

"She's acting weird," Ava Mae says, wiping the tears from under her eyes.

Taking a step back from Ava Mae, I yell back to her. "In the kitchen."

Hearing footsteps, I turn to face the kitchen door to see what the fuss is about and see who the surprise guest is. Watch it be my parents. Ava must spot him the same time I do as his name falls from our lips.

"Brody . . ." we say at the same time.

39

Ava Mae

I BLINK A FEW times to make sure I'm really seeing him. Brody is here, in Nate's kitchen. Holy shit! I jump off the counter and rush toward him. He opens his arms and catches me.

"Ava, I wasn't expecting to see you here." He chuckles as I hug him tight. "I missed you too, sis."

Opening my eyes, I see a beautiful girl standing behind him. She has a huge smile on her face. I release him from his death grip and step away. My back bumps into Nate, his hands grip my hips to keep me upright. Brody's eyes follow his hands and, if I'm not mistaken, I see fire there. Quickly, I step back toward Brody, so Nate has to release me. "What are you doing here? Everyone has been trying to get ahold of you for weeks." I hit his arm.

"Ow." He rubs his arm with a smirk on his face.

"Like that hurt, you're built like a damn tank. Now fess up, what's going on with you?"

The grin that spread across his face is new for him. Brody's a happy guy, don't get me wrong, but this . . . this is a new concept, this all-consuming grin. Reaching behind him, the girl grabs onto his hand and steps beside him. "Ava, I'd like to introduce you to my wife, Sara. Babe, this is my little sister, Ava."

"Wife?" I'm shocked.

"Yeah, we were married last week." He's beaming with happiness.

"And this guy,"—he points behind me at Nate—"this is my brother from another mother, my best friend, Nate. Nate, this is my wife, Sara," Brody introduces them.

Nate steps beside me, placing his hand on the small of my back. The other reaches out to shake Sara's hand. "Nice to meet you."

"Nice to meet both of you."

Brody focuses his attention back to me. "What are you doing here?"

Shit! I don't want to do it like this, not when he's happy with his new wife. If we tell him now, it's going to ruin that. "What are you doing here?" I counter.

"I came to deliver a surprise birthday hug to my little sister." He crosses his arms across his chest. "Your turn."

Damn it!

"I didn't want to be the only girl," Kara chimes in. God, I love that girl! "Brody, this is my boyfriend, Tanner," she introduces them.

I watch as Brody and Tanner shake hands, and then Brody has his attention focused on Nate. Releasing Sara, he steps toward Nate and they do that man hug thing that they always do. "Good to see ya, man," Nate says. I can hear the gruffness in his voice. This has been weighing on him. I need to figure out a way to get him alone and tell him we need to hold off. We need to wait until Brody's ready to go back to Hawaii before we tell him. I don't want his visit ruined. I don't want Sara's first impression of our family to be full of drama.

Brody steps back and reaches out for Sara. He's the same way with her as Nate is with me. Seems as if he always needs to touch her. "So what's going on tonight?" Brody asks.

"Have you talked to Mom and Dad?" I question him.

"Uh, no, not yet. My plan was to crash here tonight." He looks at Nate. "Then surprise you tomorrow for your birthday. Then talk to Mom and Dad, in that order."

"Sorry about that." Kara steps in, yet again saving my ass. "Nathan, get us a beer will you? I'll lead the way outside." Kara looks at Sara. "You need to fill us in; we need details." She links her arm through Sara's and leads her to the back deck. Brody and Tanner follow them, Brody with a big dopey grin on his face.

Love looks good on him.

"Baby, how do you want to do this?" Nate asks as soon as the patio door closes.

"Nate, we can't. Did you see how happy he is? We have to wait until it's time for him to go home. I can't ruin his announcement to friends and family that he's married by us telling him about us."

"No. Ava Mae, I can't wait this out any longer. I can't spend the week with him here, not being able to touch you. It's been weeks since I had to fall asleep without you beside me, and I don't want to start now." His voice is calm but stern.

"Nate, we can't do that to him." I have to make him understand. "And what about Sara? I don't want her to think she married into some crazy family. We have to wait just a few more days, a week at the most. He never stays longer than that."

His long legs carry him to stand in front of me. His hands hold my face as his eyes bore into mine. "I can't do it, Ava Mae. I cannot pretend for a week that you're not my world. I can't pretend you're not the very person my world revolves around." He laughs, but I can tell from his tone, it's not because of something he finds funny. "I never thought I would ever tell you no on anything, but I'm sorry, I can't agree to that."

"So, what, it's your way or else?" I ask a little louder than I should. My nerves are shot and I'm sure we're having our first official fight. Not to mention that nagging fear that I could lose him over this.

"On this, yes. I can't do it, Ava Mae. I'm not built that way. I can't pretend you're nothing to me," he counters.

"Really? That's the excuse you're going with? Years, Nate. For years we fought this and were able to keep it to ourselves. All I'm asking for is a week. One more week and we tell him the day he goes home."

"That was different and you know it." His voice is growing louder and his face is red with anger.

Welcome to the club, buddy. "How? How is that any different?"

I watch as he takes a deep breath, trying to calm down. I mimic him; we exhale at the same time. "That was before I knew what it was like to hold you all night long. Before I had the chance to kiss you whenever I wanted. That was before I knew what it was like to come home to you."

"Nate! Gah! You're making this harder on both of us. One week, I don't see what the big deal is. It's not like it's forever. Why can't you do this for me? For him, he's your best friend."

"We've talked about this, damn it! I told you, if it ever comes down to me having to choose, there wouldn't be a choice. It will always be you! You, Ava Mae! What do I have to do to make you understand that?"

I watch as he paces the floor, running his fingers through is hair. I know he's angry and upset, but so am I. He's being unreasonable.

"I won't ruin this for him, Nate. I refuse to do that. We will tell him the day he leaves."

"No!" he says through his teeth. "Why should you protect his feelings? He's been ignoring us for weeks. Weeks, I have called him, and he called when he knew he was most likely to miss me or he would text me and then not reply. He's been hiding a fucking wife from you, from us. Did he care about how you or your parents, or even how I would feel about that? He shows up here, expecting to stay with me, and any other time, I would be fine with that, but not this time. I refuse to put him or anyone else before you."

"UGH! Why do you have to be so stubborn?" I scream at him. I'm surprised they haven't heard us yet and came running to see what the deal is.

"Why?" He laughs. "Why am I so stubborn? Are you really asking me that right now?"

"Yes, you're stubborn and refuse to budge. You need to think about what I want in this too. This affects more than just you, Nate."

"Are you fucking kidding me? All I do is think about you. I can see this bothers you, but damn it, Ava Mae, I refuse to wait on this."

"Why?" I scream.

"Because I fucking love you! I love you so damn much it hurts to breathe. I cannot pretend I don't. I can't."

As soon as the words are out of his mouth, the patio door opens and in walks a very pissed-off Brody. "What did you just say?" His gaze is honed in on Nate. "What the fuck is going on here?" He comes to stand beside me, always the protector.

"Brody, it's—" Nate interrupts me before I can get any further.

"You heard what I said," Nate states.

"Yeah, but what I don't understand is, one, why you are screaming and yelling at my sister and, two, what do you mean you love her?"

Brody crosses his arms over his chest, not that his stance does anything to Nate; he's too busy looking at me.

Nate doesn't bother answering Brody. I can feel his eyes boring in on me, his voice softer. "Baby, look at me," he begs.

"Baby? You better start talking fast, Garrison," Brody seethes.

He continues to ignore Brody. "Ava Mae."

No matter how hard I try, I cannot fight the pull. Lifting my head, our eyes lock. "I love you." He takes a step toward me, his eyes never leaving mine. "Do you know I can tell when you walk into a room? Do you know that whenever I've been away from you, no matter how long it's been, the first time I get to set my eyes on you after your absence, I have to remind myself to breathe?" He takes another step toward me. "Do you know I've never said those three words before? That the only person I ever felt worthy of them was you?"

"What the fuck, man?" Brody says.

"Brody? Let's give them some space." Sara's voice draws his attention. My new sister-in-law, hopefully, she can get through to him. Please, God, let her be able to reason with him. I can't think straight with Nate's declaration of love and Brody's anger. I can't deal with both of them at once. Sara walks into the kitchen and takes his hand. "Let's give them some space, give everyone some time to cool off. Then we can all sit down and talk."

"He's—" Sara places her fingers over his lips.

"Babe, let's give them some time. Everyone needs to cool down. Come on?" She pulls on his arm, and, thankfully, he falls into step behind her.

The kitchen is quiet except for the sound of their footsteps and then the patio door closing behind them. That's all it takes for Nate to advance on me. His long legs carry him to me. He grabs my hand and begins leading me down the hall, toward his bedroom.

40

Nate

$\mathscr{M}$Y FIRST THOUGHT when I hear the door click is that we need privacy. I don't want Brody storming back in here and interrupting us. I need to make sure we're okay. I can't believe I fucking blurted it out like that. Dick move on my part. I guide her into my room, then close and lock the door. We're not leaving this room until I know we're okay. I'll risk my ape of a best friend busting the door down.

Keeping a grasp on her hand, I walk to the bed and sit on the edge. I pull her to stand between my legs. Wrapping my arms around her waist, I rest my forehead against her stomach. She runs her fingers through my hair, a gesture I've come to love, but only from her. Her gentle touch is soothing. I focus on taking deep, even breaths. Once I feel like I have myself under control from the shitstorm of emotions brewing inside me, I lift my head. "Will you lay with me?"

She doesn't answer with words. Instead, she climbs onto the bed, with me following her. As soon as I'm settled, she snuggles into me. That alone has me wanting to cry like a fucking baby. We're going to be okay.

That's the only reassurance I need to start talking. "I don't like fighting with you. I don't like seeing you upset, especially from something I've done. I love you, Ava Mae. I do. With everything inside me, I love you. I know I shouldn't have blurted it out like that, but I refuse to take it back. There is no way I could ever pretend you mean nothing to me, not anymore."

She's quiet. Her hand is lying on my chest over my heart. I'm sure she can feel it. I stay quiet, letting her process everything I've just said. I've thrown a lot at her tonight along with our first fight. I hate that's how I told her I love her.

Fuck!

It was on the tip if my tongue, a few more seconds, and I would have told her earlier, but then Kara yelled out for us, and then Brody was there and all hell broke loose. Regardless of how it happened, she knows.

My hand glides lightly up and down her back. I've said all I can say, bared it all for her, now she needs time. It's a lot to take in.

"Nate." My name on her lips is music to my ears.

"Yeah, baby." My voice is soft and low, soothing.

Lifting her head, she props her chin on my chest, bringing us eye to eye. "I love you, too."

Her words kick my heart into overdrive. "Say it again," I whisper. I need to hear it from her lips one more time.

She giggles. "I love you, Nathan Garrison."

Within seconds, I have her flipped over on her back and my lips pressed to hers. Telling her was a relief, not hiding what she means to me, but hearing her say she feels the same . . . I'll never be the same. Loving her, having her in my life has changed me.

"Never letting you go, Ava Mae," I say against her lips.

A pounding on the door causes us both to jump. "What the fuck are you two doing in there? Don't make me break this door down," Brody seethes.

I look down at Ava and smile. "He's angry, but he will adjust. If he doesn't, that's his issue. We're in this together. He can stay here, and if he throws a fit, we will just go to your place. I'm not sleeping without you."

"Okay."

"I love you." I kiss her one last time before letting Brody burst our perfect little bubble.

As I reach the door, she calls out to me, "Nate."

I stop and turn. She's sitting on the edge of the bed, a smile on her face. "I love you, too."

I wink at her and open the door. Brody pushes his way in. Stopping when he's sees Ava Mae on the edge of the bed. "What the hell? Why was the door locked?"

I'm ready to defend our actions, even though we shouldn't have to, when Ava lays into him. "Who the hell are you to barge into his home and demand anything?" she questions.

"You," he points at her, "are my little sister. He," he points at me, "is my former best friend. There is no reason for you to be in his room with the door locked," he fires back.

"You're going there? Really, Brody? Just like that, you're going to write him off? This is the same guy who's had your back since you were five years old." She laughs. "Did you hear what he said out there?" She points toward the kitchen. "Did you hear him say he loves me? Have you ever known him to say that before? This isn't a game, Brody. We're not in high school anymore."

She stands and walks past him. He reaches for her and I step next to him. "Don't," I warn. I know he would never hurt her and that is not his intention. He's just trying to stop her, but he's pissed off and stronger than he might realize. I'm not taking any risks where she's concerned.

"What the hell? You think I would hurt her?" Brody seethes.

"No, but you're angry, and I don't care who you are, I'm not taking the risk with her." I keep my voice calm.

"Brody, we have guests. You and Sara are more than welcome to join us. The guest room has clean sheets on the bed and towels in the bathroom closet." She turns to leave the room.

"Do you fucking live here?" he calls after her.

She turns to face him. "I spend a lot of time here, yes. Nate is my boyfriend; that's what couples do. Get over it, Brody. Nothing you say is going to change the fact that we're together." She turns and walks out of the room.

And then there were two. "Jesus, Nate, my little sister. How could you, man?"

I laugh. "How could I not? Not only is she beautiful, she's smart and funny and she has the biggest heart of anyone I've ever met. This isn't just some fling for me, Brod. She's it, man." I remain calm as we have the conversation that has been playing out in my mind for weeks.

"My best friend is fucking my little sister; the thought makes me sick."

"It's a good thing I'm not fucking her," I counter.

"Right. What, are you going to try and pull that 'I make love to her' bullshit? I'm not buying it."

"Nope. I'm not doing either."

"You expect me to believe that?"

"At this point, Brody, I couldn't care less what you believe. I'm in love with her. I refrained from sleeping with her until you knew about us. Out of respect for you, my best friend, I wanted you to know first. I also knew, even if you won't admit it, that when you found out I wasn't sleeping with her, you would understand what that means." I stare him down, waiting for him to deny it.

"She stays here, with you, in your bed?" he asks.

"Yes, or I'm in hers, every night, Brody. Every night I hold her while she falls asleep, and when I wake up, she's there, offering me that shy smile of hers. I know you're pissed, man, but you know me. I won't hurt her."

"Whatever, I'm done." He storms past me and walks out of the room.

I wish I could say I was expecting a different reaction, but I wasn't. It will take him a few days to process our conversation. He'll come around eventually, and if he doesn't, he will have to learn to deal with seeing us together regardless of his acceptance.

41

Ava Mae

*L*AST NIGHT WAS a disaster. Brody was stewing the entire night. Kara and Tanner didn't stay long; can't say as I blame them. I did get the chance to thank her before they left. She saved us even though in the end he ended up finding out anyway. As soon as they left, I showed Sara where everything was and told her to make themselves at home. Then Nate and I locked ourselves in his room. Brody bitched about it and stomped down the hall to the spare bedroom. I feel bad for Sara right now; poor girl probably thinks she married an ape.

I didn't sleep well, worried about how this is all going to play out. I hate that Brody is so angry about this. Regardless, I take being up before Nate to my advantage. I was able to detangle myself from him about thirty minutes ago when I needed to use the restroom. Instead of sliding back into his arms, I chose to watch him. My eyes take in his dark hair and his strong jawline covered in stubble, which I love. The sheet just barely covers him from the waist down, causing me to stare at his chest with every rise and fall of every breath he takes. He's sculpted. I don't really know any other way to say it. His abs and arms are so defined he looks as though he's been chiseled from clay when he lies this still. The icing on the cake is that he loves me.

I know he feels bad for blurting it out like he did, but I wouldn't change it, not for anything. Sure romance is nice, hearts and flowers, a room lit by candles. I'm sure he was brewing something to that effect in his mind. How it actually happened wins over all that every time in my book. The way he couldn't hold it in; he had to tell me that's why he insisted we tell Brody. It was real, honest and passionate. It's definitely a moment I'll never forget.

"You're watching me," he mumbles.

"I wake up to this God-like creature in bed with me, I decided I need to look my fill before he vanishes," I tease him.

His eyes pop open. "Not going anywhere," he says with his gruff, sleep-laced voice. "You're stuck with me. Now get over here; you're supposed to be in my arms."

"Nope, not done looking."

He props his head up on his arm and watches me. A smirk crosses his lips. "Like what you see, baby?"

"Ehh. It's not bad." As soon as the words register, a smirk crosses his face and he's on me. His hands are everywhere as he tickles me.

"Want another shot at that answer?" He's laughing just as hard as I am.

"N-No," I choke over my laughter.

His hand slips up his shirt that I slept in. His hand brushes over my breast, teasing one nipple then the next. "What about now? You want to change your answer now?"

I'm breathing heavy from his tickle attack and I can't stop smiling. I'm happy. Nate, he makes me happy. "Maybe." I grin. "I think I need to experience this for a few more minutes just to be sure."

He chuckles. Lifting his shirt, his lips latch on to my now hard peak, while his hand continues to roll the other between his fingers. This causes me to moan.

"What the fuck is going on in there?" Brody's voice comes through the door followed by his fist making all kinds of racket.

Nate releases me from his mouth, which has me whimpering in protest. He pulls my shirt back down and smiles. "Happy birthday, baby." He places a chaste kiss against my lips and hops off the bed. He's wearing nothing but a pair of his boxer briefs as he heads toward the door.

"Are you not going to put shorts on?" I hiss at him.

Looking at me over his shoulder, he says, "No. He has to accept this, Ava Mae." He winks, then turns and opens the door.

"What are you doing in there?" Brody questions him. "Where in the fuck are your clothes?" He storms past Nate into the room. I sit up in bed so he can see that I do have clothes on.

I watch as Nate makes a big deal of looking down at his boxer briefs. "I'm wearing clothes." Brody looks back and forth between the two of us. It's almost as if he can't believe what he's seeing. I guess it would be a shock to see your little sister in your best friend's bed.

"Brody." Sara appears in the doorway. "Can you help me find the stuff to make some coffee?" she asks sweetly.

His face softens. "Yeah." He doesn't say another word, or look at either of us as he leaves the room with his wife.

"You can take the first shower." Nate runs and jumps on the bed. His hand slips under my shirt and rests on my belly. His fingers begin to trace lines. "You might want to get moving, before I do all the things your brother assumes we were just doing," he tells me. His voice is husky.

"That's not a very convincing way to motivate me to get out of this bed," I tease.

He groans. Pulling up my shirt, he kisses above my belly button. His lips linger, teasing me. "Go, now, before I get carried away." He pulls my shirt back down and kisses my lips.

I don't argue with him. I don't need Brody barging back in here. That is not on my to-do list for my birthday.

42

Nate

I WAIT TO HEAR the shower turn on before I throw on shorts and a t-shirt. My best friend and I need to have a chat.

I find Brody and his new wife, Sara, in the kitchen. "Good morning," Sara says when she sees me. She seems like a really nice girl. "Ava showed me where everything was last night. I hope this is okay." She motions to the cup in her hand.

"Good morning, and yes, absolutely. I want you to make yourself at home while you're here." Stopping at the counter, I pour myself a cup. I don't bother to join them at the table. Instead, I lean against the counter. "Brod, can we talk about this?" I ask him.

"I have no desire to talk about you and the fact you're sleeping with my sister," he grumbles.

"Brody." Sara's voice is gentle yet warning. "Maybe you should hear him out."

"Listen, man. I've been trying to call you for weeks. I wanted to tell you. We didn't devise a plan to keep this from you. You made getting a hold of you impossible because you were hiding a secret of your own."

He doesn't say anything. He just sits in the chair, arms crossed over his chest, glaring at me. If this is how he wants to play it, then so be it.

"Listen, I understand you're upset. I understand the idea of the two of us together might take some time to get used to. I can deal with your anger. What I can't deal with is you being an ass and ruining her birthday. We didn't come into this relationship lightly, Brody. We

211

fought it. We thought about it and how we would all be affected. We decided, Ava Mae and I that the risks are worth the rewards. Do you understand what I'm telling you? That the risk of losing my best friend, the one person in this world who has always been there for me, the one person who is in every single one of my childhood memories, is a risk I'm willing to take. I won't choose between the two of you." He looks away. Not willing to believe what I'm saying.

"Look at me, damn it!" I wait for him to turn his head. "She owns me, Brod. I love her, and if you make this a choice, it's always going to be her." I slam my mug down on the counter. "One more thing, this is my house, and she is my girlfriend. You do not get to beat down my fucking bedroom door just because she's in there with me. I explained where I was with that last night. You either learn to deal with it or find another place to stay." I stalk off down the hall toward my bedroom.

"Hey." Ava smiles when I walk in.

I don't stop until I have her wrapped in my arms. Holding her, that's all it takes for my anger to subside. "Ready for your birthday present?" I ask.

"There's more?"

"Ava Mae, today is your birthday. Of course there's more. You know the drill, baby, close your eyes."

I watch as a smile plays on her lips and her lids close. Reaching for the box in my closet, I pull out her final gift. I had already planned to tell her how I feel today when I gave her this. No matter if we had reached Brody or not, I was going to tell her. "Follow me," I say against her ear. Slowly, I lead her by the hand to sit on the edge of the bed. Dropping to my knees in front of her, I place the small box in her hands. "Open."

Her eyes flutter open and she takes in the small box. I nod, giving her the go ahead to open it. Slowly, she pulls the ribbon free then lifts the lid. Tipping the box over in her hands, another smaller black box appears. Her eyes search mine. I nod again, urging her to continue. Biting her bottom lip, she lifts the lid.

"Nate," she whispers. "It's beautiful."

I take the box from her hands. "The day you walked into my gym with Kara, I knew. I knew in that moment I would never be the same. What I didn't know is what it would feel like to fall asleep with you in my arms. I didn't know what it would feel like to wake up the same way. I didn't know what it would feel like to share my life with you. I'm a quick learner though." I wink at her. "I learned that my love for you is infinite. I learned that you will forever be the perfect beginning and the perfect ending to my day." I remove the diamond baguette infinity ring from the box and slip it on her finger. The finger that I hope one day will bear a different kind of ring. One that tells the world the she's loved beyond measure. A ring that will tell the world she's mine. "Happy Birthday, Ava Mae. I love you."

"Thank you." She leans in for a kiss. "I love you, too."

"Come on. Let's get the birthday girl some breakfast."

We find Brody and Sara still sitting at the kitchen table. "Morning," Ava says brightly. Brody doesn't so much as grumble a reply while Sara greets her just as brightly. "We usually just eat bagels or fruit for breakfast." She's already digging the items out of the fridge. "Babe, do we still have that honey butter?" she asks.

Brody's head snaps up at her term of endearment. He glares at me and I smile back at him.

"Yeah, it's on the second shelf beside your yogurt." I added the 'your' for Brody's benefit. She's entangled in every part of my life and I wouldn't have it any other way. He needs to get used to that.

"Bagels sound perfect," Sara replies.

I place two bagels in the toaster then get to working on another pot of coffee. "Sara, what do you like on your bagel?" I ask over my shoulder.

"I can get it," she says, rising from her seat. Ava Mae convinces her to try the honey butter, which Sara claims is to die for.

I put down two more bagels and decide to cut up some fruit. Ava loves fresh strawberries, so I cut some into a small bowl with a little bit of vanilla yogurt just for her. I place the bowl in front of her on the table, bending to kiss the top of her head, before finishing making my bagel. Taking the seat next to Ava, I address Brody. "Yours is on the counter."

He doesn't acknowledge my words. I don't let it get to me as I dig into my breakfast. Ava spears a strawberry with her fork and slides it through the vanilla yogurt, then offers it to me. I don't hesitate to wrap my lips around the fork. This is what we do. I'm glad to see she's not letting Brody affect that. "Thank you, baby." I lean in and kiss her lips.

Brody pushes back from the table and leaves the room. "I'm sorry," Sara apologizes for him. "He'll come around. It's easy to see you love each other. He just needs time to let it sink in."

"He doesn't have a choice." Ava Mae shrugs.

We finish our breakfast and then move to the living room. Ava Mae takes advantage of the time to get to know Sara. Sara tells us that their decision to get married was completely spontaneous. The two of them flew to Vegas for a week to get some time away and ended up at a small wedding chapel off the strip. They were both completely sober.

"What the hell?" Brody yells as he comes barreling down the hall. "What are they doing here?" he asks.

"Who? What are you talking about?" Ava Mae asks.

"Mom and Dad. They just pulled in," he seethes.

"Shit! Brody, I forgot Mom said they might stop by today."

"Brody, it's her birthday. Did you really think they wouldn't come and see her?" I know he knows better than that.

"I assumed they would," he grits out, "but what are they doing here at your house?" He glares at me.

"They know I stay here most of the time. I talked to Mom earlier in the week and told her Nate was having a small get together tonight for my birthday. She said she and Dad would stop by sometime today," Ava explains.

"Son of a bitch. They know about you two?"

"Yes, and you would have known too if you weren't being such a jackass and trying to hide the fact you're married," Ava yells at him.

There's a knock on the door. "Come in," Ava yells as she stares Brody down.

"Where's my birthday girl?" her dad asks.

"Brody!" Their mom drops the bags in her hands and runs to him, throwing her arms around him. "When did you get here? Why didn't you tell us you were coming home?" she fires off questions one right after the other.

"Hey, Mom. It was supposed to be a surprise," he explains.

214

"Well, this is certainly a surprise, son," their dad says and he also gives him a hug.

Ava, now standing beside me, wraps her arms around my waist. I immediately pull her into me. "Mom, Dad." As soon as she says their names, I know what she's going to do.

"Baby, are you sure that's a good idea?" I say quietly against her ear. She releases a heavy sigh. Under normal circumstances, she would never intentionally out them like she was getting ready to do. She's upset with him; otherwise, she would have never considered it.

"It's good to see you," she says when she has their attention.

Her dad opens his arms and I release her. They sandwich her in a hug, which has the three of them laughing.

Brody watches, a small smile playing on his lips. This is their thing. "I guess you got your birthday hug from this big lug," her mom says, pointing over her shoulder.

The smile falls from Brody's lips. "Not yet." Ava doesn't bother to explain.

"That's all she ever asks from you," I say. Brody looks at me with a confused expression on his face. "Every year, for as long as I can remember, that's all I've heard her ask of you, until last night." He bristles at my words.

Brody opens his arms and Ava Mae moves slowly toward him. "Happy Birthday," I hear him say as he hugs her tight.

"I'm sorry, dear, I didn't see you there," their mom says to Sara. This captures Brody's attention, causing him to release Ava and move toward Sara.

Standing next to his wife, he introduces them. "Mom, Dad, this is Sara . . . my wife."

Their mom gasps. "Wife, I didn't . . . I had no idea that . . . Come here, sweet girl, and give me a hug," she says to Sara. She pulls her into a hug, followed by their dad. "When did this happen? Oh, I wish I could have seen it. I bet you made a beautiful bride," she gushes.

Just like that, Sara is brought into the fold of the family. I don't know what Brody was worried about, as long as they're happy, Mr. and Mrs. Evans are happy for them.

"Let's give them some time," I say to Ava. She agrees and we leave them to get acquainted.

43

Ava Mae

ONIGHT TURNED OUT better than I thought it would, all things considered. Sara, God love that girl, somehow convinced Brody they should spend the night at my parents.' She pulled me aside to let me know they would be back, but she thought it would do Brody some good to step away from me and Nate for a day or so. I couldn't agree more. She promised she would talk to him. I can only hope he's a smart husband and listens to his wife. My brother's married. It's hard to believe, but then again, it's not. Brody has always played by his own set of rules.

"Let's go to bed, babe. We can finish that tomorrow," Nate says, walking into the kitchen. Kara and Tanner just left and I'm trying to get the kitchen cleaned up.

"Just let me finish wiping down the counter and it's done."

I feel him step in behind me, his hands on my hips. "Leave it."

I drop the rag the same time he moves my hair to lay over one shoulder. His lips find my neck. Tilting my head to give him access, I say, "Thank you for today, for this week. I love all of my gifts." I raise my left hand to admire the ring he gave me.

He pauses to say, "You're welcome," then continues to kiss my neck, causing me to moan.

Nate turns me to face him. "Legs around my waist." I'm confused as to what he means until he tightens his grip on my hips and lifts me in the air. I do as I'm told, wrapping myself around him as his lips press to mine, and then we're moving. He pauses in the doorway. "Lights," he says against my lips. I reach over and hit the switch, and then we are once again moving down the hall toward his room.

He doesn't stop until his legs hit the bed. I release my legs from around his waist and sit on my knees on the bed. Not wasting any time, I pull his shirt over his head and place my lips on his chest, right over his heart. "Your turn." His voice is husky. His eyes filled with desire . . . for me.

Lifting my hands over my head, he pulls my tank off and tosses it behind him. His deft fingers snap the clasp of my bra and it, too, is flung over his shoulder. "Beautiful," he murmurs. He traces the swell of each breast with his finger. Bending his head, he pulls my hardened nipple into his mouth.

"Nate," I breathe his name.

He continues this beautiful torture, making sure to pay equal attention to both. "More," I beg him.

Never taking his mouth off me, he begins working on the snap of my shorts. I hear the sound of my zipper being lowered and I feel his hand dip inside my panties. "Off," I demand. "I want these off." I pull my legs out from under me and lie back on the bed. Nate grabs a hold of my shorts and tugs. One tug is all it takes for me to be naked, staring up at him. "Strip," I command and he doesn't hesitate to kick off his shorts. "All of it."

He stares at me for what seems like hours, but could only be seconds, before he slowly pulls his boxer briefs down his legs.

Satisfied, I slide up the bed and motion with my finger for him to join me. I watch as one knee and then the other bring him on the bed. "Ava Mae," he says reverently. His voice makes love to my name, and instead of the usual butterflies, I feel . . . heat, desire, need for him. So many overwhelming emotions, I don't know which is stronger. He remains in his spot, on his knees, raking his eyes over me.

Sitting up, I trace my fingers over the sculpted ridges of his abs. Leaning forward, I trace each plane, each ripple of muscle with my tongue.

"Jesus." He exhales the breath he's holding as he rests his forehead against mine. My hands roam his sides while his are splayed against my back. "I'm so in love with you." His husky voice touches my soul.

This time feels different. Maybe it's the declaration of love or maybe it's because Brody now knows, but this time his touch feels different. I want more with him. I want it all. I want to be connected as one.

"When," I utter the words, hoping that he understands the meaning.

"Ava Mae . . ." he sighs.

"When," I say again.

With a barely there nod, he climbs off the bed and disappears into the bathroom. Mere seconds later, he's lying down beside me as he tosses a strip of condoms onto the nightstand. I wait for him to question me, but he doesn't. Instead, he roams his hands and his tongue over every inch of me. He's worshiping my body, causing me to drip with need for him.

Once he's touched every inch of me, he reaches for the strip. I watch each movement, tracking his hands with my eyes. I watch as he tears a small foil packet from the strip. I watch as he places the corner of the packet in his mouth and tears it open. Leaning up on my arms, I watch as he settles back on his legs and rolls the condom on his impressive length.

Hovering over me, he rests his weight on his elbows. His hands softly brush my hair out of my eyes. "Keep them open," he breathes against my lips as he pushes his hips forward and slides inside me.

I wince in pain and he stills, lowering his mouth to mine. I get lost in his kiss, in the dance of his tongue against mine. Slowly, the pain turns to discomfort and the discomfort turns to something I've never experienced before. Soul baring passion, need, want, and love. My heart feels like it could burst from the love I feel for this man. I've imagined this moment more times than I care to admit and never once did my imagination prepare me for the real thing.

44

NOTHING I'VE EVER experienced could have prepared me for this. I literally feel like I'm a part of her, like she's a part of me. She tilts her hips, which allows me to slide in as far as I can go. "Ava," her name falls from my lips.

"More," she pleads and I rock into her, giving her what she wants.

She meets me thrust for thrust, eyes locked, bodies in sync . . . this is heaven. My heart pounds against my chest as my arms start to tremble. I'm not going to last. I slide my hands between our bodies. I need her with me. I rock into her and feel her gripping me from the inside, holding on to me, to this moment. "Nate . . ." Her head thrashes from side to side, trying to fight off the orgasm.

On trembling arms, I lean into her. "Look at me, Ava Mae." It takes her a minute to peel her eyes open, but when she does, what I see rocks me to my core. I see love, passion, and need all reflected back at me. "You with me, baby?"

She nods, not able to form words. I quicken my thrusts and just like that, we both explode with the passion we've created. We lay there trying to catch our breath. Ava Mae places her hands behind my neck and pulls me into her. "I'm too heavy." I try to lift myself off her, but she holds tightly.

"No, please don't go. Not yet." Her words stop me and I settle against her, trying to hold my weight on my arms. Her hands are gliding through my hair, and even though I know I have to, I don't ever want to move. I want to stay with her, inside of her, like this forever.

"I need to take care of the condom," I tell her. Reluctantly, she releases the hold she has on me. I roll off the bed and look down at her. "Shower with me?" I hold my hand out to her.

I've been trying to get her to do this for weeks, and she's shot me down every time. Claimed that if I wasn't going to give her what she wanted, then she was going to hold out on me as well. I'm glad we waited. This is something else we can add to her birthday week that will be unforgettable.

This week has been a blessing and a curse. Ava Mae and I are closer than ever. She's still staying at my place. She hangs out with Kara during the day, most days they stop by the gym and work out. Or as Tanner likes to say, distract the fuck out of us. Kara was in an outfit that looked painted on. He was watching every move she made, which is how Zach got in a good right hook, knocking him on his ass. Each night when I get home, Ava's there. We eat dinner together and talk about our day. At night, I make love to her until we're both exhausted. Those moments have been the blessings of my week.

The curse, well, that's my best friend. Brody and Sara are still at his parents' house and he's still pissed off at both Ava and me. She and I have talked about it and we're still on the same page. What he did was just as bad, if not worse, and it's not like we didn't try to tell him. In addition to that, this is not something we entered into lightly. He needs to suck it up and get over it. He's been into the gym a few times, it just so happened to be the exact same time Ava and Kara showed up as well. He would glare at both of us every time I would kiss her hello or goodbye, or anytime I was within twenty feet of her. I'm getting to the point where I'm over giving him time to process it. Instead, I'm pissed at him for not trusting me to take care of her. He doesn't trust me to love her the way she deserves to be loved. What does that say about our friendship? Not that there is currently much of one there.

Today is Saturday and the day of Zach's fight. I came into the gym to pick up his glove, gym banner, and a few other essentials we'll need to take with us tonight. It's about a three-hour drive to get there, so everyone is meeting up at my place at around one. As I'm making my rounds, I see Brody standing over by the mats, talking to Tanner. I decide to give it one more shot. One more attempt for me to convince him I'm what's best for her.

"What's going on, guys?" I approach them.

"Hey," Tanner greets me. "Nothing, just talking about the fight tonight."

"I was just telling Tanner here about a few times I've been in the ring while in the Marines. Kicked your ass in the ring," he scoffs.

Well, it's good to see he's still pissed off. Lucky for him, so am I. "If I recall, I've taken you a couple times myself," I reply.

He laughs. "Yeah, but not anymore, huh? You're too afraid to be in the ring. How am I supposed to be okay with my sister being with a guy who isn't willing to fight to protect her?" He pushes his finger against my chest. "A man who won't fight for her." He's now standing toe-to-toe with me.

"Brody, I'm not getting into this with you, not here. You know why I stopped that shit. And furthermore, how the fuck do you know I won't fight for her. You won't even have a fucking conversation with me about her, about us."

"She's my fucking sister!" he roars. He's so close that our noses are almost touching. "I asked you to look out for her. I never would have thought that you, my best friend, would have betrayed me like that."

I take a step back, separating us. I know that there is no use trying to reason with him being like this. He's lashing out and still needs time. I look over at Tanner. "Tanner, I'll see you and Kara at my place later?" I ask.

"Yeah, we'll be there."

"Yeah, you'll see me there, too, *friend*," Brody says.

I release a heavy sigh. "Listen, I'm sorry you're upset about this, but I will never apologize for falling in love with her. She's the best fucking part of me. I don't care how you treat me, or how big of a dick you want to be, that's not going to change. All your hatred is doing is pushing us away. Think about that. What are you gonna tell your kids, Brody? That you don't talk to their aunt because she fell in love with your best friend. A guy who worships the fucking ground she walks on? Good luck with that, asshole." I turn and stalk off before one of us says something we'll regret.

"I've never seen him fight," Tanner says.

"You won't," is Brody's reply. I don't hear the rest of the conversation as I pick up the bag of supplies by the door and stalk to the parking lot.

45

Ava Mae

THE EXCITEMENT IN the air is contagious. This is my first fight and I'm nervous for Zach, but excited to see him as he puts it, "Do what he does best." The guy has confidence in spades.

"Ava Mae!" Nate calls my name, pulling my attention from the TV screen that's currently scanning the arena.

I focus all my attention on him. "Zach's fight is the main event, so we were able to get tickets in the front row. I have to be ringside with him, as does Tanner and Trey. You, Kara, and Monica will be by yourselves while he's in the ring," he explains.

"Okay. Can we go there now and watch the other fights?" I survey the room. Zach's in the corner with Tanner and Trey as he bounces from foot to foot, punching the air. I assume Nate needs to be there as well, and I don't want to be in the way. Besides, I kind of want to watch the other fights.

"Sure, if that's what you want. I want the three of you to stay together. These fights bring a lot of muscle-head punks out of the woodwork, so I don't want any of you to be alone," he informs me.

"Got it," Kara says from behind me.

"Yo!" Nate yells to the guys. Once he has their attention, he motions for them to join us.

"What's up?" Zach asks.

"The girls are going to go ahead and find their seats to watch the other fights."

Understanding crosses their faces. They kiss us goodbye. Kara and I give Zach a hug, telling him to break a leg and we're off to find our seats.

Nate walks us to our seats, kisses me one more time, and then disappears back to the locker room. When the bell sounds to start round one of the next fight, our eyes are glued to the cage. I've seen the guys spar at the gym countless times, but this is brutal. They're beating the hell out of each other on purpose.

"Holy shit! That's hot," Kara says from where she sits in between Monica and me. Monica agrees with her, but I have a feeling if it was Zach getting the beating, she might change her mind. Then again, maybe not; to each their own.

We sit there round after round, fight after fight, and watch these guys beat on each other. I'm suddenly glad Nate doesn't do this. Training and being the one who takes the hits are two completely different scenarios. I know there is no way I could watch him if he were the one in the ring. My nerves couldn't take it.

"He's up next," Kara cheers.

Sure enough, music starts to blare and Zach begins his journey to the cage, flanked by Nate, Trent, and Tanner. Nate's eyes find mine and he winks.

"God, that man has it bad for you," Kara comments.

I watch as Zach is wiped down with what looks like Vaseline; I'll have to ask Nate to be sure. He taps his junk; I'm assuming to prove he's wearing a cup. His mouth opens wide, showing his mouthpiece as the official checks his gloves. Passing the officials inspection, he takes his place in the cage. Nate, Trey, and Tanner hang the gym banner in his corner as they wait for Zach's opponent to go through the same process. I spot Brody and Sara a few rows over. Sara waves. Brody doesn't even bother to look my way.

The bell rings, indicating the start of the first round. I find myself closing my eyes, not able to watch to see if Zach is the one leading toward victory or defeat.

"What are you doing?" Kara yells. "You're missing it."

I open my eyes and look at her. She and Monica are both screaming and cheering, waving their arms in the air. Looks as though I'm the odd one out on this one.

Fifteen agonizing minutes later, it's all over. Zach has his opponent's arm twisted on an angle that is not natural, which causes him to tap. The ref instructs Zach to release his arm and that's all she wrote. Kara and Monica jump to their feet, cheering him on with his win. I can't help but stand and cheer for him as well. Although I'm not sure if I'm cheering for his victory, that fact he seems to be fine, or that it's over.

As the crowd begins to thin out, my phone vibrates in my pocket.

Nate: Hey babe. I'm on my way back out to get you guys.

Me: We're good. We are heading your way.

Nate: Okay.

"That was Nate. I told him we would head his way," I tell the girls. We gather our trash and begin to make our way to the locker rooms. As we get close, I spy the door for the restroom. "Hey. I'm going to go." I point to the door. "You guys coming or going on ahead?" I can see the door to the locker room from here.

"I'm good," Monica replies. I'm sure she's anxious to congratulate Zach.

"Me too. You want us to wait?" Kara asks.

"No. I'll be quick and it's right there." I point to the door not fifteen feet away from us.

"I'll tell Nate so he doesn't freak." Kara laughs.

I wave over my shoulder, pushing on the bathroom door. I knew I shouldn't have drunk that second bottle of water.

46

I'M EXCITED FOR Zach and his win, and I want to celebrate with my girl. I'm anxiously watching the door, waiting for her. The door opens and in walks Kara and Monica, no Ava Mae. Pushing through the crowd, Kara spots me and waves. "Where's Ava Mae?"

"She had to use the restroom. She wanted us to tell you she would be right here."

I'm not crazy about her being out there by herself. Some of the guys who attend these fights are meatheads who drink like fish. By the end of the night, they're well on their way to alcohol poisoning.

It's been maybe thirty seconds, but something feels off. "I'm going to go wait for her," I say to Tanner. I guess he can read the worry on my face, because he yells for me to hold up and he'll come with me. I don't stop.

Just as I'm coming out of the locker room, I see her. I also see the fucker who has her pinned up against the wall.

Clint.

He has her caged against the wall with his body, his lips next to her ear. His hand is on the waistband of her shorts. She's trying to push him off her, but he's a big fucker and my girl is tiny. Red-hot rage like I've never felt courses through my veins. My legs carry me the short distance in no time as I reach for the collar of his shirt and pull him off her. I hear her release a sob as my name falls from her lips, after that I zone out. I throw punch after punch of which his drunk ass half-heartedly tries to block.

I feel two strong arms come around me, preventing me from swinging. "Let go!" I yell at whoever it is.

"Nate!" Brody's voice penetrates the rage. "You're scaring her, man. You have to stop."

Ava. I need to make sure she's okay. "I'm good." I twist out of his arms. I search the crowd and that's when I see her. Her face is ghost white and stained from her tears. My heart drops at the sight of her. Within seconds, I'm standing in front of her and she throws herself in my arms, burying her face in my chest. "Shhh." I try to soothe her by running my fingers through her hair. As bad as I want to comfort her, I also need to make sure she's okay. Gripping her shoulders, I pull her away from my body so I can get a good look at her. "You okay, baby? Are you hurt?" My eyes rake over her body.

"No, I'm fine. Just shaken up. I didn't think I was going to be able to get away from him, and then you . . . you hit him over and over. I've never seen you like that." She sobs. "It scared me."

Pulling her back against me, I hold her tightly. "I'm sorry, baby. I saw his hands on you, and then when he tried to unbutton your pants, I lost it. I didn't mean to scare you." I step us back against the wall, away from Clint where the security guards are hauling him to his feet.

"Hey, sis, you okay?" Brody asks. Looking up, I see him standing there with Sara tucked against his side.

"She's good," I answer for her. Ava doesn't even attempt to respond to him.

I kiss the top of her head and she looks up at me. "Can you take me home?"

"Yeah, baby. Anything you want." I spot Tanner standing a few feet away. "Hey, man, Ava Mae wants to go home. Are you all staying at the apartment tonight?"

Before he can answer, she stops me. "No, Nate. I want to go home with you, to your house. If that . . . if that's okay?"

Her words are music to my ears. "That's more than okay. Let's get you home, baby."

"Tanner, we need to go. Do you think you can find a ride home?"

"We can take you," Brody chimes in.

I nod. I hand Tanner my keys. Reaching down, I lift Ava Mae into my arms and head toward the parking lot. I'm thankful Brody pulled me off when he did. I'd more than likely be dealing with the law right now, and then Ava would be alone.

The drive to my place is quiet. Ava Mae is in my lap, neither of us ready or willing to let go.

"Thanks, man," I say when Brody pulls into the drive. He surprises me by hopping out of the car and opening the door for me.

"Keys?" he asks.

Shit! I forgot to get my key. I'm just about to tell him where the spare is when Ava Mae speaks up. "In my purse," she tells him.

Brody grabs her purse from my hand. "Side pocket," she instructs him. I watch as he reaches in and pulls out the infinity key ring I gave her. It sparkles in the moonlight. Realization washes over his face when it registers that this is, indeed, her personal key to my place. He doesn't comment; instead, he laces his fingers with Sara's and they lead the way to my front door, opening the door for us. I carry Ava to the couch and sit down with her in my lap.

Brody takes a seat in the recliner and pulls Sara into his lap. Their position mirrors ours.

"You okay, baby?" I ask Ava. I don't bother keeping my voice low for just her. If he wants to stick around, he's going to have to deal with it.

"Yeah. I've never seen you like that."

"I know. I'm sorry, I lost it when I saw his hands on you. I didn't mean to scare you."

Ava sits up and reaches for the box of tissues on the coffee table. "Your ring is beautiful," Sara compliments. I'm sure she's trying to help get tonight's events off Ava's mind.

"Thank you. Nate gave it to me for my birthday week," she says.

"Birthday week?" Sara asks.

Ava Mae laughs. "Yeah, this lug decided I needed to have a birthday week. I got a present every day for seven days and then he gave me this," she holds her hand out for Sara, "on my actual birthday." She proceeds to tell her about each of her gifts. I stroke my fingers through her hair as I listen to the girls talk.

"I thought you didn't fight?" Brody says to me when the girls are finished.

"I do for her."

"Infinity," he says.

"Yeah," I sigh. I can see he finally gets it.

"Good to know," he says as his arms wrap around his wife.

The four of us spend the next several hours talking. Sara and Ava Mae actually have a lot in common and Brody and I catch up on his plan to leave the Marines as well as their plans to move here once he does.

The night, no matter how shitty the middle was, ended with two best friends, a brother and a sister, and a new wife getting to know each other. Brody doesn't apologize, but he doesn't need to. The smile on Ava's face at the four of us getting along, making plans for visiting again soon, that's all I need.

epilogue
Ava Mae
two years later

*F*INALLY!

I walk across the stage when they call my name. I can hear Nate, Brody, and the rest of the guys in the crowd cheering for me. I smile as I accept my certificate. I shake the President of the university's hand while holding my degree in the other. We smile for the camera as instructed, and just like that, it's official.

I'm a college graduate.

Nate has been working on a business plan over the last year for me to provide dietician services to the fighters at his gym. It's really a great plan for many reasons. It's hard for new graduates to find a job with the market, and this will allow me to slide right into my new role. It's also a huge selling point for his gym. Fighters can have a dietician help them create meal plans to fit their training. Another perk of the job is getting to work side by side with Nate every day.

For over two years, we are still going strong. I moved in with him after our one-year anniversary. I more or less lived there anyway, but he was insistent we make it official.

As soon as the last name is called and the final hand is shaken, me and two-hundred plus of my fellow graduates throw our caps in the air.

We did it.

I search the crowd for my friends and family. They're not hard to spot. If the noise they're making isn't enough to draw attention to them, the sheer size of them is. Nate spots me first and he barrels toward me. Picking me up, he swings me around. "I'm so damn proud of you."

"Stop mauling my sister, Garrison," Brody grumbles, causing us to laugh.

Nate doesn't even bother setting me on my feet as he passes me to my brother. This same pattern continues until I've made it down the line and am set on my feet in front of my dad. He and Mom also wrap me in a hug, telling me how proud they are. Last but not least is Kara. She changed her major, so she still has another year to go. She's going to make an amazing Physical Therapist Assistant. We joke with the guys, telling them we're taking over the gym. This causes them to grumble, something Kara and me find amusing.

"So we'll meet you at your place," Nate says to my parents. Mom was adamant she be the one to throw me a graduation party. She was the same way when she found out Brody and Sara were expecting baby Braden. She claims if she doesn't make it known, we'll run off and do it without her.

"Yes. I have everything ready," she says.

"I just want to run home and change and we'll be right over." I give her and my dad another hug and allow Nate to lead me to his Tahoe.

Nate

This ring is burning a hole in my pocket. I didn't think I would ever get her out of there. I should have filled them in on what I'm about to do, but I didn't want any of them to slip. I talked to her dad a few months ago, on purpose. I knew it would get back to her and I wanted to keep her guessing. Her mom told Sara, who told Kara who let it slip. This time, no one knows but me.

I knew Ava Mae would want to change before heading to the party. The plan went off without a hitch as we pull into the driveway.

"I'll be quick," she says, digging her keys out of her purse and running toward the door. I let her get a little ways in front of me before

I follow her. I want to give her time to find our room and let in sink in. Let what I'm about to do register.

I find her standing by the bed, letting the soft pink rose petals fall through her fingers. Every surface of our room is covered in them. However, it's the ones on the bed she's most interested in. The soft pink of the roses stand out on our black comforter. The words 'Marry Me' are easy to make out.

I step in the room and drop to my knees. "Ava Mae." She follows my voice and her eyes land on me, or more specifically the black ring box I'm holding out for her. I had this huge speech prepared, but my mind is suddenly blank. I've waited for this moment for what seems like a lifetime. The moment where she agrees to take my last name and spend the rest of her life with me.

There's one phrase that keeps running through my head and it's the one I rehearsed at the very end of my speech. "Will you do me the incredible honor of becoming my wife?" I speak the only words my brain remembers.

"Yes!" She yells her answer as tears run down her face. I stand and remove the ring from the box, slipping it on her finger, next to the infinity ring I gave her for her birthday, the first one we were together.

"Looks like you'll need to start wearing this on the other hand," I tell her.

She doesn't hear me. Her eyes are fixed on the two-carat diamond solitaire that is encased in the diamond infinity band I just slipped on her finger.

"Infinity," she whispers. "It's beautiful, Nate."

I capture her lips with mine, tasting the saltiness of her tears on her lips. Breaking our kiss, she studies me. I'm starting to get a little nervous. Is she changing her mind? I want to yell 'no take backs.'

"When do you want to do it? Can we do it soon?" she asks, excitement in her voice.

"Just say when, baby. Just say when."

Facebook:

https://www.facebook.com/pages/Kaylee-Ryan-Author

Goodreads:

https://www.goodreads.com/author/show/7060310.Kaylee_Ryan

Twitter:

@author_k_ryan

Instagram:

Kaylee_ryan_author

Website:

www.kayleeryan.com

Other works
by
Kaylee Ryan

With You Series
Anywhere With You
More With You
Everything With You

Stand Alone Titles

Tempting Tatum

Levitate

Acknowledgements

My family. You make it possible to follow this dream. I continue to receive nothing but love and support from you. There is no way that I could do this without out. I love you!

I have met some amazing friends throughout this process. The indie community is amazing and I am proud to say that I am a part of it. Every time I see a fellow author share my work or that of our peers I can't help but be honored to be a part of this Indie Family.

To my author BFFS—you know who you are. I love the support that we give one another and I am thankful every single one of you.

Louisa—LM Creations. You're amazing. Thank you so much for being so patient with me. The cover is beautiful!

Tami Intergrity Formatting you make my words come together in a pretty little package. Thank you so much for making Just Say When look fabulous on the inside!

Saoching Moose I'm going to keep things simple this time. I love ya girl! I value the friendship that we have created and I cannot wait to meet you in person!

Give Me Books, thank you for hosting the release day blitz.

To all of the bloggers out there . . . Thank you so much. Your continued never ending support of myself and the entire indie community is greatly appreciated. I know that you don't hear it enough so hear me now. ***I appreciate each and every one of you and the support that you have given me.*** Thank you to all of you! There are way too many of you to list . . .

To my Kick Ass Crew, you ladies know who you are. I will never be able to tell you how much your support means. I will never forget all that you have done for me. Thank you!

Kaylee, Stacy, Lauren, S, and Jamie you ladies gave up so much of your time to Beta read for me. New scenes, re-worked scenes you ladies were all over it and I cannot tell you how much I appreciate your time and support of my work. Thank you so much for all that you do.

Kaylee (2) I never thought it possible to meet someone online with common interests, name, personalities and become such fast friends. I am blessed to have found the friendship that we have formed. I value our daily talks and messages. You have talked me through scenes and provided support in all aspects of my work as well as everyday life . . . I love ya girl!! Thank you for being you.

Last but not least, to the readers. Without you none of this would even be worth the effort. I truly love writing and I am honored that I am able to share that with you. Thank you to each and every one of you who continue support me, and my dream of writing.

With Love,

Kaylee Ryan
BEST SELLING NEW ADULT ROMANCE AUTHOR